MY FAVORITE BAND DOES NOT EXIST

MY FAVORITE BAND DOES NOT EXIST

ROBERT T. JESCHONEK

 CLARION BOOKS + HOUGHTON MIFFLIN HARCOURT + BOSTON   NEW YORK + 2011

CLARION BOOKS

215 Park Avenue South, New York, New York 10003

Copyright © 2011 by Robert T. Jeschonek

For information about permission to reproduce selections from this book,
write to Permissions, Houghton Mifflin Harcourt Publishing Company,
215 Park Avenue South, New York, New York 10003.

Clarion Books is an imprint of Houghton Mifflin Harcourt Publishing Company.

www.hmhbooks.com

The text was set in Platin Std. and Coldstyle.
Book design by Sharismar Rodriguez

Library of Congress Cataloging-in-Publication Data
Jeschonek, Robert T.
My favorite band does not exist / Robert T. Jeschonek.
p. cm.
Summary: Sixteen-year-old Idea Deity, who believes that he is a character in a novel
who will die in the sixty-fourth chapter, has created a fictional underground
rock band on the internet which, it turns out, may actually exist, and whose members
are wondering who is broadcasting all their personal information.

ISBN 978-0-547-37027-9

[1. Fantasy.] I. Title.

PZ7.J55312My 2011 [Fic]—dc22

2011008150

Manufactured in the United States of America
DOC 10 9 8 7 6 5 4 3 2 1
4500297703

TO WENDY,
MY FAVORITE REALITY

ONE

IDEA

WHEN Idea Deity first met Eunice Truant, he thought that the back of her head was the front of it.

He saw her while trying to escape the men who were chasing him on the Canadian side of Niagara Falls. Idea was pushing through the crowd of cheering tourists gaping at the fireworks going off on the American side. After squeezing past a fat man in a red T-shirt, Idea found himself staring at what seemed to be a dark-haired girl in black coveralls.

In that first glimpse, he got an impression of narrow green eyes with long dark lashes . . . a thin angular nose . . . sharp cheekbones and chin . . . and full red lips . . . all of it framed by jet black shoulder-length braids.

A heartbeat later, Idea realized that the face in front of him was not three-dimensional. He was actually looking at the back of someone's head, on which a girl's face had been painted or tattooed. Only the black braids were the real thing.

As much of a hurry as he was in, Idea couldn't look away, the sight was so weird. Lifting his shiny black bangs from over his eyes with the edge of one hand, he leaned in for a closer look. Then someone pushed him from behind.

Idea stumbled forward. He bumped into the person with the painted face, who turned around, giving him a look at another face altogether.

This face was real. It had all three dimensions.

Like the face on the back of the head, this was also a girl's face. However, other than sharing the same head, the two faces had nothing in common.

The three-dimensional "front" face had wide blue eyes, an upswept nose, round chin, and thin pink lips. This face was framed by silky blond hair, which fell freely to chest level, accented by a single skinny braid on one side, threaded through beads of alternating black and white.

Idea also noted another big difference in the two faces: the one on the front of the girl's head was smiling, and the smile was beautiful.

It was a crooked little smile with a double dimple to the left side but none to the right. It was kind of snarky, almost a smirk, but the gleam in the girl's eyes was pure gold.

As Idea drank it in, the girl flared red in the light from a burst of fireworks.

"There you are!" The light faded, leaving her standing before him in pink coveralls. "Fancy meeting *you* here!" When she spread her arms, he saw the coveralls were pink on one side and black on the other.

Idea frowned. "Huh?"

The girl threw her arms around him and gave him a hug. "It's great to see you!" she said. "It's been too long."

Idea took a long look at her. He guessed she was seventeen

or eighteen, just a year or two older than he was, but he didn't recognize her.

The one thing he was sure about, however, was that the men who were chasing him were still on the move. They wouldn't give up easily, and they couldn't be far away, either.

"Gotta run." Idea broke free of the hug and pushed past the girl to continue through the crowd.

As fireworks whistled and boomed in the sky, Idea weaved his way between the tightly packed spectators. He didn't realize that the girl was following him, until she spoke.

"It just occurred to me that I might have gotten you mixed up with someone else," she said. "Let me introduce myself. I'm Eunice Truant."

Idea glanced back at her and frowned. "My name is Idea Deity," he said, continuing to press forward.

"Are you a *good* Idea or a *bad* one?" Eunice said playfully.

"Depends on your point of view, I guess," he replied.

"When you have an idea," Eunice continued, "do you say, 'I've just had a great *me*'?"

"Look," Idea said over his shoulder. "I really can't talk right now, okay? I'm in the biggest hurry ever."

Idea's stomach twisted. He had a feeling that trouble was near. Nervously, he rubbed the three moles arranged in a triangle on his left cheek.

Craning his neck, he scanned the surrounding crowd. In the yellow light of another bursting shell, just as a bunch of people raised their hands to applaud, he caught sight of a familiar face.

Idea saw brown skin and thick black hair slicked back with

what looked like motor oil. He saw a nose like the beak of a cockatoo, and an Adam's apple that was more like a gourd.

As soon as he spotted that face, Idea ducked down. He was pretty sure that his pursuer hadn't seen him, but he didn't want to give the guy a second chance to catch sight of him.

"What's the big idea?" Eunice said with a chuckle. "Either that last firework scared you, or you don't want someone to see you."

Idea decided it wouldn't do any good to lie to her. "He's just a few people back from us."

The crowd cheered as a series of booms and flashes rocked the street. "Come on." Eunice grabbed him by the hand and pulled him away from the gorge.

They kept going till they reached a cobblestone plaza where the crowd was thin. Most people were passing through on their way to the rim.

Eunice stopped in front of a cement bench, one of several arranged in a ring around the plaza. "Now, just stand here." She yanked a folded-up circle of yellow plastic from the pocket of her coveralls.

Eunice shook out the folded circle, which became a big, round sheet, held taut by some kind of flexible frame. Idea saw that a huge smiley face had been painted on it.

He also quickly realized that the giant smiley was two layers, as Eunice pried the rim apart at the bottom, raised the whole circle over Idea's head with both hands, and pulled it down over him with a single tug. It covered him from his head to just above his knees.

"Over here." Eunice guided him by the frame of the circle two steps to his left. "Get up on the bench."

Idea bumped his leg into the seat of the bench. He fumbled around for a moment until Eunice grabbed hold of his arm through the plastic sheet.

"Step up," she said, and he did. His toe found the edge of the seat, and then he slid his foot onto it and boosted himself up to a standing position. Eunice steadied him, then let go.

"Don't move, Movie," she said. "Not till I tell you to."

The thin yellow sheeting was smack against Idea's nose. Fortunately, a pair of pinprick eyeholes had been cut in the vicinity of his eyes, and he could look through one at a time with little shifts of his head.

Peering down through one of the eyeholes, he saw Eunice pull on a curly green wig and giant red-framed glasses. Next, she pointed a finger directly at Idea, opened her mouth wide as if gaping in surprise and wonder . . . and froze.

Shifting his head the tiniest bit, Idea looked out over his surroundings. From his vantage point atop the bench, he had a good view of the passersby. Those who were closest shot looks of annoyance or amusement in his direction, or else they ignored him.

Further away, he spotted his pursuers.

The two men were walking away from the rim, straight toward him. The brown-skinned man with the motor oil hair was Bulab Magnificat. The other man, Scholar Wishburn, had wavy silver hair, chiseled features, and an expensive-looking business suit.

Bulab and Scholar crossed the plaza, looking grim . . . and then they caught sight of him. They stopped about twenty feet away and stared at him in the flashing light of the fireworks, eyes focused like laser beams on his disguise.

As Idea squinted at them through an eyehole, he had the urge to run. Then he remembered that although they were looking right at him, they couldn't see who he was through the yellow smiley face.

For a long moment, Bulab and Scholar stared up at him. Scholar pointed at him and said something. Bulab laughed and nodded.

Then they moved off through the crowd.

Minutes later, when his pursuers were blocks away, Idea told Eunice that he thought it would be safe to move again.

Eunice was still holding the same pose that she'd assumed when Idea had stepped up onto the bench. She was still pointing at him, with her mouth open in surprise; as far as Idea could tell, she hadn't moved a muscle.

For a moment, he thought that she wasn't going to move one anytime soon, either. Eunice remained perfectly frozen, as if she were a mannequin.

Then, she returned to life. With the hand that she'd used to point at Idea, she reached up and helped him down off the bench. As soon as his feet touched the sidewalk, Eunice lifted the giant smiley face up over his head.

"Where did you come up with that plan?" Idea asked, patting down his black hair.

"It's what I do for a living," said Eunice. She froze in place again for a moment, posing with the smiley face held flat over-head as if to keep off rain. Then she broke the pose and lowered the yellow circle to her side. "I'm a human statue."

Idea smoothed out his rumpled black T-shirt with the pic-ture of dice on the chest, one with a six facing up, the other with a five. "You really make money doing that?"

Eunice nodded. "For *stars* like me, people will walk right up and drop cash in my hat." She took off the green Afro wig and monstrous red eyeglasses and shook them at him. "Good props are key."

"I'm glad you had those props handy," he said. "I'm lucky I ran into you when I did. Thanks."

"*De nada.*" Eunice stuffed the wig and glasses down the front of her coveralls. "Just try to remember my Christmas card this year, okay?" With practiced movements, she twisted the frame of the huge smiley face, folding and compressing the plastic sheeting until it was reduced once again to a yellow disk about the size of her hand.

"Well, I'd better get going," said Idea. "Thanks again. Goodbye." He turned and started walking, eager to get moving now that he'd ditched Bulab and Scholar.

Ditching Eunice, however, wouldn't be so easy. When Idea stopped at the edge of the street to wait for traffic to pass, she appeared alongside him.

"So where are we going, Go-Go?" she asked casually.

"Huh?" Idea frowned.

"I'm guessing you could use some more help," said Eunice.

"Unless there's nothing but totally blue skies in your world from now on."

Idea looked at her. Though he'd only known her for a half-hour or so, he didn't seriously consider telling her to get lost.

She was on the odd side, but other than the face on the back of her head, she was pretty hot. Plus, Idea hadn't been having much luck eluding Bulab and Scholar on his own, and Eunice seemed to have some good tricks up her sleeve. He would have to be a complete moron, he thought, not to let her come with him.

"San Diego, California," he said.

"Cool," said Eunice. "And why are we going to San Diego?"

"To stop my mom and dad from killing themselves on the Internet."

TWO

IDEA

AT a coffee shop in Buffalo, New York, where Idea and Eunice stopped after escaping Niagara Falls, Idea tinkered with the website that he was using to hoax the world.

"Any news on your parents?" Eunice asked between gulps of black coffee.

"That's not what I'm working on." Idea didn't look up from the screen of his smartphone. He was trying to get as much done as he could, as quickly as possible. Buffalo was still awfully close to the last place he'd seen Bulab and Scholar. Idea and Eunice had crossed the border only an hour ago, in Eunice's green vintage Volkswagen Beetle.

"So what's with the killing themselves on the Internet bit?" asked Eunice.

Idea glanced up at her. "Have you ever heard of Vengeful and Loving Deity?"

Eunice thought for a moment, then shook her head. "Not that I can remember . . . and I'd *definitely* remember names like *those*."

"They're my parents." Idea returned his gaze to the phone's

screen. "Vengeful Deity is my father. Loving Deity is my mother. They set up an e-ligion site that totally took off. Tons of hits and millions of dollars—all tax-free, since they have nonprofit status as a church."

"Sounds like they have a lot to live for," said Eunice.

"But they let the religion stuff go to their heads." Idea furiously thumb-typed on the phone's onscreen keyboard. "They started believing they could die for the sins of the world."

"On the Internet," said Eunice.

"Yeah," said Idea. "And maybe they *will* save the world. You *know* they'll get the most hits ever in the history of the Web."

Eunice gulped some more coffee. She drummed her fingers in high-speed rhythms on the tabletop in counterpoint to Idea's typing. "So why are you in Buffalo, New York, if your parents are about to kill themselves in San Diego, California?"

"They knew I'd try to stop them, so they sent me away to a camp of followers in Newfoundland. I escaped not long before you met me. The guys who are chasing me have orders to stop me from going west and to take me back to the camp."

"Cool," said Eunice. "You're a fugitive."

"Pretty much," Idea agreed, typing away.

Eunice got up from her chair and circled the table to look over his shoulder. "Whatcha doin'?"

"It's a website I created." He nodded at the flashing screen. "A home page for a rock band that's really taking off right now."

"What band?"

Just then, a skinny twenty-something guy paused on his way

past. "Hey, it's Youforia!" He pointed a finger at the phone. "I hear those guys are awesome."

Idea flashed Eunice a smirk. "Me, too," he said. "I would *kill* for a download of one of their songs."

"I thought I downloaded one last week." The twenty-something guy combed his fingers through his shaggy blond hair. "It was supposed to be a copy of 'Corpuscle Porpoise,' but it turned out to be a three-minute broadcast of the Emergency Alert System."

Idea shook his head sympathetically. "Keep trying. I hear there are Youforia song files out there somewhere."

"There'd better be," said the guy. "Otherwise, there're gonna be a lot of pissed-off people around." He snorted, then headed for the door of the café.

As he walked away, Eunice tapped a fingernail on the screen of Idea's phone. It was then that he noticed her nails were painted with the Chinese yin-yang symbol, a circle with a curved line down the middle, one half black with a white dot in the center, the other half white with a black dot. On the nails of her right hand, the black half was closest to the tip, while the white half was closest on her left hand.

"'Corpuscle Porpoise'?" said Eunice. "Never heard of it."

Idea made sure that the guy was too far away to hear what he said next. "It's a made-up song."

"All songs are made up by someone," she observed.

"Yeah, but no," said Idea. "What I *meant* was"—his voice dropped to a whisper—"none of Youforia's songs are real."

"What are you talking about?" Eunice didn't bother to whisper.

He leaned closer to her and lowered his voice even more. "Youforia does not exist."

"And this is a big deal *why?*"

"There's a lot of buzz," said Idea. "People are hitting the website like crazy. I did such a good job of making up the band that people actually think it's real." He scrolled through the site's home page. "Take a look. The site's got fake band member biographies and photos, fake tour schedules, fake discographies and reviews. Youforia's on YoFace and Yapper, too. I'm yapping as we speak, pretending to be the lead guitarist, Wicked Livenbladder."

"So you're not real, then?" She rapped her knuckles on his head. "You seem solid enough to me."

He shot her a dirty look. "You know what I mean. They all think I'm Wicked Livenbladder instead of who I really am." A fresh line of text appeared in the Yapper window, and Idea read it with a grin. "Look at this! Thiefaroni109 is talking about seeing the band play a legendary secret gig at Humpy's in Hotknee, Nebraska."

"A *secret* gig?"

"The lead singer's got stage fright issues. He'll only let the band play out in disguise." Idea smirked. "The *made-up* singer in the *make-believe* band, that is."

Eunice grinned. "Which Thiefaroni109 couldn't have seen because, like you, they aren't real."

"Exactly!" said Idea. "The gig never happened. There's no

such place as Humpy's or Hotknee. In my original story on the website, Youforia played their gig at Hump Day's in Hotfoot, Florida. Now, you watch; other people will say the gig was at Humpy's in Hotknee, and Thiefaroni's mistake will become the new truth. I might even change the website to match."

"Interesting," said Eunice. "This stuff takes on a life of its own, doesn't it?"

He nodded. "That's a good way of putting it."

"Too bad you can't make up your own life the same way," she said. "Make things happen the way you want them to."

"Yeah," said Idea. "Too bad."

THREE

YOUFORIA

WHEN Eurydice Tarantella emerged from the bathroom, bass player Chick Sintensity was trying to stop lead guitarist Wicked Livenbladder from smashing the laptop.

"They did it again!" With his grizzly bear face twisted into a snarl, Wicked tore the laptop out of Chick's hands. "They did it *again!*" He swung the laptop across his huge belly, using his girth to prevent bony, bald Chick from retrieving it.

Just as Wicked pulled the computer away from Chick, drummer Gail Virtuoso took it away from Wicked. Before he could make another grab for it, Gail ran across the beds and dove through the door into the adjoining room. She slammed it shut behind her and locked it from the other side.

Wicked stomped across the room and pounded on the door with both fists, shouting for Gail to bring back the computer. She responded by cranking up the volume of the TV to drown him out.

After a few moments, his pounding faded. He went from two fists to one, then from one fist to one open hand.

Chick tapped him on the shoulder and offered him a bottle

of beer. Wicked looked pissed, but he took the beer and had a long drink from it.

As he lowered the bottle from his lips, he shook his head and pawed at his shaggy mane of brown hair and beard. "How do they keep *doin'* it? How do they know so much about us?"

Chick had a drink from his own beer and shrugged. "It's weird, all right. We haven't exactly gone public. This is supposed to be a *secret* tour we're on."

"Yeah," said Wicked. "But at the rate these guys are goin', pretty soon there won't be anything secret about it."

"That's no secret, man." The scars on Chick's cheek, chin, and nose folded into the lines of his broad toothy smile.

"Everything's on the website," Wicked continued. "All over YoFace and Yapper, too. Everything you ever wanted to know about Youforia."

Eurydice blew a green bubble with her chewing gum, then popped it and sucked the gum back into her mouth. "Look on the bright side. Maybe nobody cares enough to *want* to know your secrets." Though she'd stayed back during the action, she stepped forward now and checked herself in the mirror. After adjusting one of her long black braids, she helped herself to a bottle of beer from the six-pack on the dresser.

"I wish." Wicked winced. "I mean, I want people to care about us, but I don't want 'em finding out all our secrets on the damn Internet before our big debut!"

"They were yapping about the Hotfoot, Florida, show, back

in Jovember," said Chick. "They even knew we played in disguise, under a different name."

"Scowling Linda," said Wicked.

"Not that it would've made any difference if we'd played as Youforia," Chick added. "No one but *us* is supposed to know that we call our band Youforia, anyway!"

"Us"—Eurydice sat down on the edge of the bed—"and everyone who hits the Youforia website, YoFace page, and Yapper feed."

Wicked let loose a loud growl of frustration. "How the hell did this Youforia website even get started? We're a *secret band*, for cryin' out loud!"

"Must be Sty." Gail, who'd eased open the door from the adjoining room and slipped in unnoticed, sat in one of the blue vinyl chairs by the window.

"You think so?" said Wicked.

"Is the sky green?" Gail tossed her head emphatically, shaking her choppy red bangs out of her eyes.

"Yes, the sky is green," said Wicked. "Are we done stating the obvious?"

"Maybe it's his way of speeding things up," Gail said. "Maybe he figures the publicity will finally force Reacher to get over his freaky stage fright and play in front of people without wearing a mask."

Eurydice cracked her gum loudly. "Sty wouldn't do this."

Gail flashed her a dark look. The two of them didn't get along at all, and it wasn't just because Gail had once dated

Eurydice's current boyfriend, Reacher Mirage, the band's lead singer.

"So who else would know all our personal information?" asked Chick. "Other than one of us in this room, that is."

"I don't have any answers for you," said Eurydice.

"What about Rebacka?" Gail said with a sneer. "She's being awfully quiet about all this."

Without taking her eyes off Gail, Eurydice took a drink from her beer.

"Come on, Eury," said Gail. "Turn around so I can ask Rebacka a couple questions."

Eurydice lowered her beer. Slowly she turned her back on Gail.

And turned another face toward her . . . a face that was drawn on the back of Eurydice's head.

This two-dimensional face had big blue eyes, a pug nose, and thin pink lips. These features were framed by free-falling blond hair with a single thin braid on one side, threaded through black and white beads.

Eurydice further accentuated the impression that a second person looked out from the back half of her by wearing clothes with two front halves stitched together. Tonight, on her front side, her blouse was black silk with a brown fur collar; the black half of the blouse ended along the sides of her body, where it joined to the pink and white striped top on her back. On her front half, she wore black jeans, but in back, her pants were red.

It was Eurydice's trademark look, and of course it drew

stares in public. Among the band members, though, it was old news. No one in the band brought it up anymore, except Gail, who'd nicknamed the back side Rebacka and made fun of it whenever she was drunk.

"Hey, Rebacka!" Gail said with a nasty laugh in her voice. "How much did they pay you for our personal secrets?"

Eurydice cracked her gum twice. "They were going to pay me plenty." She said it in a high singsong, as if Rebacka were the one speaking. "Except they already got all *your* secrets for free off a men's room wall."

Everyone laughed except Gail, who jumped off the chair and stormed out of the room again.

With that, Chick folded his hands behind his head, stretched, and yawned. "On *that* note"—his voice, after the yawn, was high-pitched—"time for bed, I'd say. Doesn't look like we're gonna catch the traitor tonight."

Wicked yawned, too. "I'm with you."

Eurydice threw herself down on one of the beds and picked up a fat paperback from the bedside table. The book belonged to Reacher, who'd been reading it between band gigs.

It was a fantasy novel titled *Fireskull's Revenant,* by Milt Ifthen. True to the title, the cover was splashed with a painted image of a man with a flaming skull. He wore black leather, rode a jet black horse, and brandished a gleaming sword that dripped blood.

With nothing better to do while she waited for Reacher to get back, Eurydice opened to the bookmarked place—the start of Chapter 39—and began reading . . .

Fireskull's Revenant

MILT IFTHEN

Constant Books

CHAPTER THIRTY-NINE

AS the echo of the final sword strike faded over the battlefield, Lord Fireskull stomped among the dead, handpicking the corpses that would decorate the walls of his keep. His ever-burning head and black, leathery wings gave him the appearance of an angel of death, collecting the souls of fallen warriors under the blazing orange sky.

Two newly taken slaves and a slave driver followed, throwing bodies on a cart as Fireskull selected them. In some cases, *parts* were chosen and tossed onto the cart, severed forever from the bodies to which they had once been attached.

"Oh, *here's* a good one," said Fireskull, kicking the mangled corpse of a blond-haired man. "When this traitor's head has been picked clean atop the highest pike, I shall use it to adorn my bedpost."

Gripping the man's hair with one hand, Fireskull lifted him from the muck. With his other hand, he used his sword to hack through the man's neck.

The body fell free. Fireskull heaved the head over his shoulder, and it landed on the ground. Neither of the slaves caught it, drawing whip strokes from the slave driver for both of them.

As the slaves scurried under the cracking whip to retrieve the prize, Fireskull continued onward through the misty field of gore. Though he was the victor, he was restless and seething with rage.

As satisfying as it was to mutilate dead traitors, Fireskull knew that he would not find the one corpse he most wanted. With his own fiery eyes, he had seen his lifelong enemy ride off toward the borderland at battle's end, alive and whole.

These other bodies were no substitute for Johnny Without. Many of them had been followers of Johnny's and so deserved whatever defilement Fireskull chose to lavish upon them. But none could draw the boiling torrent of vengeance from Fireskull's pseudoheart and absorb his full and terrible wrath.

Only Johnny could do that.

Just the thought of Johnny hurtling away, on goose back, was enough to make Fireskull kill a twitching survivor at his feet. He heard someone groaning a few corpses away and stormed over to kill her, too.

Neither murder did a thing to relieve his fury. After a

blistering battle, Johnny Without was still alive and safe within the borders of his neighboring kingdom.

That would have to change. It had happened too many times before, in spite of shifting alliances and ever more brilliant plans that had seemed to confer unbeatable advantages upon Fireskull. Again and again, his opponent had escaped, even when his death had seemed certain, and returned to resume the blood feud.

It was a vicious circle that had to end. Perhaps the time to act was now.

Now, so close to a just-ended catastrophic battle, could be the best time for an all-out strike. Perhaps, instead of pulling back to rebuild and retrench and rescheme, Fireskull should hurl everything that he had left into an assault on Johnny's domain.

It would be something that Fireskull had not tried before. It might turn out to be completely unexpected and boldly successful.

Fireskull disposed of another survivor in the mud, then searched the drifting mist for General Shunjoy Undercut. With each passing moment, Fireskull liked his plan more, and he wanted his chief military commander to set it in motion.

When Fireskull spotted Undercut, however, his focus shifted. Red-plumed war helmet in hand, Undercut approached from the forest's edge with a stranger. Without saying a word, the stranger declared himself to be a person of significance.

The stranger wore a robe of tattered brown sackcloth, his face mostly hidden by the hood, but he carried himself with a regal bearing, stiff and imperious. Though Fireskull did not know who the stranger was, he sensed that the man possessed some kind of power and authority. In spite of the carpet of disemboweled corpses at his feet, the stranger seemed as at ease on the battlefield as General Undercut.

As usual, Fireskull's instincts were accurate, although he did not realize just how historic a meeting this would be and how important a role the stranger would play in his future. If he had known those things, Fireskull would have dismembered the prophet on the spot, before a single word had left his mouth.

"Excellency." Undercut drew ahead of the stranger and fell to one knee with head bowed before Fireskull. "I have brought a holy man who seeks an audience with you."

Fireskull tapped the flat of his black sword on Undercut's shoulder. "Rise, faithful warrior. Tell me . . . is this man friend or foe?"

"Most assuredly, I come as a friend." The stranger swept forward and dropped to one knee just as Undercut was getting to his feet.

"My lord, this man is Highcast," said Undercut. "A

great prophet. He is said to have predicted the Plague of Nothing, Premageddon, and the Day/Night Wars."

Fireskull nodded and said nothing. He had heard the man's name before, although he did not wish to admit it and confer additional status upon Highcast.

"Brother Highcast," said Undercut. "You are in the presence of the Ultimate Destroyer, the Ebon Angel of Suffering and Slaughter, the most exalted and terrifying Lord Righteous Fireskull of the Unrepentant Kingdom. Make peace with whatever gods or devils you serve, for you might not survive to tell of this rapturous and terrible experience."

"On your feet, wretch," snarled Fireskull. "Tell me why I should not rend you into ten thousand pieces for setting foot in my kingdom uninvited."

Smoothly Highcast rose from the bloody ground and spread his arms wide. "The end of the world is upon us. And *you* will set it in motion."

Fireskull cocked his head to one side. "Who says so?"

"I have seen it in a vision," said Highcast. "I have seen the vision three times. There can be no mistake."

"So, tell me." Fireskull leaned close to Highcast. "How do I do it? How do I end the world?"

Highcast glowed red in the light of Fireskull's flames, but he did not seem a bit nervous. "You do not do it alone. The prophecy is this: If Lord Fireskull and Johnny

Without should ever again meet face-to-face, the world will be destroyed in a cataclysm of devastating explosions."

Fireskull smirked and leaned back. "Explosions?"

"And that day, when all life ends and the world is reduced to cinders and dust, shall be called Boomsday."

"'Boomsday.'" Fireskull looked at Undercut, whose expression was quite serious, and laughed. "The world will blow up unless I stay away from Johnny Without."

Highcast nodded. "As you say, lord."

"Good one." Fireskull laughed some more. "And what a coincidence that you show up with this prophecy just when Johnny's back is against the wall."

"It is no coincidence," said Highcast, "that I have come just as you are about to launch an attack that will bring you face-to-face with Johnny, fulfilling the prophecy and ending the world."

Fireskull did not show it, but he was surprised at Highcast's mention of an impending attack on Johnny. No one but Fireskull himself could have known that a fresh assault was imminent. Yet the self-proclaimed prophet, Highcast, had mentioned it as if it were common knowledge.

However Highcast had come up with the information, whether by mind-diving or guesswork, Fireskull would not give him the satisfaction of confirming it—especially since he thought that he knew whose hands were pulling Highcast's strings.

"How much is Johnny paying you?" asked Fireskull. "How much to save his miserable hide?"

"I am in no one's employ but my own." Highcast bowed. "The truth itself is my only reward."

With a sigh, Fireskull turned his back on the prophet. Spreading his leathery wings wide, he took several steps away, walking over sprawled corpses as if they were paving stones.

"You must not value your life much, trying to trick me into sparing your master," said Fireskull. "*He* must not value your life much, either."

"My life is not an issue," said Highcast. "I have foreseen that I will leave here alive and unharmed."

Fireskull laughed loudly and flapped his wings. "Then perhaps you're not much of a prophet, after all."

"My visions are never wrong," said Highcast. "I foresaw the destruction of the Second Sun seven years before it happened. I warned of the return of the Consumptive Legion a full decade before they crossed into Carcassia.

"Five years before the Milkmen escaped the Bleak District, I prophesied every detail before the Kings of Psalivir. I saw it all before it happened."

Fireskull spun and jabbed a clawed finger at Highcast. "According to *you,* and *Johnny,* who's putting words in your mouth."

"He is not my master," said Highcast. "In fact, when

I leave here, I will go to him and tell him exactly what I have told you."

"You will report back to him on the outcome of the mission he sent you on, you mean," Fireskull snarled.

"Please," said Highcast. "I beg you. Do what you will, but do not meet him face-to-face. The world *will* be destroyed, and you along with it."

Fireskull flapped his wings and rose several feet into the air. He had heard enough. Whatever amusement value Highcast had provided had long been exhausted.

"General Undercut," said Fireskull. "Shall I give him a ten-second head start, or no head start at all? Better yet, should I let him keep his head, or leave him with no head at all?"

"Lord Fireskull." Undercut looked nervous, but his voice was firm. "As always, I shall obey your orders without fail in this matter. I do humbly suggest, however, that we release the prophet and allow him to continue on his way."

"And why would we ever do that?" said Fireskull.

Undercut cleared his throat. "In the event that the prophecy is accurate, perhaps Highcast will discourage Johnny from hastening a face-to-face meeting with you and ending the world."

Fireskull thought it over for a moment and understood what Undercut was getting at. If Johnny bought into the prophecy, he would be less likely to move out to the borderlands, where he might have a greater chance of encountering Fireskull. Therefore, Johnny would be less prepared to repel an invasion by Fireskull's forces.

"I see your point." Fireskull nodded. Stilling the movements of his wings, he drifted down to the bloody ground in front of Highcast. "You're a lucky little man, prophet. You get to live another day."

Highcast steepled his fingers together and bowed deeply. "Many thanks, magnificent one. And thank you for saving the world."

"If I choose to do so, you may thank me then," said Fireskull.

"But I already know you will save it," said Highcast, his voice nearly a whisper. "I have foreseen it."

Fireskull's sunspot eyes narrowed in an angry glare. "None may fathom or predict my glorious and mysterious ways."

Highcast, leaning close to Fireskull, whispered, "In my vision, you realize that it is sometimes wiser to kill an enemy from afar, without setting eyes or hands upon him yourself. In this way, you avoid a trap that Johnny has set for you, a trap baited with your own stolen soul."

"Ah, I see." Fireskull leaned even closer, so that his flames singed Highcast's hood. "I, too, have had a vision. In it, I saw a man suffering through weeks of unending torture.

"It did not take long for the man to beg to be put out of his misery, but his torturer would not end the pain so soon. The man screamed for days and nights on end as one torture device after another cut and pierced and bruised and split him. Pieces of him were removed and fed to wild beasts while he watched.

"Finally, the man was killed. His name, coincidentally, was Highcast, just like yours. His torturer, Fireskull, told him before he died that all this could have been avoided if Highcast had only known when to shut up and go away."

Without another word, Highcast turned and walked off across the battlefield, heading in the direction of Johnny's border.

Fireskull watched him go. In truth, though Fireskull would admit it to no one, the prophet's words had affected him in more ways than simply annoying him.

Perhaps Highcast was not just a charlatan working for Johnny Without. At the very least, he knew things that he should not have known.

For one, he knew that Fireskull was planning an immediate follow-up attack on Johnny, although, granted, he could have guessed that. In the wake of the recent battle, Fireskull had two choices—attack or fall back. So anyone would have had a fifty-fifty chance of guessing what he would do.

On the other hand, Highcast had known about Fireskull's stolen soul. That was something that only Fireskull knew about. Even Johnny did not remember that he had taken it.

And Johnny carried the soul within him as his own.

Fireskull wondered what else Highcast knew, and how much of his prophecy might be true.

FIVE

REACHER

WHEN Reacher Mirage threw open the motel room door, the lights were on and everyone was asleep. Chick was curled up on one bed, snoring like a horse. Wicked was sprawled on his back on the other bed, clutching a beer bottle in his right hand and a pillow in his left.

No one stirred when Reacher entered the room. However, their blissful obliviousness would not last.

"Wake up!" When Reacher shouted at the top of his lungs, Chick's and Wicked's eyes snapped open. *"Get up now!"*

"What the *hell?*" Wicked's voice was a snarl.

"Cut it out!" said Chick.

"Not till you wake up!" shouted Reacher. "It's an emergency!"

Wicked sprang to a sitting position on the bed. "Since when?"

Reacher marched to the door to the adjoining room and hammered it with his fist. "Eurydice! Gail! *Wake up! Emergency!*"

"What *kind* of emergency?" howled Wicked.

"The kind that makes us get out of here right away," Reacher replied.

"No chance." Chick rolled over and closed his eyes.

Reacher rushed to the bed, grabbed a pillow, and hit him over the head with it. "I'm not *kidding!* Pack up, people! If we don't leave in ten minutes, everything we've worked for will be destroyed!"

"Come on, you guys," Reacher urged as he carried two suitcases out of the motel room. "We have to hurry!"

Youforia's fifty-something manager, Sty Latherclad, stood just outside the door. His face, with its chiseled features, looked tense as he lowered the cell phone from his ear. "My source says Hiya's on his way."

"How does he keep finding us?" Chick marched out of the room with his bass guitar case in one hand and an amplifier in the other. The amplifier cord dragged through the patch of pink grass between the front door and the parking lot.

"How do you think?" Wicked pushed past Chick into the room. "He watches the website and YoFace."

Sty snapped his phone shut and waved it at Reacher. "He's going to be here any second now." Sty's wavy silver hair fluttered in the breeze, as did the tail of his unzipped navy blue jacket.

In response, Reacher cupped his hands around his mouth and yelled at the band. "We leave in one minute! Whoever's not in the van by then gets left behind!"

"Where's your girlfriend?" Gail said sarcastically as she slouched past with an armload of stuffed animals. "I bet you won't leave *her* behind."

"Whatever it takes." When Reacher smiled, the star-shaped port-wine stain on his right cheek bunched up into a crescent. Some people thought that the plum-colored stain was a tattoo meant to symbolize imminent stardom, but in reality, it was just a birthmark that had never faded.

"The natives are restless," Sty said quietly, for Reacher's ears only. "They're worked up about that damn website."

Reacher shrugged. "So what else is new?"

"They're pointing fingers at each other," said Sty. "And at me. And, by the way, I have nothing to do with it."

"I know." Reacher ran his hand over the white stubble on his scalp the way he did when he was nervous. The color of his hair was unusual, because he was only eighteen years old, and he'd never bleached it.

"That's not to say I think it's a bad thing, necessarily," Sty continued. "The website, YoFace, and Yapper traffic is building interest in you. You already have fans, yet you've never released a recording or played a single gig under your own name."

"Yeah." Reacher fiddled with the middle button of his white bowling shirt. "I hear what you're saying." He always wore untucked bowling shirts with cool designs, straight out of the 1950s. A seven-ten split was embroidered on the breast pocket of this one, with a bowling ball rolling toward the seven pin.

"You're already being chased around by a reporter from *Tuned* magazine, for Pete's sake. Hiya Permaneck's a household name in his own right, and he wants to write an article about you." Sty spread his arms wide and grinned. "The undercover band thing has paid off! Don't you think it's time to end the secret tour? Imagine the publicity when you play out for the first time without being in disguise."

"Time's up!" shouted Reacher. Then he turned to Sty and spoke in a low voice. "We're not ready."

Sty frowned. "Pretty soon, you might not have a choice."

"Not. Ready." Reacher growled.

"When *will* you be?" asked Sty. "Two Jovembers from now? Three Junuarys? Ten Faugusts?"

Wicked and Chick raced past, arms loaded with belongings, and dove into the band's "tour bus," a twenty-year-old black Studebaker van. Eurydice followed, wearing a backpack and lugging an overstuffed duffel bag.

Reacher shook his head grimly. "*I* say when we go public. That's the rule."

"All right, then." Sty opened the driver's door and climbed in behind the wheel. "Just so you know, a secret band isn't really a secret if everyone already knows about it from what they read online."

Reacher hopped into the van's passenger seat. "*I* say when we go public. End of story."

SIX

IDEA

IDEA sat on the Lake Erie beach under a sky full of stars and tried not to make it too obvious that he was closely watching Eunice walk back from the water's edge.

Though he still thought that the whole face-on-the-back-of-her-head thing was weird, he was attracted to her. More accurately, he liked the front half of her, the half with the blond hair and real face.

He liked the front half of her clothes, too. She had changed from the coveralls into another two-sided outfit. He preferred the formfitting pink and white striped top and red pants on the front side to the fur-trimmed black top and jeans on the back side . . . although that might have had something to do with the fact that clothes designed for the *front* of a girl's body didn't look normal when worn on her *back*.

Either way, as he watched her walking toward him, Idea wished that she would invite him to share the sleeping bag she'd brought along, which was spread out on the sand nearby. It looked to him like it was big enough for two.

"Earth to Idea," Eunice said as she approached. "Who's on your mind? Could it be *me?*"

Idea felt the heat of a blush climbing into his cheeks. "Just thinking about my website," he lied. "Planning what the band will do next."

"Well, *I'm* thinking about *you*." Eunice came to a stop and looked down at him. "You should really think about adding a face on the back of *your* head, you know."

Idea laughed and stared out at the surface of the enormous lake. After hours of driving, he and Eunice had stopped at a campground on the shore in Pennsylvania. Lake Erie stretched off in the distance, its rippling skin shimmering in the moonlight.

"Let me know if you decide to go for the double face," said Eunice. "I can totally hook you up. Whatever you need."

Idea lifted his bangs out of his eyes with the edge of his hand as he looked up at her. "Whatever I need? How about telling me why you're going all the way to California with a complete stranger."

Eunice shrugged. "Maybe I'm bored. Maybe I'm a sucker for strays. Maybe I'm going to rip you off." She reached into a pocket of her red pants and pulled out a strange-looking smartphone. It had a black and white striped body with a rubbery texture. When she touched the screen, a cloud of fine, twinkling glitter appeared over it. "Maybe it was my digihoroscope."

Idea gaped at her cool phone, wondering where she'd gotten it. "Your what?"

"The most advanced and accurate electronic horoscope ever developed," said Eunice. "I created it myself, using a customized astrological algorithm to predict events on an hour-by-hour basis instead of a daily or weekly one. I've been living my life by it religiously for the past two years."

"And this thing told you to come with me?"

Eunice shook her head. "Based on certain data—my astrological sign, the current date, my geolocation, environmental conditions, et cetera—the digihoroscope predicts likely outcomes. It's up to me to choose which actions to take."

"So what's it say is going to happen next, then?"

Eunice tapped the screen. The glittering cloud swirled gently around her fingertips. "You won't *believe* this."

Idea stared, mesmerized by her strange phone. He'd never seen anything like it. "What does it say?"

"Are you sitting down?" she asked, although she could see that he was indeed sitting down. "According to the digihoroscope, in the next hour, you and I will . . ."

Eunice paused and shook her head in stunned disbelief.

"What?" Idea said impatiently.

"Sleep," said Eunice. "We'll be sound asleep. And get this: we'll sleep for several hours to come."

Idea snorted and shook his head. "Wow. That horoscope thing is more amazing than I imagined. It'll sure come in handy on the road."

"No kidding," said Eunice. "By the way, what's your sign?"

"Gemini," he said. "What's yours?"

"Virgitarius." She resumed tapping the phone's screen.

Idea frowned. "Do you mean Virgo or Sagittarius?"

"Yes." Eunice sat down on the sleeping bag. "And what are your parents' signs?"

Idea was annoyed that she'd avoided answering his question. "What do you care?"

"I have to enter all your data for the digihoroscope to chart your future," she said. "And now that our futures are connected, I have to chart yours in order to chart mine with any accuracy."

Idea liked what she'd said about their futures being connected. His annoyance level suddenly dropped. "My mother's birthday is February twenty-third. My father's is October fifteenth."

"Pisces and Libra." Eunice nodded and kept tapping away. "It figures."

"What do you mean, 'It figures'?"

"That ought to do it for now." She shut off the phone, and the cloud of glitter faded. "At least we've gotten started."

"Started with what?"

"I think we should get some sleep." She slipped the phone into her pocket and lay back on the sleeping bag.

Idea was annoyed again. "Can't you give me a straight answer to *one question*, at least?"

Eunice sighed. "All right, all right. Ask me one question."

Idea thought it over for a moment. It was like being given a wish by a genie; so many possibilities rushed into his head that he had to struggle to choose the best one.

Finally, he said, "When I first met you, where were you going, and why were you able to just pick up and run off with me like you did?"

"That's more like two questions put together, but okay. I

+ 38 +

was going to meet someone else who was also being chased, but you were more interesting." Eunice rolled over on her belly and winked at him. "As for the other part of your question, I was able to pick up and run off with you because I lost everything and everyone I loved a long time ago, and now I have nothing and no one to slow me down."

Idea stared at Eunice as her words sunk in. As he considered and reconsidered what she'd said, he began to feel funny. His stomach clenched and twisted. In spite of the campfire's heat, he began to feel a chill.

Sick feelings rose up in him, and he recognized them. He'd experienced these symptoms before, and he knew what caused them.

Idea rubbed the three moles on his left cheek with the tip of his index finger, the way he always did when he felt like this. "So what you're saying is that you were meeting someone else who was being chased for some reason when I just *happened* to bump into you?"

Eunice boosted herself up on her elbows and grinned at him. "Ding, ding, ding! That's exactly right! You were paying attention!"

"That's quite a coincidence." Suddenly, although he was out in the open under an infinite starry sky, he felt as if walls were closing in around him. He jumped to his feet and paced back and forth in the sand.

The chill he felt continued to grow, and his stomach continued to twist in knots. A dizzy nausea oozed into his head, making him weave and stumble.

"What is it?" Eunice pushed herself to her knees on the sleeping bag. "What's wrong?"

Idea stopped, bent over, and planted his hands on his knees. "Did you ever feel . . . like someone else is pulling your strings?"

Eunice got to her feet and went to him. "Like God, you mean?"

He shook his head. "It's like you think you're doing things because *you* want to . . . but it's only because someone else *makes* you want to. Someone controls your every move." Idea gulped deep breaths, trying to calm himself down. "Maybe . . . yeah, maybe it *is* God . . . and ninety-nine percent of the time, you don't even notice. But then once in a while you *feel* it . . . and it's the *worst* feeling in the world."

"Sounds like you're having an anxiety attack." Eunice lightly touched his shoulder.

"Not just . . . an anxiety attack," Idea said. "They named it . . . after me."

"Named what after you?"

"This disease," said Idea. "The doctors named it . . . Deity Syndrome. I'm the first person diagnosed with it, so they named it after me."

"Come on and sit down." Eunice took his hand and pulled him toward the sleeping bag.

Idea let her guide him. "It's too much of a coincidence. I'm running from someone, and I meet you, just when they're closing in on me. You just *happen* to be looking for someone else . . . who's on the run, too."

Eunice helped him sit down on the sleeping bag and kneeled

beside him. "Try to relax." She pressed the back of her hand to Idea's forehead, as if she were feeling for a fever.

"What are the chances?" Idea tipped his head back and looked up at the starry sky. "How stupid do you think I *am?* I *know* you're using me!"

He glared upward for another moment, then let Eunice help him lie back on the sleeping bag. He closed his eyes, slung an arm over his face, and tried to get control of his shallow, quick breathing.

After a few minutes, he began to feel better. The nausea and chills eased, and the ache in the pit of his stomach began to subside. He lifted his arm from over his eyes and smiled weakly up at Eunice.

"Could you get the book from my backpack?" he asked. "I'd just like to lie here and read for a little while."

"Sure." Eunice retrieved the thick paperback from Idea's pack. She read the title before handing it to him. "*Fireskull's Revenant*. Any good?"

"I can hardly put it down." Idea pulled his phone out of his pocket, switched it on, and opened an app that made the screen glow with enough light for him to read by. Then he opened the paperback to a dog-eared page and waved the book at Eunice. "This is what Deity Syndrome's all about, you know."

"How so?"

Idea met Eunice's gaze and recited from memory a passage from a medical textbook. "'Multisystemic symptoms resulting from a psychosomatic manifestation of the unshakable fear that the patient is a character in a novel.

"'Psychological complex may include the conviction that an omnipotent author has doomed the patient/character to die in the novel in which he appears.'"

"Hmm." Eunice cocked her head and frowned. "So what's this novel about? The one you're a character in?"

"I don't know. All I know for sure is that it's not *Fireskull's Revenant*." He raised the book to read by the light from his phone. "Or maybe I just haven't gotten to that part yet."

CHAPTER FORTY

WHEN Highcast had finished delivering his prophecy to Johnny Without, Johnny had his aide, Shut Stepthroat, throw him out of Castle Vanish.

Although Shut did not argue with Johnny in front of the prophet, he spoke up when he returned to the throne room. "My lord." Shut's towering blocky body stood at stiff attention in the middle of the vast chamber. "I have heard that Highcast is an authentic prophet."

Johnny looked up from the ancient dusty book in his lap. As always, thanks to Fireskull's theft of the Talisman of Integrity, the parts of Johnny's body changed shape often, remaining constantly out of synch. One moment his amber eyes were magnified compared to the rest of his face; then one arm was slightly larger than the other, one leg much smaller than its partner. Looking at him was like looking through a patchwork magnifying lens, with his head, torso, and limbs all seen at different degrees of enlargement or reduction.

Johnny wore a white tunic and bottoms that were loose enough to stay out of the way of his body's changes ...

usually. As forgiving as the clothes were, they still bore rips and tears from his more extreme and sudden shape shifts.

"Clearly, he is working for Fireskull." Johnny's voice, like the rest of him, was fragmented. Each syllable sounded as if it had been spoken by a different person, jumping from bass to soprano to whisper to shout to child to adult to woman to man. "He wants to buy time to rebuild his forces by discouraging us from attacking."

"Humbly, I offer a question, my lord," said Shut. "What if his prophecy is true?"

"*My* world already ended the *first* time I met Fireskull face-to-face," said Johnny. "When he stole the talisman and lost my sons in the distant future."

"But if there is even a chance that Highcast is right . . ."

"Why would he wait until now to tell us?" Johnny asked. "Why not warn us *before* the huge battle in which there were who knows how many close calls of Fireskull and me bumping into each other?"

Shut shrugged. "Maybe he didn't have the vision in time to get here before the battle."

Johnny shook his head. With each shake, one side of his face ballooned as if passing through a bubble of magnification, then popped back to its original size.

"Remember the last time someone told us a prophecy?"

Johnny raised an eyebrow, which swelled and skated up off his forehead.

Shut sighed. "The Lady Acrimony."

"And how did things turn out when we listened to what *she* said?"

"We were fed to sky sharks," Shut replied.

"And what else?" Johnny asked.

"Your subjects were turned to stone."

"By whom?" Johnny glared.

Shut flushed with embarrassment and shuffled his feet on the red carpet. "The Lady Acrimony." He dropped his voice and turned away as he spoke.

Johnny slammed the book shut. "Case in point. The moral of the story is do not always listen to prophets."

"But we're talking about the end of the world here," said Shut. "Maybe it would not hurt to err on the side of caution this time."

Johnny tossed the heavy book aside, and it hit the marble floor with a satisfying *thoom*. "Look," he said. "If you can figure out a way to retrieve my sons and my talisman and destroy Fireskull without involving me, maybe I'll never again have to meet him face-to-face and bring on Boomsday. So gather up the war council and get cracking!"

Shut nodded. "Yes, lord." He bowed deeply. "Thank you, lord." Then, he spun and marched briskly out of the room, leaving Johnny on his own.

It was only then that Johnny could relax completely and slump down into his throne. It was only then that he could allow the weight of Highcast's prophecy to press upon him like a giant thumb. Because, truthfully, Johnny was not as sure that the prophecy was a lie as he had led Shut to believe.

Highcast had said things that implied supernatural insight, referring to facts that only Johnny could possibly have known.

Johnny was certain that the comments had gone right over Shut's head, as he could not have known what to make of them. Johnny, however, had recognized the significance of each one.

No one but Johnny, for example, knew that he and Fireskull were distant cousins; not even Fireskull knew that. Highcast, however, had mentioned Johnny's struggles against his "cousin next door."

No one but Johnny knew that some of the soldiers defending his kingdom were illusions, but Highcast had referred to Johnny's "mirage warriors."

And no one but Johnny knew that he had given up his sons to save his kingdom. Not even Fireskull knew that Johnny had sacrificed them voluntarily—giving up two lives for five thousand—but Highcast had begged him to abandon his plans for revenge on Fireskull, just as he had "let those children go for the good of the kingdom."

So, contrary to what Johnny had told Shut, he did not really reject Highcast's prophecy as an outright lie.

The problem was, in order to comply with the prophecy's restrictions, Johnny would have to abandon his sole purpose in life. In other words, he would not be able to tear the talisman from Fireskull's throat—the only way that he could restore his body to an undistorted state—and he would not be able to use torture to compel Fireskull to return his sons from the time warp. Contrary to what Johnny had told Shut, both tasks required Johnny and Fireskull to meet face-to-face. And according to Highcast, that would set Boomsday in motion and end the world.

For decades, the only things that had kept Johnny going were thoughts of restoring his body, retrieving his children, and personally making Fireskull suffer. After all the years of sacrifice, he could hardly imagine giving up on those goals.

Still, Johnny could not deny that it would be wise to proceed with caution. Highcast had given him enough reason to suspect that the prophecy had some truth to it. Saving his sons and restoring his natural form would not do him much good if in the process he destroyed the world and himself along with it.

Johnny had been planning a daring new strike at the heart of his enemy's stronghold, following up on the battle just concluded. After hearing Highcast's prophecy, however, he would postpone the planned strike at Fireskull and his Unrepentant Kingdom. Perhaps he could even turn the change in plan to his eventual advantage.

Meanwhile, he would try to think of a way around the prophecy. Maybe, if he inhabited another person's physical form or altered himself in some way, he could still face Fireskull without triggering Boomsday. Better yet, perhaps an investigation of Highcast's word would cast doubt on its accuracy and untie Johnny's hands altogether.

To pursue these avenues, he would need magic, which only one adept in all his kingdom could wield. He would need to turn to the sorceress.

He sprang from his throne and marched across the chamber. As he walked, one foot became enormous—as big as a leg—while the other foot grew and shrank and spun around all at the same time.

"Shut!" He flung open the door to the room where the war council was meeting. "Bring me the witch! Bring me Scrier Inevitas!"

EIGHT

REACHER

REACHER barely looked up when Eurydice walked in the door of his motel room. He was busy writing a song for his rock opera, *Singularity City,* alternately strumming chords on his acoustic guitar and scribbling in a notebook on one of the twin beds.

"Lunch is served." She dropped onto the other bed and plunked a bag of fast food down beside her. "I'm starving."

"Thanks, Eury." Reacher was hungry, too. The band had driven twelve hours from the last hotel, where Hiya Permaneck had almost caught up with them. They'd stopped only once, five hours in, for gas and vending machine junk food.

"Please remember to tip your waitress," Eurydice said with a wink. "The lyrics you're looking for are 'Eurydice, Eurydice. She is the perfect woman.'"

"Okay, yeah," said Reacher. "Let me see if I've got that." Strumming his fingers over the guitar strings, he smiled beatifically and sang, *"Eurydice, Eurydice. Her middle name's insanity."*

Eurydice opened the fast food bag and pulled out a french fry. "Just for that, you don't get any of these."

"Well, if you don't give me any fries," Reacher said, "I *will* write a song about you."

"Anything but that!"

"Maybe I've already written one," he continued. "Maybe I'm saving it for when Youforia goes public."

"You better watch it," said Eurydice. "I might start pushing for the band *never* to go public."

Reacher sighed and strummed the guitar. "At the rate we're going, there's not much chance of that, what with the website posting our secrets and Hiya Permaneck chasing us around and everyone in the band ready to string me up if I don't give the go-ahead."

"Don't let them rush you."

"I just don't want the band out there till we're ready. Till *I'm* ready," said Reacher. "I don't want to fail. I don't want to fall apart onstage in front of everyone."

Eurydice nibbled a french fry and sucked soda from the straw in her fast food paper cup. "So when will you know if you're ready?"

He strummed a chord and stared at the floor. "I'm waiting for that magic feeling. Chills up my spine. Like, we're in the middle of a practice, and I'll get this feeling and I'll just *know*. I'll know I'll never have to wear a mask again. I'll be able to play in front of people as myself, and they'll accept me for who I am."

"But you're not getting that feeling yet?" Eurydice pulled a dodo bird burger out of the bag and tossed it on the bed beside him. Then, she unwrapped a burger of her own and took a bite.

Reacher shook his head. "Maybe I'm trying too hard to find it. I don't think the others will stick around much longer, so I keep hoping I'll get the feeling and we can go public before everyone quits."

Eurydice finished her burger, then balled up the paper wrapper and threw it at Reacher. The wrapper bounced off his chin and landed in his lap. "You can always make Youforia a duo," she said. "I'm not going to leave you."

"I might just take you up on that." He put his guitar down on the floor, then leaned toward the nightstand to grab the thick raggedy paperback he'd been reading. He flipped through it absently before tossing it aside on the bed. "Or maybe I'll just give up music and be done with it."

Eurydice tilted her head and smiled. "You try it, and I'll kick your butt." Then she snatched a pillow from the bed and walloped him with it.

She got in three swings before Reacher yanked the pillow away from her. He threw it over his shoulder, then grabbed her wrist and pulled her onto the bed with him.

"Why don't you pick on someone your own size?" he said with a grin.

"I'd rather pick on someone I know I can beat," she said. "Like you."

He tickled her, sending her into twitching, giggling spasms. When he stopped, the two of them lay tangled on the bedspread, face-to-face.

Reacher gazed into her eyes. "You crack me up."

Eurydice stroked the white stubble on his scalp. "And you love me because of it."

Both smiling, Reacher and Eurydice drifted together and their lips met. When the long kiss finally ended, they stayed in each other's arms, gazes linked and breathing synchronized.

"Reacher," Eurydice said softly. "You won't fail."

"You make me *feel* like I can do it."

"Your band's already a success, even in disguise, even as a secret. You haven't even introduced yourselves and people already know your name."

"But what if it's all for nothing?" Reacher asked. "What if we let everybody down?"

"You won't." Eurydice caressed his cheek with her fingertips. "Trust me." Her fingernails were painted with yin-yang symbols. On the nails of her right hand, the white half of the symbol was nearest the tip; on the nails of her left hand, the black half was nearest the tip. "You're so talented, and your rock opera is incredible. They're going to love you."

"All my life, people told me I couldn't do anything right," Reacher said.

"And here you are, on the verge of making your dreams come true." Eurydice tweaked the tip of his nose. "I guess they were wrong."

Though they were alone in the room, Reacher dropped his voice to a whisper. "I'm afraid I'll come so close and it'll all fall apart."

"Well, guess what? You know that magic feeling you've

been waiting for with the band? The chills up your spine, and you just *know?*"

Reacher nodded.

"I've had that feeling since the first time I saw you," said Eurydice, and then she kissed him again.

NINE

IDEA

WHEN the girl wearing a T-shirt with the name of Idea's made-up band on it walked by, Idea was happy to see her . . . at first.

He and Eunice sat in a booth at a burger joint west of Cleveland, Ohio, where they'd stopped for lunch. While waiting for their food to arrive, Idea used his phone to work online, updating the band's Yapper feed and posting on YoFace as Wicked Livenbladder.

Across the table, Eunice was working on her own phone. "Time to update my digihoroscope. Gotta input data on the dorks who were chasing you."

"*Are*," corrected Idea. "*Are* chasing me. Chasing *us*. And it's only a matter of time till they catch up."

"Not if we use the digihoroscope," said Eunice. "It's like magic, I'm telling you."

"I could use some magic," he said.

Eunice waved a straw like a magic wand. "Abracadabra! Presto disco!"

It was then that the girl walked in the door of the restaurant.

At first, he didn't pay much attention to her. She was a

skinny redhead who looked like she'd just stepped out of a vat of freckles. Her hair was pulled back in a ponytail, and her glasses had dark red frames. Idea thought she was about the same age as Eunice, seventeen or eighteen.

The redhead wore white pants and a pink T-shirt with YOU printed in bright yellow across the chest. As she walked past, Idea looked back down at his phone.

Eunice's eyes, however, stayed glued to the girl as she walked away. "Did you see that?"

"See what?"

"Turn around," said Eunice. "Look what's on the back of that girl's shirt over there."

Idea twisted around, lifted the bangs out of his eyes with the edge of his hand, and read the letters on the back of the girl's shirt. It took an instant for what he saw to fully register.

Then his heart began to pound and his eyes shot wide open. "The front said *YOU*."

"Plus *FORIA* on the back," added Eunice.

"Equals *YOUFORIA*." As Idea watched, the redhead sat down in a booth across from another girl, a blonde who looked about the same age.

"So is that T-shirt real?" asked Eunice. "Or is it imaginary like your band?"

"Both." Idea turned back around to face her. "It's what you said about this thing taking on a life of its own. I made up this fantasy band, and the next thing I know, people in the real world are wearing T-shirts with the fake band's name on them."

Eunice pretended to hold out a pen and a piece of paper. "Can I have your imaginary autograph?"

"I wonder where she got it." Idea glanced over his shoulder at the redhead. "I wonder who's making them."

"And what else are they making?" Eunice asked. "Imaginary posters? Imaginary ball caps? Imaginary underwear? Is there an entire imaginary factory somewhere, *not* cranking these things out?"

"I have to talk to her." Idea slid across the bench and out of the booth just as the waitress brought their food to the table.

Eunice jumped up and intercepted him a few steps from the redhead's table. "Allow me." She said it with a wink and a smirk, then swooped around him and planted herself smack in front of the two girls.

"Youforia!" Eunice shifted from her usual snarky self to the voice and mannerisms of an excitable teenager. "*Where* did you get that *shirt? Tell* me!"

"Some T-shirt stand at the mall," the redhead said with a friendly smile. "I'm Youforia's *biggest* fan."

"*Second* biggest," said Eunice.

"*Biggest* biggest." The redhead looked around, then leaned toward Eunice and lowered her voice. "Who else do you know with an actual Youforia download on her phone?"

"No *way*," said Eunice.

Suddenly Idea shoved in between Eunice and the redhead. "That's impossible!"

The redhead drew back, looking annoyed. "I downloaded it this morning from this bizarre website. I can't remember the address, but it's called Talisman-something. The site comes and goes, so you can't always find it."

"It's an actual track by Youforia?" Eunice asked.

The redhead nodded smugly. "It's called 'Chapter 64.'" She raised her phone and tapped a few onscreen controls.

Idea felt a twinge of Deity Syndrome but forced it down. "Not possible. It must be someone claiming to be Youforia."

"It's *Youforia* claiming to be Youforia," said the redhead. "And this song is *unbelievable*."

"I'm telling you, it *can't* be them." The more Idea thought about it, the easier it became to replace the panic of Deity Syndrome with rising anger. "Someone's taking all of Youforia's hard work and name recognition and *stealing* it by calling themselves Youforia."

The redhead looked at her blond friend and sighed. "Here." She held out her ear buds to Idea and Eunice. "Listen for yourself."

Eunice and Idea each took a bud. As they placed them in their ears, the redhead tapped her phone's screen.

Idea's eyes widened. Eunice bobbed her head along with the beat of the song.

The redhead and her friend shared a laugh at their expense.

"See?" said the redhead. "*Now* who's the biggest fan?"

An hour later, Idea and Eunice were back on the highway. They were still listening to the song, which the redhead had sent to Idea's phone.

And Idea was brooding. As Eunice drove onward, he glared out the window in silence.

Eunice made a game of trying to draw him out, with no success. "I'm going to pull over and rip off all my clothes now. What do you think of that, Pat?"

When that didn't get a rise out of him, she tried this: "I'm secretly an eccentric billionaire, and I'll give you a million dollars in cash *right now* if you'll just tell me what you plan to spend it on."

That didn't work, either. She tried again.

"So does this mean you liked the song or hated it? I thought maybe you'd be happy that your made-up band was taking on even more of a life of its own."

Idea didn't say a word. "Chapter 64" continued to play.

He couldn't decide whether he was more angry, worried, or amazed. Angry because someone out there was taking advantage of all his hard work, and not just to sell a few T-shirts. Worried because the title, "Chapter 64," had an ominous ring that fit right in with his Deity Syndrome fears of being stuck in a novel.

Amazed because the band he was listening to sounded *exactly* the way he'd always imagined Youforia would sound.

TEN

REACHER

IT wasn't enough for Gail Virtuoso to quit playing her drums in the middle of Reacher's new song. Apparently, the only way she could adequately express her feelings about it was to kick over half of her drum kit and throw her drumsticks across the barn where Youforia was practicing.

"I can't play this piece of suckage!" she yelled. "What the hell is 'Chapter 64' supposed to *mean,* anyway?"

"I already told you," Reacher replied. "It's part of the rock opera. The main character, Impulse Devilcare, thinks he's trapped in a book, and he's doomed to die in Chapter 64."

"But you never *mention* Chapter 64 in the damn lyrics," said Wicked Livenbladder, flopping his shaggy mane around as he shook his head.

"That's because Impulse wants to be in any chapter other than 64," explained Reacher. "He imagines himself jumping through chapters out of sequence to avoid Chapter 64. Then, he imagines jumping out of the book he thinks he's in and jumping into another one, where he won't die at all."

"A *book* song!" Gail marched out from behind the parts of

her drum kit that were still standing. "Now, *that'll* get the teenagers worked up on the dance floor."

"It's not really about books, though," Reacher said as Gail stomped past. "It's about God and fate and life. Impulse is like a god, because he creates this world of his own on the Internet, right? But he's still at the mercy of *the* God in the *real* world. Impulse wants to write his own life, but forces beyond his control won't let him."

Gail spun to face him. "Oh, Reacher, your song is just so *deep* and *meaningful*."

Chick Sintensity plucked some notes on his bass guitar and laughed. "Eurydice seems okay with it, Gail. Or doesn't the *Reacher-stealer's* opinion count?"

Gail glared across the barn at Eurydice, who was sitting on a hay bale, watching and listening. "It's not stealing if you take what somebody else already threw away."

"Oooo." Wicked grinned at Reacher. "She just called you garbage, man!"

Suddenly Reacher stuck two fingers in his mouth and let loose a shrill whistle. Everyone fell silent and looked at him.

"We've only got the barn rented for another hour," he said. "I still think the song'll grow on you, Gail, but let's take a vote. Who wants to quit rehearsing songs and just jam for an hour?" Reacher raised his hand.

Wicked's hand shot up, too, followed by Chick's.

Gail glared at them for a moment with arms folded across her chest. She cast her vote by stomping back to her drum kit and picking up the pieces that she'd kicked over.

"All right, then." Reacher smiled, and the star-shaped port-wine stain on his right cheek dented into a crescent. "When in doubt, jam."

Wicked churned out a wild lick on his guitar. "Jam early and often!"

Chick hammered the strings of his bass. "Make jams, not war!"

Gail pounded out a thundering beat on the kick drum. *"Shut up and play!"*

Sty Latherclad nodded at Eurydice on his way into the barn, then stopped in front of the band and pointed at his wristwatch.

Youforia was in the middle of a careening jam and kept at it for another minute before winding down. Chick dropped out first, then Wicked, then Reacher. Gail got in the last word with one more full-throttle blast across her drums.

"Yeah!" Wicked unplugged his guitar from an amp. "*There's* the fun part!"

"I was wondering where it ran off to," said Chick as he packed his bass in its case.

Sty cleared his throat loudly. "I've got news."

"Let me guess," said Wicked. "They're charting my bowel movements on the website."

Chick laughed. "We've been nominated for best nonexistent band, nonexistent record of the year, and best nonperformance in a nonexistent category."

"None of the above," said Sty. "You have a *price* on your heads."

Reacher scowled as he adjusted his red and black bowling shirt with a shrug of his shoulders. "You're kidding."

Sty held up a magazine. "*Tuned* has posted a reward for your capture. They'll pay fifty thousand dollars to anyone who delivers the whole band. Individually, each of you is worth ten grand . . . except Reacher, who's worth fifteen."

"Unbelievable." Reacher took the magazine from Sty and stared at the page it was folded open to.

"I could really use that ten K." Wicked cast an evil look in Chick's direction. "Could you step outside and help me with something, Chick old pal?"

"Only if I can bring that there pitchfork."

"Whoa," said Gail. "We really *have* hit the big time. What will people do when we go public?"

"Speaking of which"—Sty locked eyes with Reacher—"I think it's time."

"You've been saying that since last Junuary." Reacher slapped the magazine against Sty's chest. "This doesn't change anything."

Wicked and Gail laughed out loud. Chick winced.

"You're kidding, right?" said Gail. "Everybody and their cousin's uncle's *grandniece* will be out looking for us now!"

"Hiya Permaneck isn't the only one chasing you anymore," Sty agreed. "The band has been outed. Secrecy is no longer an option."

Eurydice cracked her gum loudly. "That's not entirely true." She boosted herself off the hay bale and walked over to join the others. "The only pictures they have of you are the artist's renderings on the website, which suck. As long as you don't walk around wearing T-shirts with 'I'm in Youforia' printed on them, no one will know who you are."

"The van's been described on the website," said Sty. "And whoever's been feeding information to the site keeps leaking our whereabouts."

"Not always," said Reacher. "This barn seems to be off the radar. No one's found us here yet."

"It's *time*," Sty insisted. "How's this for a photo opportunity? For their first official public appearance, the members of Youforia turn themselves in for the reward!"

Reacher walked away from the group and began coiling microphone cables. "It's not time yet."

"They're going to get us!" said Gail. "Isn't it better to go public while we have a choice, rather than be hauled in by some moron with a gun?"

Sty left the group and stood in front of Reacher. "I'm telling you, it's *time*. This is a real no-brainer."

Reacher looked around at everyone and nodded. "If the rest of you want to do this, be my guest. That's your call. But I won't go with you. Not yet. I'm going to see this thing through."

Sty shook his head. "This *is* the 'thing.' This is how it's *supposed* to work out. Now that you've been on your secret tour for a year, you take your secret band and go public in the most attention-getting way possible."

Reacher glared at him with icy contempt. "Is *that* how it's supposed to work? Thanks for explaining it to us, Sty."

Chick stepped forward, rubbing his chin. "You really think this'll get us big-time attention?"

"How much more attention-getting can you get?" Sty continued. "And it's all being handed to you! Free buzz, man! Do you know how hard that is to come by?"

"What's the problem here?" said Reacher. "I already told you to do what you want."

"We need everybody," said Sty. "The whole band."

"No, you don't," Reacher replied. "Chick can sing. Let *him* be your lead singer."

"No way, man," said Chick. "This is your band, Reacher. Your *dream*."

Reacher smirked. "Well whatta you know? Somebody remembered."

Sty snorted. "Yeah, great. Like no one else has any stake in this. Like none of us has anything to lose when you let your dream shrivel up and die because you're too scared of *failure* to put it out there! Because you're too scared to perform in front of an audience without a *mask* on."

"Maybe if we worried less about going public and more about the music, we'd be ready by now," said Reacher.

Sty laughed humorlessly. "Here's something to think about, gang." He looked around at the members of Youforia. "Maybe he's more afraid of *not* failing. Maybe the band's been ready for a while now, and he's holding you back because he's terrified you'll *succeed*."

With that, Sty spun on his heel and marched straight out of the barn under a sky that was the perfect shade of emerald.

ELEVEN

IDEA

"**SINCE** when are you the boss of me?" Eunice Truant asked as she drove her Beetle down a street in Chicago, under the bright blue morning sky.

"Left at the stoplight." Idea watched their progress on a GPS app on his phone. "Then a quick right on Lincoln."

All he could think about were the tickets they were on their way to buy. Somewhere between Cleveland and Chicago, he'd found them online. He *had* to check them out, since they were tickets to an impossible show.

No way could Youforia be playing a concert anywhere but in his imagination.

Unfortunately, Eunice didn't seem to be as interested in the impossible tickets. She grumbled and sighed as he called out directions.

"Remind me again why we're doing this?" she said. "Obviously, the guy selling the supposed tickets is a con artist. Wouldn't it be more important—"

"Left here," Idea interrupted. "Then go three blocks and make a right."

+ 65 +

"Wouldn't it be more important for us to stop your parents from killing themselves?"

"Uh-huh." Idea leaned forward to stare out the front window with the fixed attentiveness of a kid on the way to a toy store.

"Then, why are we doing this right now?"

"Don't worry about it," said Idea. "Make a right."

Eunice turned, then slowed to a stop behind cars waiting at the red light. "Let's see." She raised her hands, palms up, as if they were the trays of a scale. "Parents"—she wiggled the fingers of her right hand—"versus supposed tickets to a Youforia show." Her left hand shot downward while her right stayed up. "What was I thinking? Of *course* bogus Youforia tickets outweigh your mom and dad."

Idea poked an index finger between the two dice on the chest of his black T-shirt. "Someone's trying to make money from *my* hard work."

"Hard work fooling people with a phony band, you mean?"

Idea glared. "This guy's either ripping people off by selling tickets to a nonexistent concert, or he's selling tickets to a show by a band calling themselves Youforia. Maybe the same band that cut that phony 'Chapter 64' track."

The light turned green and Eunice rolled the Beetle forward. "A nonexistent concert. I wonder if the tickets are nonexistent, too."

Idea checked the GPS map on his phone's screen, then pointed ahead. "There it is. That's the place."

+ + +

"Bud System?" Idea said as the apartment door opened.

A fat man with messy brown hair and a bushy beard to match looked out at them. He wore stained red sweatpants and a white T-shirt with a spaceship on the chest. "What do you want?" He frowned briefly at Idea but reserved most of his attention for Eunice.

"We're here about the Youforia tickets," Idea said.

Immediately Bud brightened. "Tickie-tickies." He turned his back on them and walked into the apartment. "Why didn't you say so?"

"Actually, he just did," said Eunice, but Bud either ignored or missed her comment and disappeared through a doorway.

Idea took two steps forward and looked around. Although Bud's personal appearance was sloppy, his apartment was immaculate. His living room sparkled right down to the last dust-free figurine on his bookshelves.

"Where did you find these tickets, anyway?" Idea took another step forward. A figurine in a curio cabinet across the room had caught his eye and he wanted to get a closer look at it.

"I saw an ad in a magazine." Bud lumbered back into the living room with a white business envelope in his hand. "I sent a check to a post office box, and the tickies came a few days later."

At that moment, Idea was only half listening. The figurine on the top shelf of the curio cabinet had come fully into focus; it was a painted sculpture of a man clad in black leather whose head was engulfed in flames.

"Fireskull." Idea pointed at the figurine.

"Oh, yeah," said Bud. "I love that book."

Eunice cleared her throat and gestured at Bud's envelope. "Are those the tickets?"

Bud frowned as he looked her over. "Yeparooni." He untucked the flap of the envelope and tugged out two tickets without taking his eyes off her. "Here be me beauties."

Idea reached for the tickets, but Bud pulled them away. "No touchy-touchy till you give me greeny-greenies."

Idea lowered his hands, and Bud eased the tickets forward. Everything about them looked authentic, from the typeface and logos to the background holograms. What most fascinated Idea, though, was the name of the star attraction printed in large type in the middle of the ticket.

He lifted his bangs with the edge of his hand so he could be sure of what he was seeing. "Youforia," he said, and then he read what was printed below. "'Stowe Amphitheater, Maysville, Pennsyltucky. Seven p.m.'" He frowned. "Where's Pennsyltucky?"

"Look at the date." Eunice squeezed in beside him. "Saturday, July thirty-second?"

Idea read it for himself. "I think you've been scammed, Bud."

"What kind of Youforia fan *are* you?" scoffed Bud. "That's the date they've been advertising all along. They always have to give things a twist."

"Yeah, okay," Idea said irritably. "I guess I'm not a *true* fan of Youforia. It's not like I followed them from the start or anything."

Eunice elbowed him in the side. "It must just be a clever way of saying the show's on August first. The day after July thirty-first."

"You ordered these through a post office box?" Idea asked. "What city and state?"

Bud chuckled. "I don't know how they did it, but it was pretty cool." With a flourish, he held up the white envelope, tapping a finger on the return address.

"'PO Box sixty-four,'" read Eunice. "'Gauntlet, Oklarado.'"

"'Oklarado'?" Idea repeated.

Bud laughed. "I *know!* How would the postal service even *deliver* something like that? And look at the cancellation stamp. The state abbreviation is OO, as in Oklarado. Apparently there's a post office in a state I never even knew existed!"

"So much for finding whoever's making the tickets," said Eunice. "Tickets to see a nonexistent band were mailed from a nonexistent state."

"Box sixty-four," said Idea. "Like that song 'Chapter 64.'"

"Anyway," said Bud. "The tickies are three hundred fifty bucks apiece, and you *know* that's a bargain. This is Youforia's big debut show, their first official concert ever."

"Thanks, anyway," said Idea. "Not interested."

"How 'bout three hundred apiece, then?" said Bud.

"Save them for a true fan."

Idea sat on the steps in front of Bud's apartment building and tapped away on his phone, adding text to Youforia's website. His fingers flew over the keypad with a speed born of anger, throwing down a storm of thoughts as fast as they came to him.

Eunice watched over his shoulder, reading the text as it

flowed onto the screen. "Look at *you*. Is this national Burn Your Bridges Day or something?"

Idea's only answer was an annoyed nod as he kept typing.

"I mean, this will be the end of your make-believe band," said Eunice. "People will know the truth about Youforia."

. . . like to thank everyone for their interest and support, typed Idea. The most important thing I've learned from all this is how the Internet can enable us to share a dream and make it a reality . . .

Revealing the truth about Youforia was *exactly* what Idea had in mind. As proud as he was of the hoax he'd created, he now believed the time was right for him to confess online and thwart the opportunists who were taking advantage of his brainchild.

Idea had decided to end the charade after seeing Bud's tickets and realizing that people were cashing in on the buzz he'd generated, making hundreds of dollars a pop on phony tickets, or tickets to see a band of impostors.

And please don't be fooled by anyone claiming to be Youforia, typed Idea. There is no Youforia!

Youforia only exists on this website and in my imagination. If you hear music by a band calling themselves Youforia, it's fake. If someone tries to sell you tickets to a concert by Youforia, that band is not Youforia!

If anyone tries to trick you or rip you off by selling Youforia merchandise or claiming to be Youforia, please contact me at the e-mail address on this home page.

From now on, instead of featuring news, information, and chat about Youforia, this website will be dedicated to exposing frauds related to the imaginary band.

"Now, there's an interesting twist," Eunice commented. "Creating the fake band was kind of a fraud in the first place, wasn't it?"

. . . and I will travel to Maysville, Kentucky, on the date of the supposed debut concert, to confront the individuals who stole the name of my creation . . . if, in fact, a band shows up to play there at all.

"Wait a minute." Eunice's voice quickly shifted from teasing to serious. "I thought it was Maysville, *Pennsyl*tucky."

"No such place," muttered Idea. "But there's a Maysville, Kentucky, according to the GPS."

In this way, I hope to put an end to the lies and abuses that have become associated with Youforia.

"We're going to Maysville on July thirty-second? But that's two days from now," said Eunice. "What about your parents?"

Idea ignored her. To anyone who has suffered because of the thieves and impostors who have exploited my well-intentioned creation, I apologize.

"I thought we had to hurry to San Diego to stop your mom and dad from killing themselves," said Eunice. "Kentucky's kind of out of our way, isn't it?"

I will try to make it up to you. And maybe someday, if there is enough interest, Youforia will return in a new incarnation. Yours truly, Idea Deity.

+ + +

As the green VW Beetle rolled down the interstate, headed southeast toward Indianapolis—and Kentucky beyond—Eunice punched Idea in the arm.

"Hey!" Idea grabbed his bicep. "What'd you do *that* for?"

"Here's the deal, Big Wheel," said Eunice. "Do I seem like the kind of girl who likes a good mystery?"

Idea stared at her, wondering if she was going to hit him again if he said the wrong thing. "Yeah. Sure."

"Good guess." Eunice smiled. Then, her smile snapped into a scowl. "I am *not*, however, a fan of bullshit. Being lied to is *not* a turn-on for me.

"So here's the thing. If you want me to keep driving to Kentucky, you're gonna have to tell me why all of a sudden it's okay for us to take this big detour instead of getting to San Diego as fast as possible."

Idea rubbed his arm and watched her for a moment. Then he blew out his breath and threw his hands in the air. "All right. You got me."

"How so?" Eunice asked.

"My mom and dad aren't going to kill themselves on the Internet. Okay? Now can I read my book for a while?" He grabbed his copy of *Fireskull's Revenant* from the dashboard and opened it to the page that he'd dog-eared to mark his place.

Eunice's hand darted over and plucked the book from his grip. "We're not done yet. If your parents aren't going to kill themselves and they're not trying to stop you from stopping them, then why are those guys chasing you?"

Idea looked out the side window. His original, made-up

story was much more interesting than the truth, he thought. He was afraid Eunice wouldn't be as impressed by the truth, but he realized he had to tell her or risk losing her help, along with whatever chance he might have to get closer to her.

He sighed. "They aren't trying to keep me from my parents; I ran away from home and those guys are trying to take me back."

"Much better." Eunice sniffed loudly. "Now *that* has the whiff of truth to it."

"Well, enjoy it. I'm done talking." With that, Idea snatched *Fireskull's Revenant* back and folded it open. As Eunice returned her full attention to the road and kept the car rolling, he started reading again.

CHAPTER FORTY-ONE

T would have been inappropriate in the presence of a witch, but Johnny Without was seized by an urge to laugh as Scrier Inevitas delivered her warning.

She floated in front of him, her diaphanous white gown flowing and rippling as if she were underwater. "Your only chance for survival is to join with your neighbor. You must combine your forces, else both your kingdoms shall be lost."

Johnny shook his head. "Damned if I do," he said, his voice changing with every syllable, "damned if I do something else." As his head turned from side to side, it distorted, compressing and stretching into a ceiling-high vertical bar when it turned right, then flattening out like a plank on his shoulders when it turned left.

With a sigh, he slumped on the throne. His arms swelled to the size of tree trunks, and his legs became as tiny as fingers. "No offense, Scrier, but when are you going to bring me some *good* news for a change?"

Scrier hung in midair and said nothing. As often as her guidance had helped him, Johnny never had the feeling that she cared if he lived, died, or turned into a shower of confetti. The only expression that he had ever seen on her face was one of disinterest, as if even the small amount of attention that she paid to him was barely worth the effort.

It was probably better that way, though. Her impartiality seemed to guarantee that her predictions were truthful.

Still, her latest offering seemed pretty hard to believe. Stacked up alongside Highcast's Boomsday prophecy, it was especially disturbing.

According to Highcast, the world would end if Johnny and Fireskull came face-to-face. Scrier, on the other hand, claimed that Johnny's kingdom would be lost if he did *not* join Fireskull.

It was enough to make Johnny's head spin. Actually, his head *did* spin when he tilted it to one side and back again, staring at Scrier.

"Sorceress," he said. "I have heard a prophecy that the world will be destroyed if Fireskull and I should meet. How am I to know what to believe?"

"The prophecy is a sham." Scrier's voice sounded like it was engulfed by rushing winds. "It was meant to keep you from your destiny."

Johnny liked what the witch was telling him. Highcast's prophecy would have kept him from fulfilling his mission in life. "My destiny is to rip the Talisman of Integrity from Fireskull's throat and force him to bring back my sons from the future. My destiny is to retrieve all that I have lost."

"Among other things," said Scrier.

Johnny had folded his arms over his chest. When he unfolded them, his right arm was where his left should have been, and vice versa. . . . But he was distracted and did not notice.

For him, the question of whom to believe required little consideration. Time and again, Scrier's predictions had proven flawlessly accurate, and her advice had been excellent. Further, Johnny liked the repercussions of what she had to say far more than what Highcast had prophesied.

He liked *most* of the repercussions, anyway. One thing did bother him, and made him wonder if he might have been better off believing Highcast's take on the future.

"Joining forces with Fireskull." Johnny rubbed his chin with fingers that had suddenly become stacks of flesh-colored cubes. "I do not know if I can do that, after all that has happened between us. I cannot see *him* doing it, either."

"It is time to change," said Scrier. "Or perish."

"What if Fireskull does not believe you?" Johnny asked.

"I know how and when the world will end," she said. "And I tell you, it will not end on a so-called Boomsday when you come face-to-face with your enemy neighbor."

"I'm just saying, Fireskull might have me killed before I get too close to him."

Scrier's face darkened. Her black hair whipped, and the roaring wind of her voice grew louder. "Ignore me at your peril. The universe will go on without you."

Johnny held his hands up in front of him, palms facing the witch. One inflated like a knobby balloon the size of his torso, and the other disappeared except for an outline of dim yellow light.

"I need that talisman to stabilize my form," he said. "And I need my sons back. I *want* to believe you."

"You have been warned." With that, Scrier's body started to turn and rise toward the ceiling, spinning faster the higher she got.

Realizing she was about to leave, Johnny rushed out some final questions. "What about the threat to my kingdom?" He raised his voice to reach her as she ascended. "I mean *our* kingdoms. What should we be on the lookout for? What else can we do to prepare?"

Inscrutable as ever, Scrier did not answer. "We shall meet again," was all she said.

With that, she whirled even faster and leaped upward, plunging through the ceiling of the throne room as if it provided no resistance whatsoever. She left behind no trace, no disruption of the solid stone through which she had passed.

Far below, Johnny gazed after her, his eyes drifting slowly apart and sliding off his face. As he stared at the ceiling, he thought of one more question that he would have liked to have asked.

Johnny knew *what* he was supposed to do, but he did not know *when* he was supposed to do it. Did he have hours, days, weeks, or months to forge an alliance with Fireskull? Was the danger to the kingdom so near that he ought to leap into action at that very instant, or did he have enough time to plan and prepare properly?

He sighed. "Just get it over with," he said to himself, rising from the throne and crossing the chamber to find Shut Stepthroat. "The sooner I see Fireskull, the better."

AS his captors bound and gagged him, Reacher found himself wishing that he hadn't left his motel room to get ice.

He knew now that he should have been more careful, but he hadn't taken the price on his head seriously. What were the chances that anyone would pick him out based on the poor likeness posted on the Youforia website and YoFace?

Apparently, the chances were pretty good.

Reacher's luck wasn't *all* bad, though. Instead of ruthless bounty hunters or lowlifes, his captors were five of the most courteous abductors he could imagine.

As they took him from the motel under the dimming light of a deep green sunset, they handled him with care. They gagged him, tied him up, zipped him into a garment bag, and slung him over someone's shoulder. But they seemed to go out of their way not to hurt him.

Even as they captured and whisked him away, they consistently addressed him as either Reacher or Mr. Mirage. They told him what to expect each step of the way, explaining, "Now we're going to take you on the elevator," and, "We're crossing the parking lot now, on the way to our vehicle."

When the five kidnappers had first approached him in the ice machine nook, before they'd taken him prisoner, Reacher had had a chance to take a good look at each of them. He hadn't thought that any of them had looked especially dangerous.

In fact, after the conversation that he had gone to the ice machine to get away from, he felt like he might actually be in friendlier hands with the kidnappers than with his manager and bandmates back in his room.

It had all started with a disagreement over disguises.

Since Reacher was set against going public, and Sty still thought it was long past time for it, Sty had proposed a compromise. To capitalize on the wave of publicity over the bounty on the band members, he'd suggested that the band keep playing gigs in disguise, but under their own name.

"It won't work," Reacher had said as he strummed chords on his acoustic guitar. "As soon as we announce we're Youforia, we'll be mobbed and captured."

"So we don't announce it up front!" Sty's silver hair, which was usually impeccably combed, had gone unruly, and he'd rolled up the sleeves of his dress shirt to the elbows. "We don't tell 'em until after the show!"

"After the first time or two, word will get out," Reacher had said. "People will know."

"But that's a good thing. Once we're out of town and back on the road, we *want* them to know." Sty's voice had gotten progressively louder, and his gestures had become wilder. "Who was that masked band? It was *Youforia*."

"Forget it," Reacher had said. "It'll never work."

"It *will* work," Sty had insisted. "It'll build excitement and let you keep playing in disguise."

"It'll get us caught and turned in for rewards," Reacher had said. "I won't do it."

With that, Sty had stepped up to stand toe to toe with Reacher and glare in his face. For a long moment, Sty had remained silent, teeth clenched, shoulders rising and falling.

And then . . .

"You selfish *jerk!*" Sty had shouted. "How much longer do you think you can keep us all living in your little fantasy world?" His face had turned deep red as he let Reacher have it. "They *trust* you, man! They *believe* in you! Now, when everything's in place for this band to succeed, you won't *let* it!"

"If you feel that strongly about it, succeed without me," Reacher had replied calmly. "I sure won't stop you."

"That's exactly what they *should* do," Sty had said. "But they won't! You're their so-called leader. Too bad you don't know how to *lead.* This buzz you've got right now won't last forever! Are you going to be a man and take advantage of it, or are you going to let down everyone who believes in you? Are you going to get over this messed-up stage fright of yours, or are you going to let it ruin your friends' big chance at fame? Maybe their *only* chance?"

Reacher's face had darkened at that. For most of his life, until Youforia and Eurydice, no one had believed in him at all. "I'm not going to let anyone down," he'd said to Sty, lowering his voice menacingly.

It was then that Sty had jabbed Reacher in the chest with

his finger. "You already have! You're perfectly happy being a coward and a failure, and you're going to drag the rest of us down with you."

Jaw clenched, Reacher had glared at him. Sty's words had cut so deep that he'd wanted more than anything to shut him up with a punch to the chin.

It hadn't helped that no one in the room had come to his defense. Eurydice was out somewhere, and the band members had melted into the wallpaper in a way that had suggested they didn't disagree with Sty. Even Chick, who was always an ally, had remained silent during Sty's tirade.

In that moment, Reacher had felt like they were all ganging up on him. He'd felt trapped, betrayed, resented, and rejected. Worst of all, he'd had a terrible feeling that the others were right and that he was wrong.

Maybe, on another day or in a different world, Reacher would have reacted by talking things over with the band. Perhaps he could have arrived at a compromise and resolved the problem without resorting to violence.

Instead, without a word, he'd shoved Sty out of his way, knocking him backward onto a bed. Then he'd grabbed the ice bucket and stormed out of the room, slamming the door shut so loudly that it had sounded as if it had been dropped ten stories flat into a parking lot.

From there, Reacher had marched to the ice machine nook at the far end of the hall. The kidnappers who'd caught him there just might have done him a favor; he was pretty sure that if he'd gone back to his room, he would have ended up quitting or being thrown out of the band. There might even have been a fistfight.

"We're going to put you in the vehicle now," said one of his captors, a young man. Sure enough, whoever was carrying Reacher lowered him onto what felt like the floor of a vehicle.

Someone got in beside him and tugged down the zipper of the garment bag a few inches. "That'll let in some more air for you." He tried to catch a glimpse of her through the unzipped opening of the bag, but all he could see was dark gray ceiling.

Reacher heard the rear door of the vehicle slam shut. People threw themselves onto seats, and someone started the engine.

"Don't worry a bit," said the girl beside him. "We'll take good care of you." She patted his shoulder through the garment bag. "We're Youforia fans. You know, 'Youfers.'"

More doors slammed shut, and the vehicle started moving.

The girl leaned closer to Reacher and lowered her voice to a whisper. "I'll tell you a secret now. It's *our* secret. The others think they're going to turn you in for the reward . . . but not me. I've got other plans for you, Reacher Mirage."

FOURTEEN

IDEA

"THEY don't believe you?" Eunice frowned from across the table in the shopping mall food court in Indianapolis, Indiana.

Idea closed the Internet browser on his phone and stuffed it in the pocket of his new shirt, a black button-down. He'd just bought it at a store in the mall; his dice T-shirt, which he'd worn for days, had been getting kind of ripe. "I don't think *anyone* believes me."

"They think you're lying about making up Youforia?" said Eunice.

"They think Youforia is real." Idea grabbed his soda from the table and took a sip, gazing down at the people on the ground floor below. He and Eunice had a bird's-eye view from where they were sitting, along the second-floor railing. "I told them the truth about the hoax, and they won't believe me."

"It really took on a life of its own, didn't it?" said Eunice. "It's broken away from you now."

"It's been *stolen,* you mean," said Idea. "Someone took what I created and is cashing in on it."

"Maybe you should stop worrying about it. Just see what it all turns into."

"I can't." Idea looked at her with an expression somewhere between anger and helplessness. "It's like it's part of me. I can't let them ruin it." He sighed, then drank some more soda as he stared back down at the shoppers on the ground floor.

He choked when he spotted familiar faces in the crowd. Most of what he drank went down the wrong pipe, and he started coughing loudly, which was the *last* thing he wanted to do at that moment.

"Are you okay?" Eunice asked.

Idea fought to stifle his hacking. "They found us." Peering between the bars in the railing, he got another look at the men he wished he'd never seen.

One was brown-skinned and big-nosed, with thick black hair that looked like it had been combed with motor oil. The other was a silver-haired executive type with chiseled features and a flashy tailored suit.

"I see them!" said Eunice. "The ones who were chasing you at Niagara Falls."

"Bulab and Scholar." Idea nodded. "I can't let them find me."

Eunice took a quick look around. "Come on." She grabbed his hand.

The two of them jumped up and darted away, leaving their food on the table. Eunice pulled him toward the nearest department store, the one they'd passed through when they'd come in from the parking lot.

"How did they find us?" she said. "Some kind of tracking device?"

Idea pulled out his phone. "They must be watching the website and YoFace. They know we're heading for Maysville."

Eunice dashed through the perfume department, ignoring the saleswomen waving sample atomizers at her. "And they just *happened* to stop at the same mall in Indianapolis? Isn't that a pretty big coincidence?"

"Yes, it is!" He laughed bitterly. "Now do you see why I think I'm trapped in a book?"

Eunice led him to the left, down the aisle through Housewares. "If this *was* a book, what would happen next?"

Idea thought about it. "Bulab and Scholar would see us, I guess. There'd be a dramatic chase scene."

At that moment, Eunice lurched to a sudden stop.

Idea ran right into her. "What the—?"

"Over here!" Without explaining, she hauled him off the walkway, into the women's clothing department. She dragged him behind a circular clothes rack, loaded with short-sleeved tops, and ducked down, pulling him with her.

Idea looked at her and she put an index finger against her lips, signaling for silence. He caught himself before saying a word.

Looking away, she slowly rose behind the rack. She stopped when her eyes were just barely above the level of the clothes.

Idea did the same and instantly realized why she'd bolted. At that very moment, Bulab and Scholar were strolling past, not six feet away. Luckily, they weren't looking in his direction.

But they *did* stop in front of the rack. They stood there,

talking about where to go next . . . and just when Idea thought his heart was going to pound its way out of his chest, they continued walking.

He blew out a sigh of relief. "That was close," he whispered.

Eunice frowned, looking lost in thought. Then she stood up straight. "I'll be right back."

Idea grabbed her elbow. "Get down! They'll see you!"

"I certainly *hope* so." Eunice shook off his hand. "This is a golden opportunity." She cleared her throat and patted her hair. "You stay here, okay? I'll just be a minute."

Idea made another grab for her arm, but she dodged and kept moving. Crouching behind the clothes rack, he watched her march toward Bulab and Scholar.

His stomach twisted as he wondered what she was up to. Was she planning to hand him over in hopes of getting a reward? Maybe he should make a run for it while he still could.

Or maybe she was up to something else altogether.

Eunice pulled a piece of paper and a pen from her pocket and scribbled something down. When she was a few steps from Bulab and Scholar, she spun around. Her eyes met Idea's as she walked backward, away from him, approaching the two men.

Why she was walking backward, Idea couldn't imagine. He became even more baffled when she stopped, and Bulab and Scholar turned to face her.

The two men seemed to listen for a moment to something that she was saying. Idea wondered how she could possibly be saying a thing, since she was facing him and her lips weren't moving.

Bulab said something, then Scholar, and then they both listened some more. Idea couldn't hear a word.

As he watched, Eunice stretched her arm out behind her, holding up the folded slip of paper. Bulab took it from her hand and opened it.

Scholar read over Bulab's shoulder, then said something to Eunice, who shrugged. To Idea, whom she was facing, it looked as if she were shrugging at him . . . but Scholar reacted as if *he* were the focus of her attention. With a frown and a shake of his head, he looked back down at the note in Bulab's hands.

At that point, Eunice waved and started to move away from them, walking forward toward Idea. Scholar asked her a question, and Bulab asked one, too, but her only response was a shrug and a shake of the head, both of which incongruously seemed to be directed at Idea.

As she continued to walk away from them, Bulab said something to Scholar, who nodded. Then, they bolted in the direction of the exit that led to the parking lot.

Eunice grinned as she approached Idea. "Thank you for your applause, ladies and gentlemen. For my next trick, I will saw my lovely assistant, Idea Deity, into fourteen pieces and turn each piece into a white rabbit chewing on the ace of spades."

Idea stood up from behind the clothes rack and stared at her, unable to process what he'd just seen her do. He couldn't quite believe it had happened the way it had seemed to.

"What?" Eunice tilted her head to one side. "What's wrong?"

"I thought you just . . . Did you just . . ." His voice trailed off. He rubbed the triangle of moles on his left cheek with the tip of his index finger.

"Seize a golden opportunity to throw them off your trail?" A hint of a playful smile twitched at the corners of her mouth. "The answer is *yes*."

Idea decided to stick with a part of the incident that at least made sense according to the laws of nature. "The note. What was on the note you gave them?"

"It was from *you*, actually." Eunice grinned. "You told them they'd just missed you. You dared them to try to catch up to you. Oh, and you said they were so colossally incompetent that they make complete morons look like world-class geniuses."

"No wonder they rushed off," said Idea.

"My guess is they'll head for Maysville, Kentucky, since they know from the Youforia website that's where you're going."

"Wait a minute," said Idea. "That *is* where we're going. Why is it good that they're headed for the same place?"

"Maybe they'll get to Maysville first, have a look around, see you're not there, and go someplace else," said Eunice. "At least we'll have a better idea of where they are from now on. We'll know they're up ahead, between us and Maysville, and we can keep an eye out for them."

Idea scowled as he thought it over. "I don't know."

Eunice sighed. "Come with me." She grabbed his arm and pulled him out of the women's clothing department into the main aisle.

As Idea walked behind her, he stared at the face that

was tattooed on the back of her head. He'd mistaken it for a three-dimensional face once, but only for a second when he'd first met her. How could two grown men who'd gotten a good look treat it like the front of a person, right down to *talking* to it?

Eunice led him to the glass double doors of the store. Looking around nervously, he tried to dig in his heels—afraid Bulab and Scholar might see him—but she managed to haul him through the first set of doors, anyway.

Once inside the vestibule, she let go of him. Walking up to the second set of doors, she tapped one yin-yang–painted fingernail on the thick glass. "There they go."

When Idea looked, he saw Bulab and Scholar jogging across the parking lot outside the mall. They jumped into a black BMW, backed it out of its space with a jolt, and sent it hurtling toward the exit.

"See ya later, suckahs," said Eunice.

"Thanks," said Idea. "That's the second time you helped me get away from them."

"All part of the service." Eunice pretended to brush dirt from her hands.

"I just have one question." He hesitated. "How did you—if you were looking at *me*, why were they acting like you were looking at them?"

"Well . . ." Eunice smiled at him with a sheepish expression. "It's like ventriloquism."

"Oh." Idea nodded.

"Only it's not," she added. "And we know who the *real* dummies were."

Idea grimaced in confusion. "Wait a minute—"

But Eunice waved off his questions. "Let's get going."

She herded him out the door, across the parking lot, and into the Beetle before he managed to formulate another question.

"Are you trying to tell me you can talk through the back of your head?" he asked Eunice as she started the car.

The Beetle's tires squealed as she backed it out of its space. "Worry about that later. We've got a Youforia show to catch."

"But—"

Eunice pitched *Fireskull's Revenant* at him, and he caught it.

"Read that," she said as they lurched out of the parking lot onto the street. "We've got a lot of driving to do."

Idea opened the book and started reading, but he was thinking more about Eunice than the story.

CHAPTER FORTY-TWO

FIRESKULL could not believe what he was hearing.

The witch Scrier Inevitas floated in front of him, her diaphanous white gown flowing and rippling as if she were underwater. "Your only chance for survival is to join with your neighbor," she said. "You must combine your forces, else both your kingdoms shall be lost."

Fireskull smiled and raised an index finger. "Excuse me. Did you know that a prophet told me the *world* will end if I do exactly what you're telling me to do?"

Scrier did not answer his question. Her long blond hair waved like fronds of seaweed in a current.

Her eyes were fixed on Fireskull with languid, distant apathy. It was always that way with Scrier; she freely dispensed information but never gave Fireskull the impression that she cared what he did with it, or even cared who he was.

Folding his hands behind his back, he paced a few steps across the stone floor of his enormous throne room.

He gathered his thoughts, then turned on his heel and paced back to the sorceress.

"I called you here for advice on how best to exploit the current state of affairs," he said. "I do not care about mending fences with my worthless neighbor."

"The prophecy you were given is a sham. It was meant to keep you from your destiny."

"And my destiny is to join forces with Johnny Without?"

"Among other things," said Scrier.

Fireskull lowered his head and breathed out a wisp of black smoke. "You must know that Johnny is my mortal enemy. I have sworn never to rest until I have destroyed him and taken back what is mine."

"It is time to change," said Scrier. "Or perish."

"And how can I be sure that Highcast's prophecy is a sham?" said Fireskull.

"I know how and when the world will end," said Scrier. "And I tell you, it will not end on so-called Booms-day when you come face-to-face with your enemy neighbor."

"I suppose I have only your word for it," said Fireskull.

Scrier's hair whipped and snapped like a nest of striking cobras. "Ignore me at your peril. The universe will go on without you."

Fireskull smiled. "That's too bad. I had always hoped it wouldn't."

"You have been warned." With that, Scrier's body began to rotate and drift upward. "We shall meet again." She spun faster and rose higher with each turn.

"See you then!" Fireskull said with a bow. Although he had many more questions, he knew from experience that it was fruitless to try to convince her to stay. "Thank you for your counsel, Sorceress."

As he watched, Scrier launched straight up to the vaulted ceiling and shot through it like an arrow.

When she was gone, Fireskull resumed pacing. He thought about what she had told him, measuring it word for word against what Highcast the prophet had told him.

On the face of it, Scrier's advice went against Fireskull's every desire and instinct, not to mention Highcast's prophecy. Of the two seers, however, Fireskull trusted Scrier more; he had seen her predictions come true again and again.

In addition, the longer he thought about it, the more he came to appreciate Scrier's advice. Although it had at first seemed the opposite of what Fireskull would ever consider doing, he began to see that it could allow him to do *exactly* what he wanted.

"Ilk!" he shouted suddenly, his voice filling the throne room. "Come here!"

Fireskull's chief minister, Ilk Sugarcoat, lunged into the chamber at a dead run, her red robes flapping behind her.

"Your malevolent perfection shall burn away all deception and weakness!" Ilk flung herself to her knees at his feet. "The world awaits your wicked kiss. I mean bliss."

Fireskull tipped his head back and breathed out a jet of golden flame, which for him was like a roar of triumphant laughter. "Rise and obey me, maggot food."

Ilk sprung to her feet and stood there, shivering and panting. She was tiny, barely half as tall as Fireskull, with short red hair and freckles. He had always thought of her as a small dog, jittery and neurotic at the hands of her master and viciously cruel when set loose on a stranger.

"Order General Undercut to mobilize the armies," said Fireskull. "Today we march on the kingdom of Without."

As he snapped out his orders, Fireskull's body rushed with the heat of impending action. For nearly a day, since hearing Highcast's prophecy, he had held back his forces. Now, the way he saw it, Scrier had given him permission to move against Johnny.

"We are putting *everything* into this push," said Fireskull. "I want every able-bodied man, woman, and child in the kingdom armed and marching."

"They shall kill each other for the honor of serving you first and best," said Ilk.

"Hold nothing in reserve," said Fireskull. "We will not leave behind a single arrow, blade, or torch."

Ilk bowed deeply. "Shall I schedule the victory celebration and raise a fresh pike on the castle walls for Johnny's head?"

Fireskull considered her question. He knew better than to tempt fate needlessly, but he had a feeling that after years of stalemate with Johnny, things were finally looking up.

According to Scrier, Highcast's prophecy was a sham and the end of the world was out of the picture. Instead of staying away from Johnny, Fireskull had to join forces with him to fulfill his destiny.

What better way to join forces, Fireskull thought, than to conquer Johnny's kingdom and absorb his military might? After all, Scrier had not specifically forbidden such action.

At least, that was what Fireskull wanted to believe, which was enough to convince him of the outcome of his new war.

Laughing, he thumped Ilk's shoulder with his enormous gauntlet. "Schedule a *month* of celebrations and raise the highest pike in the kingdom! Mark my words! They shall sing epic ballads about our triumph for centuries to come!"

Ilk shivered, gaping up at him with bloodshot eyes.

"D-does that mean you want me to commission the m-minstrel to write a ballad?"

Fireskull walked to the window and gazed out at the landscape, its rolling hills writhing with red-tentacled trees under the bright orange sky. Leaning back, he roared up another jet of flame. "Do it! In fact, tell him to make it an *opera!*"

SIXTEEN

"IDEA Deity? Never heard of him." That was what Reacher said when he heard the name for the first time.

One of his abductors, a girl named Sundra, had just freed him from the garment bag in which he'd been trapped. She'd taken off his gag but hadn't untied his hands, and now she was feeding him a dodo burger in the back of a Tucker van on the move.

"He claims he created Youforia?" Reacher asked between bites.

Sundra was the girl who'd told Reacher she had different plans in mind for him than the other kidnappers did. She was slim, in her early twenties, and had sandy brown hair that reached to her knees. Her fingernails were painted with alternating suns and crescent moons. "What he actually wrote was that Youforia only exists on the website and in his imagination."

Sundra rolled down the paper wrapper and pushed the dodo burger toward Reacher's mouth. Just as he was about to take a bite, the van hit a pothole, jolting the burger out of reach.

She giggled. "Whoops! Let's try again."

This time, Reacher got a bite, a *big* one, squeezing ketchup onto his sky blue, black striped bowling shirt. The dollop landed between the two dominoes embroidered on the left breast of the shirt.

He sat on the floor of the van, leaning against the back seat. He had no idea where they were, since he'd spent most of the trip zipped into a garment bag, but he guessed that they'd been on the road for about two hours.

"This Idea guy said that if you hear music by Youforia, it's not Youforia," said Sundra. "According to him, there *is* no Youforia, so buying tickets to a Youforia concert is just throwing your money away."

"Interesting," said Reacher.

"You better believe it." Sundra held out the burger for him again. "Especially since Youforia's big official public debut concert is set for July thirty-second in Maysville, Pennsyltucky!"

Reacher took another bite and nodded while he chewed.

"There oughtta be some real fireworks," she continued. "Idea posted on the website that he's going to Maysville to confront the impostors posing as Youforia. He said he's going to end the lies."

"If the band doesn't exist," said Reacher, "how can there be impostors? And why would this Idea guy care if there are?"

"He said he doesn't like people exploiting his creation to rip off other people," said Sundra. "They're using Youforia's name in vain."

"*They* are?" Reacher chuckled and shook his head.

Sundra rolled down the dodo burger wrapper to expose the last bits of meat and bun. "The funny part is, since Youforia's a real band, everything this Idea guy says about making it all up is a complete lie, anyway!"

Reacher snapped up the last bite from the wrapper. Sundra lifted a cup of soda from the cardboard takeout tray and moved the straw within reach of his lips.

"Hey, Reacher, man," the van's driver, a guy named Barry, called from the front seat. "Is it true that you're thinking about cutting 'Hieroglyphic Scream-Laugh' and 'Land of the Freak' from the rock opera?"

Reacher was shocked. What Barry was saying was absolutely true, but Reacher had told no one about it.

"Where did you hear that?" he asked.

"A little birdie told me," Barry replied. "A birdie on YoFace, that is."

Reacher frowned. It was impossible that his plans for the rock opera had appeared on YoFace. Even if a band member or someone from the band's inner circle had been feeding facts to an outsider, no one could have leaked this information, for one simple reason.

No one but Reacher himself had known that he was considering the changes.

Another guy was sitting up front, in the passenger seat. His name was Rondo, and he had a nasally voice. "Was Youforia planning to play the *Singularity City* rock opera at the debut show?" he asked. "Before their lead singer got kidnapped, that is?"

Barry laughed. So did the other two kidnappers, Sam and Liz, who were sitting in the back seat, but not Sundra.

"I'm as much in the dark as you are," said Reacher, and he was telling the truth. Until a few moments ago, he hadn't even known that Youforia was supposed to play a debut show in Maysville, Pennsyltucky, on July 32.

"Whatever you say, Reacher," said Rondo. "I know you have to keep the band *secret* and all."

"You really don't have to pretend with us, Mr. Mirage," said Liz. "We know all about Youforia, and we totally love your work."

"Every one of us is a Youfer," said Sam.

Reacher thought for a moment. "If you guys are such fans, why would you want to kidnap Youforia's lead singer right before the band's official debut concert? Wouldn't you want the concert to happen?"

"Sure," said Rondo. "But we're guessing that once *Tuned* magazine is done getting an exclusive interview with you, they'll make sure you get to the show in time."

"Meanwhile, we pocket fifteen thousand dollars," said Barry. "It's a win-win situation."

Reacher sighed and slumped against the seat. In his opinion, the situation was more like win-lose, and he was the loser.

All of his plans were falling apart. He'd sworn not to unveil his secret band to the world until he got the magic feeling that they were ready. But now he was on the verge of being handed over to *Tuned* magazine. Because of the online revelations, Youforia's secrets were widely known; when Reacher was exposed, the fans would have concrete proof of the band's existence.

Unless, of course, Reacher wasn't handed over.

Recalling what Sundra had said earlier, he leaned toward

her and whispered in her ear. "What did you mean when you said you have other plans for me?"

"Nobody's getting a reward," she whispered. "You're not going to *Tuned* magazine."

"Where *am* I going, then?"

"Maysville, Pennsyltucky," said Sundra. "Because there's no guarantee the *Tuned* magazine people will get you to the show on time once they're done with you. You don't think I'm going to let anyone risk ruining the official world debut concert of Youforia, do you?"

"What can I do to help?"

"The only thing that'll get them to risk losing fifteen thousand dollars by untying you," said Sundra. "Tell them the truth about Youforia and offer to play a private show for them."

"Oh," said Reacher. "Is *that* all?"

CHAPTER FORTY-THREE

JOHNNY Without was meeting with his war council, trying to decide how he could cross the border of Fireskull's Unrepentant Kingdom without being killed outright. That was when he first learned of the unexpected attack.

A messenger girl burst into the council chamber without knocking, wide-eyed, sweating, and gasping for breath. "*Invasion!* The Burning . . . Legion!"

The mood in the room immediately darkened. Johnny shot to his feet, as did everyone else around the council table.

"Fireskull is invading?" Johnny hurried to the girl and helped her into a chair. "What of our troops?"

The messenger shook her head. "Not . . . good. Heavy . . . losses. General Fairforce requests reinforcements . . . immediately."

"But the border was already secure," said General Knell. "The line was three men deep from end to end."

"It was," gasped the messenger. "It . . . was."

Everyone in the room took a deep breath at once.

Johnny broke the mood by bringing his fist down hard on the table. "Again he tests us! We men and women of war must fight once more!"

All eyes locked on Johnny. He pounded the table a second time, ignoring the way his fist liquefied when it hit.

"I was told that we would have to ally with Fireskull to save this kingdom." Johnny's shifting voice made every syllable sound like it was spoken by a different person. "In my soul, I knew all along that he could not be trusted. Sure enough, while we planned to offer peace, he attacked us like the night snake that he is.

"But he will not find us lacking!" Johnny hammered the table once more, and his fist shattered like glass. "As often as he has struck at us in the past, we have pushed him away. This time, let us go forth with one common goal. Let us see this as an opportunity to achieve that which we have ever dreamed of!"

Johnny jumped onto a chair and then stepped up onto the council table. "To hell with the prophecies!" He drew his sword from the scabbard at his side and shook it skyward. Orange light streamed in from the windows, surrounding him with a dramatic aura. "Let this be the day we crush Fireskull for good and all!"

EIGHTEEN

IDEA

I T was a beautiful blue-sky day, not that Idea noticed. He was too busy keeping his nose stuck in *Fireskull's Revenant*.

"What's going on in there?" asked Eunice, looking over from the driver's seat. "It must be pretty juicy, because you haven't said a word for the past hour."

"A major battle," Idea said without looking up from the book. "All-out war between archenemies."

"Just like you," said Eunice. "You're heading for a fight with the Youforia impostors."

"Not a fight, unless they make it one."

Eunice swung the Beetle into the passing lane to get around a tractor-trailer. "You do realize you don't have a leg to stand on, right?"

"What are you talking about?" said Idea.

"With the impostors." She zipped past the truck and back into the right-hand lane. "You don't own any rights to Youforia, do you? Anyone can use the band's name if they want."

Idea looked up from *Fireskull's Revenant*. He thought about what she'd said, and realized she was right. Youforia had been a completely imaginary creation intended as a hoax, so Idea had never considered trying to copyright anything.

"How can you even prove you're the one who made up the band?" Eunice continued. "Anybody could say that."

Since leaving Chicago, Idea's anger at having Youforia stolen from him had propelled him toward Kentucky. Now, on the interstate between Indianapolis and Cincinnati, Ohio, about three hours from Maysville, Eunice was making him realize he hadn't thought his plans through. He had no real strategy for what he was going to do when he reached his destination, other than a vague notion of finding the Youforia impostors and shutting them down.

"You know, you're right," he said. "So how do you think I should handle this?"

Eunice laughed. "What makes you think I have any better ideas than you do?"

"Because *you* have the digihoroscope. It predicts events on an hour-by-hour basis, remember?"

"It *is* about time we checked the digihoroscope," said Eunice. "Thanks for reminding me."

"Let's see what this thing has to say. Not that I believe in horoscopes, computerized or otherwise."

"Prepare to have your mind changed," said Eunice. "Or should I say blown?"

Sitting in a booth at a truck stop, Idea watched as Eunice typed on her strange striped phone. Her fingernails with their black and white yin-yang symbols danced in the little cloud of glitter swirling over the screen.

She brushed her blond hair from her eyes and tucked it behind her ears, which Idea thought made her look prettier. "Okay." She reached for her chocolate milk shake and took a sip. "All the data has been updated. What question do you want to ask the digihoroscope?"

"What should I do when I meet the phony Youforia in Kentucky?" said Idea.

Eunice typed the question into the phone. Then, she held it up with the screen facing Idea.

A single word was displayed there for him to read. "'Unite.' That's it?"

"'Unite' is the keyword. There should be more." Eunice turned the phone around and tapped the screen. "Here it is. 'To succeed, you must unite with your enemies. You must not face the coming threat alone.'"

Idea frowned. "What threat?"

She tapped the screen a few more times and shook her head. "That's all it's giving us."

"It's kind of general, isn't it?"

"Maybe," said Eunice. "But doesn't it seem like a huge co-incidence that it fits your situation perfectly?"

"Horoscopes are designed to make as many people as possible think they apply specifically to them."

"The digihoroscope's different," Eunice insisted. "It applies a statistical algorithm to a set of real-world data to generate accurate predictions. Think about it. Seems to me the Youforia impostors qualify as 'enemies.'"

Idea rubbed the three moles on his left cheek. His stomach twisted, and a familiar chill rushed through him.

"Maybe we're on to something here," she continued. "What if you team up with the impostors and make them the official 'real' Youforia? This could be exactly what you need to take your make-believe band to the next level."

Idea was glad he was sitting down, because his head started to spin. As a wave of nausea rolled over him, he realized why Deity Syndrome was rearing up at that moment.

"You could bring Youforia to life, have a voice in what they do, and share in the profits," said Eunice. "You wouldn't have to sit back and watch someone else exploit the buzz you've whipped up while you get nothing."

Idea shivered. Her words were dovetailing with the book he'd been reading.

Eunice had advised Idea to join forces with his enemy. In *Fireskull's Revenant,* Scrier Inevitas, the witch, had given Johnny Without and Lord Fireskull the same advice.

Once again Idea was confronted with what seemed like incontrovertible proof that he was a character in a novel. It seemed like a plot device: the book he was reading was paralleling the book in which he was living. It was just the kind of thing that made Idea feel like he could see behind the curtain of his world, straight through to another where his fate was being devised by a malevolent mind of questionable imagination.

"Are you all right?" Eunice stared at him with a concerned expression.

He pushed his milk shake aside, nearly knocking it over, and put his head down on the table. "I know you're out there," he said under his breath. "Nobody else seems to know, but I do."

"What did you say?" Eunice asked.

"I'll be okay in a minute." As the dizziness, chills, and nausea continued to rage, Idea's thoughts swirled around *Fireskull's Revenant*. Certain events in the book were coming too close to his reality. What if the pages he had yet to read foretold his future?

And what if that future had already been foreshadowed in his life? For example, the number 64 kept popping up. "Chapter 64" was the title of the Youforia song he'd downloaded from the girl in the coffee shop. Bud System had ordered Youforia tickets from P.O. Box 64.

Since coming down with Deity Syndrome, Idea had suspected he was trapped in a book and would someday be killed off in its pages. What if the number 64 was foreshadowing his greatest fear? Maybe it was going to play a role in his death in the novel.

Maybe the song title said it all. Maybe he was doomed to die in Chapter 64, and the same chapter in *Fireskull's Revenant* would tell the tale.

Did he dare skip ahead to that part of the book to find out? No way.

Not yet.

THE three men and two women sang and danced around a campfire in North Tenneginia, acting not at all like kidnappers. Their captive, Reacher, who was no longer bound, gagged, or zipped up in a garment bag, sat on a picnic table in a wooded campsite, surrounded by lush pink trees and a carpet of thick pink grass. He sang and played an acoustic guitar that one of his abductors had just happened to have in the van.

Sundra had been right about what it would take to get her partners to let Reacher out of his bonds. He'd barely finished offering to play a private concert for the Youfers before they'd freed him and thrust the guitar into his hands.

But Sundra hadn't been quite so clear about how she would get him away from the others. "Wait for my signal," she'd told him. "You'll know what to do."

Reacher wondered what the signal would be and if in fact Sundra had any plan at all beyond getting him to perform.

The fact that he was playing a concert at all without being in disguise was a minor miracle. He was nervous, as he always was when performing for an audience. But it helped that there were only five of them, and he didn't really have a choice in the matter. It was the only way to escape being turned in to *Tuned* magazine.

The lack of options forced him to focus and calmed his nerves. So did the fact that the kidnappers were blowing his mind.

He was stunned when he launched into "Coming to Life" from *Singularity City* and all the kidnappers sang along. He'd never performed the song in public, had never released a recording of it, and had never posted the lyrics on the Internet . . . yet the Youfers knew every single word by heart.

"Come to life," he sang. *"Come to life and eat the sun. D-don't you know that two-two heads are better, much better than one?"*

Reacher played a version of the big screaming guitar solo that came next. It didn't quite sound the same on the acoustic.

"Step right up," he sang after the solo. *"Tell me what to do. There's a man at the center of everything laughing . . . but I know a way out and I'll take you."*

Everyone continued to sing along, matching him word for word. The whole thing was completely unnerving, which was what gave him the idea to try an experiment.

"Upside downside," he sang. *"My side your side."*

Then instead of the lyrics that should have come next, he improvised. Instead of singing "Come to life, your life will come," he sang, *"Come to see, don't criticize me."*

And the Youfers sang along. Though Reacher had made up the new words on the spot, the Youfers sang them exactly as he did. Their mouths moved in perfect time with his own; they were anticipating him, not mimicking him.

He tried it again. Instead of singing "I'll put you on, but I'll follow through," he sang, *"Never again will I dream of you."*

Just like before, the Youfers sang the improvised lyrics as if they were old favorites they knew by heart.

Even as Reacher continued to play and sing, he wondered how they did it. The only explanation he could think of, which seemed pretty far-fetched, was that they could read his mind. If that was the case, though, why hadn't they tied him back up yet? If the Youfers could read his mind, they would surely notice his thoughts of escape.

Although Reacher hadn't been mistreated, apart from being bound and gagged and zipped into a garment bag, he'd had enough of being a captive. Breaking away from the others with Sundra would give him his best shot at winning his freedom. But she just kept singing and dancing around the campfire.

Realizing that she might go back on her promise to help him, Reacher decided he would take action alone if he had to. If Sundra didn't initiate an escape attempt before long, he would try one himself. Although he was outnumbered five to one, he was a great sprinter and would try to make the most of the element of surprise.

Two songs after "Coming to Life," as he started into "Magic Feeling," he lost sight of her. She'd been dancing with everyone else around the fire, but when he looked up from the guitar after playing the intro, she was gone.

She showed up again midway through the song, although Reacher couldn't get a good look at her because she was behind him. He heard her voice in his ear and felt her arm sling over his shoulder and chest.

And he felt the flat edge of a knife blade touch his throat, cool and solid against his skin.

Later, with the hunting knife stowed in a sheath strapped to her thigh, Sundra raced the Tucker van across the border into Pennsyltucky, driving like a maniac. Reacher sat in the passenger seat beside her, watching the nighttime scenery flash by in the bright beams of the triple headlights. His right foot kept stepping on an imaginary brake pedal, as if that could keep them from crashing.

Miles behind the van, the other four kidnappers were stranded in the Tenneginia woods, their shot at a fifteen-thousand-dollar reward speeding away like a loose helium balloon spitting into the sky.

Now that Reacher had escaped the rest of the kidnappers, he was glad Sundra had threatened to slice his throat, although he hadn't thought it was such a great idea at the time.

In particular, he hadn't been a fan of the part where she'd actually *cut* him to prove how serious she was. When the other Youfers had expressed doubts that she would follow through with her threat, they'd closed in around her . . . only to back off again when she nicked Reacher's left cheek with the knife.

The sight of blood had seemed to convince everyone that she meant business, because they'd all cooperated perfectly from then until she'd driven off with her hostage. She'd told them to hand over all their cell phones and the keys to the van, and they'd done it. They'd said a lot of nasty things to her, but no one had made a single move to stop her.

Reacher hoped the next phase of his getaway—escaping from Sundra—would go as smoothly.

"I told you I'd rescue you." She smiled over at him from behind the wheel.

"Thanks." Nervously, he rubbed the white stubble on top of his head. He wished she would keep her eyes on the road, given the van's high rate of speed—eighty-five the last time he'd checked. "Do you think the others will send the cops after us?"

Sundra shook her head. "They *kidnapped* you, and I *saved* you. I don't think they'll be calling the cops. Plus which, they're out in the woods without phones or a car." Reaching over, she patted Reacher's knee. "Don't worry. You'll make it to Maysville for your show."

The way she was driving, Reacher had his doubts about that, but he kept them to himself. "I think it'll be a good one. I had a great warm-up back at the campfire." He had no intention of performing in Maysville, but he thought it best to say what she wanted to hear.

"That's wonderful." Sundra chuckled. "Hey, it just occurred to me . . . maybe you'll write a song about all this."

"Why not?" Reacher laughed along with her. "At the very least, I'll dedicate one to you at the show."

Sundra gasped. "Really? You'd do that?"

"Without you, there wouldn't *be* a show, would there?" said Reacher. "Of course, there *is* one problem yet."

"What's that?"

Reacher sighed. "I'm not sure if my band will be there. They probably don't even know if I'm alive or not."

"Whoops," said Sundra. "You're right."

"The last thing they knew, I was going to the ice machine."

Sundra reached into the console tray between the seats and drew out one of the four cell phones that she'd taken from the other Youfers. "Here. Call and let them know you're okay."

Reacher took the phone and activated it with the press of a button. "No service," he read from the glowing green screen.

Sundra stomped on the accelerator, and the Tucker sped up even more. "We need to get out of the boondocks. Get in range of some cell towers."

Reacher tried not to watch the speedometer needle as it climbed past ninety. His heart pounded as the van hurtled through the night.

Seconds later, his hands clenched the dashboard as the triple headlights of an oncoming vehicle flew around a bend in the road, rushing straight at them.

TWENTY

IDEA

EUNICE wrenched the steering wheel hard to the left, racing head-on toward the white van.

"Watch out!" said Idea. "It's heading straight for you!"

"No prob, Rob." At the last possible instant, she yanked the wheel hard right, veering away from the oncoming vehicle.

Tires screaming, the van spun and stopped in the middle of the road. Eunice's car tumbled into a ditch. From her point of view on the screen of the video game, the world was canted at a cockeyed angle, seen through a rising cloud of smoke and steam.

"GAME OVER" flashed red across the middle of the screen.

"You tried to hit him," said Idea. "You *tried* to wreck."

"I thought that was the object of the game." Eunice smiled.

Idea blew out his breath in frustration. "*They* try to hit *you. You* try to keep from being *hit.*"

"Now, where's the fun in that?" Eunice abandoned the console and headed for a soda machine on the other side of the rest stop building. She carried a white plastic grocery bag full of clothes with her. She'd just changed in the bathroom, switching to a different two-sided outfit: a light green T-shirt with a white bull's-eye and faded blue jeans in front; a floral-print black and purple top with dark blue jeans in back.

Idea followed her to the soda machine. "You were driving like a maniac."

"Better in a video game than real life." She pulled a dollar bill and some coins from her pocket. After counting out the money, she reached around into a pocket on the back half of her jeans and drew out a dime.

"You told me you were an expert at that game," said Idea.

Eunice fed her dollar and coins into the soda machine. "Maybe I lied." She turned, then raised an eyebrow at him. "Good thing *you* never lie."

She hit a button on the front of the machine. A bottle of cola shot down the chute and landed with a thump.

Idea shrugged. "I don't think I'm the only one with secrets around here."

Eunice grabbed her soda and walked out the door. The night air was warm, and a light breeze carried the scent of freshly mown grass. Clouds of moths jittered around the bright lights spaced along the sidewalk and parking lot.

"You're the only one with secrets *I* don't know." She opened the soda and had a sip.

Idea frowned. "Like what?"

"Hmm." Eunice strolled along, head tipped to one side, looking thoughtful. "Well, for example, you've never told me why you ran away from home."

Idea sunk his hands in his pockets and sighed. "Too much pressure, I guess. Mom and Dad wanted me to be president. Or at least a multibillion-dollar CEO or a Nobel Prize–winning scientist."

"They pushed you too hard, huh?"

Idea laughed ruefully. "I even had a greatness coach, if you can believe it."

"Really?"

Idea nodded. "Scholar was my greatness coach. Bulab was my tutor. So imagine how much fun *my* life was."

Eunice offered him the soda. "Fun enough to make you run away?"

Idea took a drink and handed it back to her. "It was Bulab and Scholar, twenty-four seven. Tutoring, followed by workouts, followed by studying, followed by goal-oriented lucid dreaming. No sleeping in, no TV, no video games, no junk food. The only friends I was allowed to see were handpicked by my parents and Scholar, to maximize my potential.

"I wasn't even supposed to use the Internet unsupervised," he continued. "Luckily, I got so good with computers that I could make Scholar see one thing on his spy screen while I looked at something else on *my* screen."

"Ah." Eunice nodded. "That's where Youforia comes in."

"It was the only thing I could do for fun," said Idea. "When it caught on with so many people, it was, like, not only was I doing something I wasn't supposed to be doing, but I was succeeding at it. I could succeed on my own, without someone telling me what to do."

Eunice sat down on a bench, and Idea sat beside her. They

watched traffic race past on the highway toward Cincinnati, Ohio, which was just a few miles away.

"When you finally left home, did something happen that made you do it?" Eunice asked.

Idea snorted. "They got divorced. Six months ago."

"Sorry to hear that."

Idea laughed. "And guess what? I didn't know about it until last week."

Eunice grimaced with disbelief. "How is that even *possible?*"

"Anything's possible for two high-powered attorneys."

"They didn't tell their own son?" Eunice shook her head slowly. "That is so sad."

"You know what's even sadder?" said Idea. "I didn't notice."

Eunice met his gaze. Gently, she placed her hand over his.

"I saw them about as often after they divorced as before," he said quietly. "In other words, hardly at all. Apparently their idea of joint custody was for Bulab and Scholar to watch me as usual."

"Wonderful." Eunice offered her soda again, and Idea took another sip.

"They still expected great things from me, though," he went on. "They kept planning my future and e-mailing me encouraging quotes from Machiavelli and Sun Tzu. And when Bulab finally let it slip about the divorce, I decided I'd had enough. I made my plans, and then I ran." Idea stared fixedly at the traffic rushing by through the darkness. "And if I have my way, I'll never go back."

Eunice patted his hand. "I don't blame you."

He shook his head. "I feel nothing for my parents. Absolutely nothing." He paused. "Maybe that's how they want it. They always drilled into me that I should never let emotional attachments prevent me from reaching my destiny. But I don't know. It doesn't seem like that's how it ought to be. I just don't see what's wrong with caring about people."

Eunice folded his hand between both of her own. "Nothing." She leaned toward him. "There's nothing wrong with it."

Her eyes locked with his. Idea's heart pounded, and this time it had nothing to do with Deity Syndrome. He felt a nervous chill mixed with a flutter of pure excitement.

Eunice drifted closer. Idea held back, surprised by what was happening, and then he pressed toward her.

She closed her eyes, and he did the same. Their lips met lightly and parted, then fused again and held.

Idea's senses seemed to amplify a thousandfold. He was overwhelmed by waves of feeling—the soft touch of her mouth, the smell of her skin, the firmness of her grasp. Every bit of him rushed with warmth, and everything but the experience of the moment was swept from his mind.

Her lips floated away from his, breaking the dreamlike contact, only to light upon his cheek with a pressure that was at once soothing and electrifying. She lingered for a moment, her breath warm on his skin.

Then, although he wished it would continue forever, she pulled away.

She brushed one finger along his jaw and stopped at the

middle of his chin. "It'll be all right. This is a new beginning for you."

Idea wasn't sure if she meant the beginning of a better life or the beginning of a romantic relationship, but either one would be okay with him. "I'd like that."

"Maybe together we can make it happen," said Eunice. "Maybe that's why we met."

"I'm glad we met."

"I think everything happens for a reason," she said. "Maybe a good reason. Maybe, if someone *is* pulling the strings, it's not such a bad thing."

Idea nodded.

"Maybe we can be happy." Eunice leaned forward and kissed him again.

TWENTY-ONE

REACHER

REACHER recognized the victim of the crash. When the door of the car on its side in the ditch flew open and the driver looked out, Reacher was so surprised that he nearly fell down in the middle of the road.

Just moments ago, the car had nearly slammed head-on into Sundra's speeding van. Its headlights had streamed around a bend, seemingly too close to avoid, and then had veered off at the last second, barely missing them.

Sundra had slammed on the brakes, and the van had slid down the road, completing a one-hundred-and-eighty-degree spin. The other vehicle had careened off the pavement and landed on its passenger's side in a shallow ditch.

Both Sundra and Reacher had been wearing seat belts and were fine. As soon as Reacher had made sure she was uninjured, his next thought had been of the other driver. Quickly, he'd unbuckled his seat belt, thrown open the door, and run for the other vehicle.

That was when the driver's side door of the car in the ditch flew open.

Reacher couldn't believe his eyes. The person rising out had been full of surprises in the past, but this surprise was the most amazing of all.

Before he could call out her name, she surprised him again. She pressed an index finger to her lips, signaling him to be quiet.

And then she winked.

"I'm so sorry, sir," she said in a thick Southern accent. "I just lost control of my car."

Reacher nodded slowly, a stupefied look on his face.

"Could you give me a hand?" she asked. "This is kind of an awkward position."

He hurried over and helped her climb out. She lowered herself into his arms, and he turned to deposit her on the ground.

"I'm a stranger," she whispered as he put her down in the pink grass at the side of the road. "Let's have some fun with this."

"Are you all right, miss?" asked Sundra, rushing over. "Is there anything we can do?"

"I have a *killer* headache," Eurydice said emphatically. "And as a matter of fact, I could use a little ol' ride right now."

Soon, the three of them were in the van, rolling into the night.

Sundra was still behind the wheel. "So what's your name?" she asked over her shoulder.

"Elizadeath," Eurydice said from the back seat. "But you can call me Deathy."

Sundra's eyes flicked up to the rearview mirror for a glimpse of her passenger. "That's an interesting name," she said slowly. "Is there a story behind it?"

Eurydice blew a big purple bubble with her gum. When it popped, she peeled the gum from her chin and stuffed it back in her mouth. "You might say that. *Lots* of stories."

"For instance?" said Sundra.

"Let's just say the name suits me," said Eurydice, "and leave it at that."

In the front seat on the passenger's side, Reacher struggled to keep a straight face. He still had no idea how Eurydice had managed to pop up at his exact location in the middle of no-where, but for now he pushed his questions aside and enjoyed her performance.

"Where're you two headed, again?" Eurydice asked.

"Maysville, Pennsyltucky," Sundra replied. "You're sure you don't want us to take you back in the other direction? That was the way you were going before the accident, after all."

"This is fine," said Eurydice. "I wasn't so much headin' somewhere as lookin' for someone. Some*ones,* actually."

"Who's that?" asked Sundra.

Eurydice cracked her gum loudly. "We'll know 'em when we see 'em, I reckon."

Reacher had to turn to the window to hide the grin on his face. He wondered what she would come up with next.

Sundra frowned in the rearview mirror. "Where did you say you were from?"

"Death Valley."

"And your name is Deathy." Sundra sounded skeptical.

"Nah," said Eurydice. "I mean, that's my name, but I'm from Laidlow, Louisibama, not Death Valley."

"Laidlow," said Sundra. "Never heard of it."

"You wouldn't've," said Eurydice. "It ain't there no more."

Reacher couldn't resist participating any longer. "Why is that?"

"No one knows," Eurydice deadpanned. "There was only one survivor, and she ain't talkin'."

"Who's the survivor?" asked Reacher.

Eurydice blew a bright green bubble with her gum, then popped it and stuffed it back in her mouth. "Me."

Sundra cast a worried frown in Reacher's direction. He just shrugged.

"So, Deathy." Sundra's voice had a nervous edge to it. "Would you like us to drop you off anywhere in particular?"

"Not really," said Eurydice. "I'd rather just tag along with y'all for a while."

"Okey-doke." Though Sundra's voice sounded light and friendly, Reacher could tell her tension level was rising.

"Say." Eurydice leaned forward between the front seats. "You two seem like open-minded types."

"Sure." Sundra nodded a little too emphatically.

"You got any hobbies?"

"Music," said Reacher.

"I love music, too," said Sundra. "Listening to it, I mean."

"What about you, Deathy?" asked Reacher.

"Taxidermy," said Eurydice. "And dressing exotic meats."

Reacher nodded and hid a grin behind his hand. In the driver's seat, Sundra noticeably stiffened.

Eurydice was silent for a long moment. "Hey, buddy," she finally said to Reacher. "What's the biggest thing you ever killed?"

He didn't have to pretend to be surprised by the question. "Who's the *what* now?"

"Well, you hunt, don'tcha?"

"No, I don't," said Reacher. "Why? What's the biggest thing *you've* ever killed?"

"Hmm. I'm gonna have to get back to you on that one," said Eurydice, cracking her gum.

Humming softly, she pulled a paperback book out of her purse and settled back to flip through it. She turned the pages as if reading in the dark wasn't a problem, then tossed it over Reacher's shoulder into his lap.

It was his copy of *Fireskull's Revenant*.

"Check out the book," she said. "It's one of my favorites. *Tons* of bloodshed, especially in the part I've got marked."

"Cool." He smiled and flicked on the dome light. The bookmark was right where he'd left it. "Maybe I'll read just a few pages."

CHAPTER FORTY-FOUR

THE arrow was streaking toward Fireskull's chest when a screaming man dove in front of it.

"Fiercely!" said the man as the arrow pierced his naked flesh, puncturing his heart instead of Fireskull's. "Winner! Reward!"

The man was part of the Lunatic Guard, a gaggle of maniacs whose sole purpose was to give their lives to protect Lord Fireskull. Simultaneously pampered and driven insane, the Lunatic Guardsmen wore maroon velvet robes in the field and painted their faces with dung and blood. It was well known throughout the Unrepentant Kingdom that they were Fireskull's favored warriors, members of a caste that superceded even the Priestlings in terms of stature.

As the Lunatic dropped to the ground, Fireskull whirled and belched flame into the forest. The archer who had shot the arrow was already on the run, staying barely a step ahead of the blast scorching the trees behind her.

Calmly Fireskull dug a handful of living bullets from a pouch on his belt and tossed them in the air. Forged from the boiled-down brains of murder victims, the bullets were known to kill with the single-minded savagery of vengeful ghosts.

Blood-red and dripping, they turned their corkscrew tips toward Fireskull. Each one blinked its single yellow eye at him as he pointed after the fleeing archer.

Then the bullets spun and flashed away into the smoking trees. An instant later, Fireskull heard the sweet screams of the archer as they struck and slowly worked their way through her, tearing her to shreds in torturous slow motion.

Fireskull laughed. "When they are done with her, I will have her made into a bullet herself!" His voice rang with cruelty.

"Glittering!" said the Lunatic with the arrow through his heart, squirming on the ground at Fireskull's feet. The Lunatic grunted and moaned in pain, clutching the arrow shaft as blood pumped out around it. "Entrails! Bludgeon!"

Other Lunatic Guardsmen crowded around, clucking and gaping vacantly like chickens at the dying man. "Ruined! Ruined!" shrieked a gray-bearded Lunatic with mushrooms growing all over his body. "Hero's funeral?"

Fireskull patted the mushroom man on the head, then wiped his hand on his trousers. "Yes, very good." Fireskull's voice was full of affection. "Give him a hero's funeral."

With a swirl of his black cape, Fireskull stomped away

from the dying Lunatic. The others crowded around the mortally wounded man, and his screams soon joined those of the archer in the cool twilight air.

A messenger stood nearby, helmet in hand, newly arrived from the frontline of the battle against the forces of Johnny Without. He looked extremely nervous, which was the reaction of most ordinary people who saw the Lunatic Guard in action. Fireskull went to him, eager to hear the latest good news.

"What say you, fleet foot?" he asked.

"General Undercut sends word of more victories," said the messenger. "Johnny Without's garrisons at Farcry and Plainday have been annihilated. Fort Skein, Fort Lightway, and Fort Tributary have fallen. General Leverage outflanked the Shining Regiment at Distance and cut down every last man."

"Wonderful!" The flames that made up Fireskull's head flared from red to gold with pure delight. "At this rate, we shall capture Castle Vanish before the day is through."

"General Undercut said the same thing," the messenger agreed. "Taking the castle is a formality. He has already planted the flag."

"Marvelous," said Fireskull. "Then, all this is mine." He spread his arms wide to take in his surroundings. "I hereby rename this the Kingdom of Not. This land is not worthy, not wanted, and not free. It shall be removed from all maps, enclosed with walls of bones, and turned into a playground for the Lunatic Guard."

"Yes, my lord," said the messenger.

"Starting immediately," said Fireskull. "Any without my brand on their flesh shall be pitted against each other in fights to the death. Family member against family member, preferably."

"Yes, my lord."

"And tell General Undercut to send word the *instant* that the battering ram smashes the gates of Castle Vanish. I wish to hear Johnny's screams when the reanimated cadavers of his own loyalists feast on his innards."

The messenger swallowed hard, fighting to conceal his skittishness. "I will tell him, my lord." He bowed low.

Fireskull took a long look at the young man, committing his face to memory. For no good reason but utter cruelty, he decided that after the war, he would forcibly enlist him in the Lunatic Guard.

"Go now," he said. The messenger bowed and backed away several steps, then turned and ran.

Fireskull laughed. Finally, he was on the verge of complete victory. Decades of struggle had yielded a sweet reward. Let Johnny's stragglers lob arrows at him. Their puny weapons could not get past the Lunatics.

And so what if Highcast's prophecy had put just

enough doubt in his mind that he stayed back from the frontline, where he most wanted to be? Johnny and his weaklings would still go down in defeat.

The sweetest reward that Fireskull could imagine was within his reach. The Kingdom of Not was his, and he would sit upon the throne of Castle Vanish by morning, gulping Johnny's blood from a chalice. He would allow nothing to get in the way of that.

"Come, children," he said to the Lunatic Guard. "Time to go." He spread his leathery wings wide and flapped them, rising from the ground.

Cackling and yelping, the Lunatics abandoned their project. Licking blood from their lips and picking their teeth with splinters of bone, they danced away from what little remained of their dead comrade's corpse.

While the Guard mobilized, Fireskull flapped above the treetops to reconnoiter. To the northwest, in the direction of Castle Vanish, he spied a patrol of eight of Johnny's men marching along a riverbank. Those men, Fireskull decided, would also die at the hands of his Lunatic Guard.

With a rustle of leathery wings, he turned, intending to descend and give his maniacs their orders. Instead, he stopped suddenly and darted backward.

He was not alone in the blazing orange sky.

"End your war." It was Scrier Inevitas, floating there in front of him. "Join with your enemy, or all is lost."

Fireskull laughed. "I will join with him, all right, when I devour his wretched body."

Scrier showed no emotion. Her voice roared with the sound of rushing wind. "If you and your foe do not unite, both your kingdoms shall be lost before the cock crows tomorrow."

"Not if I kill all the cocks before then!" Fireskull swung his sword with a mighty stroke that could have cleaved a man in two. "Along with Johnny and his loathsome ilk!"

"Your choice is clear," said Scrier. "Surrender."

"If surrender includes wiping every trace of Johnny Without from the face of the world, consider it done!"

"I will go to Johnny next and tell him the same thing," said Scrier.

"You do that!" Fireskull's flames burned hotter and higher with wicked glee. "Tell *him* to surrender! Then he will finally know peace . . . the peace of the grave!"

With that, Fireskull soared off toward the frontline, whistling for the Lunatic Guard to follow. Scrier hovered in place for a moment, then shot past him so fast that all he saw was a blur.

FOR a long time, the van was silent except for the noise of the engine as Sundra drove through the night. She gripped the steering wheel tightly and checked the rearview mirror several times a minute, watching for suspicious moves from Eurydice.

For her part, Eurydice calmly watched the darkened countryside slip past. Every once in a while, she shot a glance at the rearview, taking Sundra by surprise and hypnotically holding her gaze for an instant.

It was during one of those instants that Eurydice finally broke the silence.

"Get off at this exit!" she shouted, bouncing up and down. "This is it!"

"This is what?" Reacher wondered what she was up to now.

"Please!" said Eurydice. "Get off here. I have to show y'all the *coolest* place!"

Sundra swung off the highway and onto the exit ramp. "What place are you talking about?"

"At the bottom of the exit, go left." Eurydice cracked her gum three times fast.

"Go left toward what?" Sundra pressed.

"I want to see if the place is still there," Eurydice said. "I haven't stopped by in years."

Sundra made the left turn off the ramp. "How much farther should it be?"

"'Bout two miles," said Eurydice. "Go right at the blinking light."

Sundra flashed another worried frown at Reacher as she made the right turn. She frowned at him again after they passed the three-mile mark. "Okay," she said finally. "We're going on four miles now. I thought you said two."

"Give or take," said Eurydice. "I told you, it's been a while."

"No offense," said Sundra, "but we're in kind of a hurry. We have to get to Maysville ASAP."

"I know a shortcut," said Eurydice. "Just keep driving."

Sundra sighed and drove onward. Three miles later, she slowed down. "Enough of this. We have to get back on the highway." She swung the van wide over the shoulder and started to make a U-turn. "You'll have to look for this place some other time."

"Wait." Eurydice tapped Sundra on the shoulder with a yin-yang–painted fingernail and pointed straight ahead. "There."

Squinting into the darkness, Reacher saw a dim, distant glow on the left side of the road. "That's it?"

"You betcha." Eurydice blew a gray bubble with her gum.

Sundra leaned forward, peering at the light. "Looks like an old roadhouse."

"Go on now." Eurydice waved a hand with a shooing gesture to get Sundra moving. "You won't be sorry."

With another heavy sigh, Sundra gave up on the U-turn and rolled the van forward again.

As they drew closer, Reacher saw that the light was indeed coming from the windows of a dilapidated roadhouse. The squat building looked as if it had been patched together from mismatched planks and tarpaper about a century ago. An unlit neon sign topped the rippled front lip of the tin roof.

Just as they pulled up across the road from the place, the sign flickered to life. It spelled *Wigwam* in red cursive.

"'Wigwam'?" said Reacher.

"Everybody calls it Dusty's," said Eurydice. "It's been here forever."

"I can see that."

"All right, then." Sundra clapped her hands together. "You go on ahead, Deathy."

Eurydice opened the door to get out. "Come on, now," she said. "You guys have *got* to go in and see this place."

"Thanks, anyway," said Sundra. "We'll wait here."

"You'll hate yourselves if you miss this."

Reacher shrugged and unclipped his seat belt. "Why not?"

Sundra grabbed his arm. "I think you should stay here with me. I really think we need to talk."

"We will." Reacher opened the door. "Later."

"No, please." Sundra's voice held a trace of hysteria. Apparently, Eurydice's serial-killer routine had been a little too convincing. "Please stay."

"I'll be fine." Reacher peeled her hand from his bicep. He slid out of his bucket seat and stepped down onto the gravel shoulder. "I promise."

"All right." Sundra didn't look like she believed him.

Reacher shut the door and crossed the road with Eurydice. "Good job freaking her out," he said when they were out of earshot.

"She deserved it." Eurydice dropped the Southern accent. "She kidnapped you, remember?"

Reacher shook his head. "I don't suppose you'll tell me how you even knew I was kidnapped? Or how you found me?"

She shrugged. "Would you believe women's intuition?"

He sighed. "So what's going on here?"

"You'll see." Eurydice led him across the deserted dirt parking lot.

It looked to Reacher like no one had been there in a long time. He couldn't even see any tire tracks in the dirt. So who was inside with the lights on, and how had they gotten there?

A chill shot up his spine. The place was like something out of a horror movie. He had the urge to turn around and get away as fast as he could, but he trusted Eurydice. He *loved* her.

Of course, the front door *did* look like the lid of a pine box coffin.

Without batting an eyelash, she opened it for him. "After you."

Reacher stepped through into a musty vestibule with another door. Beyond it, he heard music playing.

He aimed a puzzled frown at Eurydice, who pointed at the wall behind him. Turning, he saw an ancient poster tacked to it. The ink was faded, and the paper was cracked and torn, but the images and text were still clear enough to make out.

In the middle of the poster, a man and a woman in what looked like World War Two–era clothes were dancing excitedly. The man wore a white shirt, bow tie, baggy brown trousers, and suspenders; the woman wore a knee-length red dress and a red bow in her hair. They were flushed and grinning, waving and kicking as if they were doing some kind of fast dance—a jitter-bug, maybe.

In the upper left corner of the poster, behind the dancers, a big band wearing tuxedos supplied the music, illustrated by swirling measures of jumbled notes streaming out of their high-held horns.

The lower right corner of the poster was dominated by a cutout black and white photo of a man's head attached to a drawing of a tiny, tuxedoed body. The face on the head was long and thin, with a huge oily forelock arching over one eyebrow. A pencil-thin mustache clung to his upper lip, and the teeth in his vast smile were so huge that each seemed to have a life of its own. Because he held a conductor's baton in one tiny hand, Reacher guessed that he was the band's leader.

"WHAT ALL THE FUSS IS ABOUT!" read the bold-lettered title atop the poster. In the lower left corner, in faded but still eye-catching red letters surging from the heart of a sunburst, was the band's name.

"'Donny Basquette,'" Reacher read aloud. "'And Your Favorites.' Never heard of them."

"You've got a lot in common," said Eurydice.

"Like what?"

"Come on." She smiled and squeezed past him to open the next door. "Let's go have a listen."

TWENTY-FOUR

REACHER

REACHER and Eurydice were the band's only audience. They sat on some overturned crates in the back of the room and listened as the ancient musicians performed.

They looked more decrepit than the roadhouse around them. Reacher guessed the female vocalist was the only one under the age of eighty.

As old as the musicians looked, though, they sure could play. Dressed in black tuxedos, they reeled off songs like it was 1942. Reacher hardly knew a thing about big band music, but he could tell that the codgers were pros, performing with vitality that belied their advanced years.

He pointed at the bandleader. "That's Donny Basquette?" he asked, raising his voice over the music.

Eurydice shook her head. "Donny's dead. That's Laszlo Taper. No one can replace Donny, but Laszlo's filling in."

The song ended, and Reacher and Eurydice clapped. Laszlo bowed and swept back an arm to encompass the band.

The members nodded and grinned. They each sat behind a plastic music stand, the top part of which was black, with "Donny Basquette" in white across a raised lip that faced the audience. "Your Favorites" was painted in black around the middle of the cylindrical white base of each stand. Without exception, the stands were scratched and dented and chipped, worn down from decades of use.

"Thank you," said Laszlo. He was skinny, with a hawkish nose and thick-lensed, dark-framed glasses. His shiny silver pompadour matched the silver beard on his chin. He hadn't stopped smiling since Reacher and Eurydice had entered the room. "And now, 'Take the Z Train.'"

Raising his conductor's baton, Laszlo turned to face the band. "A-one and a-two," he said, and they launched into another song.

"Hey!" said Reacher. "I *know* this one!"

Eurydice cracked her gum twice. "I know them all."

After two more numbers, the band took a break. Laszlo rushed right over and threw his arms around Eurydice.

"Enid!" he said. "It's great to see you!"

"Same here." She planted a kiss on his cheek. "You look great."

Laszlo stood back and beamed at her. "You haven't changed a bit, as always." Glancing at Reacher, he seemed to reconsider what he'd said. "Not that it's been *that* long," he added.

"This is my boyfriend, Reacher Mirage." Eurydice put a hand on Reacher's shoulder. "He's a musician, too, you know."

"Of course he is, dear," said the female vocalist as she sidled up to join the group.

"Reacher," said Eurydice. "This is Clementine Tasseltoe. Clementine, meet Reacher Mirage."

"Charmed." Clementine nodded.

"Pleased to meet you," said Reacher.

"Welcome to Dusty's." Laszlo shook Reacher's hand. "The rest of the gang will be over soon enough to say hello." Laszlo bobbed his head to indicate the musicians lined up at the door to the men's room. "Bathroom break, you know."

"When your band has fifteen men over the age of seventy, you have to take plenty of bathroom breaks," Clementine said.

"So what brings you this way?" Laszlo peered at Eurydice from behind the thick lenses of his glasses.

"Reacher wanted to meet you," she said. "He has a band, too."

"What's it called?"

"Youforia." Eurydice slid her arm around Reacher's shoulders and cracked her gum. "They're amazing."

"How nice," Clementine said sardonically. "Maybe they'll play Dusty's with us someday."

"Your Favorites have been together since 1939," Eurydice told Reacher. "The last new member joined in 1957."

"Well, you guys sound great," he said.

"Why, thank you," said Laszlo.

"Too bad no one else ever hears us," said Clementine. "But we don't exactly advertise, do we?" She cast a meaningful look at Laszlo, who nervously looked away.

"C'mon over here, Preacher." He grabbed Reacher by the elbow and pulled him toward the ramshackle bar across the room. "I've got something to show you."

Looking back over his shoulder, Reacher saw that Eurydice and Clementine weren't following him and Laszlo. "Eury?"

"You go ahead," Eurydice said with a wave.

"Have a seat, sonny." Laszlo swept a cloud of dust from a rickety barstool with the side of his hand. Releasing Reacher's arm, he scooted around behind the bar and ducked out of sight. He popped back up a second later and slammed down a fat scrapbook, sending up more dust.

"Welcome to the Your Favorites archive." Laszlo threw open the cover of the book. "There's a lot of history on these pages."

Reacher turned for a glimpse of Eurydice. He could tell she and Clementine were having a heated discussion, although he was too far away to hear any of it. As he turned back to Laszlo, one of the ancient musicians pushed in for a closer look at the scrapbook.

"That's ol' Donny Basquette!" said the old man. "Why, he don't look a day past twenty."

Laszlo jabbed the scrapbook page with his gnarled finger. "That's because he was eighteen in that picture!"

"Like I said." The old man winked at Reacher.

"Preacher, this is Spill Ringamajig." Laszlo playfully punched the newcomer's upper arm. "Spill's been with the Favorites since the beginning."

"Glad you could join us." Spill grabbed Reacher's hand and shook it vigorously.

Reacher nodded, but his attention was elsewhere. He couldn't take his eyes off the scrapbook page that Laszlo and Spill had been talking about, the page where they'd seen the photo of eighteen-year-old Donny Basquette.

"He was a handsome fella, wasn't he?" Spill pulled the book over in front of him.

Reacher rubbed the snow white stubble on his scalp as he continued to stare at the scrapbook. A chill rippled up his spine.

From what he could see, the page was completely blank.

ANOTHER musician hobbled over to the bar and joined Laszlo and Spill in laughing at a clipping in the scrapbook—a non-existent clipping, from Reacher's viewpoint.

"Mooney Claptrack," Laszlo said between chuckles, slapping the new arrival on the back. "Meet Preacher."

"Yo." Mooney was a full head taller than Laszlo and had a huge belly. His wispy silver comb-over barely covered his spotted scalp. "I'll never forget the look on Donny's face when Japanese Bill waltzed in stark naked."

"And he just sat down and started playing," said Spill.

"Donny could really think on his feet, though," said Laszlo. "Remember, he told the audience it was part of an 'Oriental tradition'?"

"Bill was only doing it to get back at Donny for insisting he wear a tux like everyone else in the band!" Mooney leaned back and roared a belly laugh at the ceiling.

"But it backfired," said Spill. "Donny got all kinds of free publicity because of the 'bare clarinetist'!"

"Pretty funny, huh, Preacher?" said Laszlo.

Reacher nodded and smiled. "Oh, yeah." With Laszlo, Spill, and Mooney acting like they all saw a newspaper clipping on the page, Reacher was afraid to tell them it looked blank to him.

"Oh!" Laszlo turned to another page. "And look at this! Our first world tour."

"World tour?" A fit-looking old man shoved his way between Spill and Reacher for a glimpse. He had neatly trimmed white hair and the handsome but fading features of an ancient movie star. "World's *shortest* tour is more like it, thanks to Montezuma's revenge."

"Oh, that was bad," said Mooney. "Twenty guys with the runs on a tour bus in Mexico."

Laszlo laughed so hard that he had to take off his glasses and rub the tears from his eyes. "And Donny wrote a song about it," he said, shaking his head. "'Montezuma' was one of our biggest hits."

"By the way, kid." The movie star slid a hand toward Reacher. "I'm Tommy Coin. Vocals and vibes."

Reacher shook Tommy's hand. "Reacher Mirage. I'm with Eurydice."

Tommy looked puzzled until Laszlo spoke up. "Enid," he said simply, and Tommy nodded with understanding.

"Speak of the devil!" said Mooney.

"Hey, guys!" Eurydice strolled around the bar, waving and smiling. "Whatcha doin'?" She cracked her gum, and then her attention was caught by the scrapbook. "Is that who I think it is?" She leaned over the bar, poking a yin-yang fingernail at the scrapbook page.

"Sweetwind Wilson," Tommy said with a grin. "The one and only."

Reacher watched as Eurydice studied the page. Since she seemed to see something other than blank paper, too, he started to wonder if *he* was the one with the problem and everyone else was seeing just fine.

Eurydice smirked. "Wasn't he the one who—?"

"Tried to get Donny Basquette fired," finished Mooney.

"Was wanted in seven states," added Spill.

"Claimed to be a Baptist minister," Tommy chimed in.

"Was the best tenor saxophonist on God's green earth." Laszlo nodded appreciatively.

"Handsome guy." Eurydice stared at the scrapbook.

"He sure was." Clementine piped up suddenly from behind Reacher. "What do you think, young man?"

Reacher looked at the scrapbook page. "Uh, sure. I guess he's handsome."

Clementine stared at him for a moment, hands on her hips. "C'mere a minute," she said to him, walking away from the bar.

Reacher looked to Eurydice for a cue, but she was busy flipping through the scrapbook while the musicians shouted out stories and laughed. With a shrug, he followed Clementine across the room.

She stopped by a framed photo on the wall, a black and white eight-by-ten that was hanging at an angle. She straightened the frame, then clasped her hands behind her back as she gazed at it. "You see this picture?"

Reacher considered his answer, then nodded. "I see it." The image in the frame was that of a big band, dressed in white tuxedos and arranged on risers behind gleaming music stands. The stands looked just like the ones in the roadhouse, with "Donny Basquette" painted along their upper lips and "Your Favorites" painted around the bases.

A beaming bandleader stood at one side of the frame, baton raised and ready to conduct. A beautiful woman in a low-cut, sparkling evening gown smiled warmly on the other side of the photo. Reacher thought she could have been Clementine, a long time ago.

"You see it?" said Clementine. "But there's nothing there!"

Reacher flashed her a look of alarm.

Clementine laughed and patted his shoulder. "Just kidding, young man. You can relax. Not only is there a photo of Donny Basquette and Your Favorites on the wall in front of you, but it is the only *actual* photograph in the place."

"Okay." Reacher nodded. He was relieved to have someone confirm what he'd seen . . . and not seen. "Then why is everyone acting like they see pictures in that scrapbook?"

"Wishful thinking," said Clementine. "They see what they want to see."

A roar of laughter erupted at the bar, and he looked over. Laszlo was holding up the scrapbook and pointing at a blank page that everyone seemed to think was hilarious.

"I don't get it," said Reacher.

"It's like this." As old as she was, Clementine still had touches of toughness and sexiness in her throaty voice. "We had the makings of a great band, maybe the best band ever, but we never made it big. The fact is, we never really tried. We never performed in public." She paused and gave Reacher a knowing look. "We were the world's greatest secret band that nobody ever heard of . . . and we were secret on purpose."

REACHER gaped at Clementine as if she'd just turned into a giant fish. "Secret?" he repeated. "On purpose?"

Clementine nodded. She ran a finger down the glass over the image of the bandleader in the photo. "Donny Basquette was what today you might call obsessive-compulsive. Back then, we just called him a perfectionist. Donny made his mind up that we wouldn't play in public until we were better than everyone else. Problem was, the band never got good enough for him."

The musicians at the bar howled with laughter.

"At first, we all thought it was a great gimmick," said Clementine. "Like a secret weapon . . . a secret band. We didn't think it would go on as long as it did. After a while, some of us got tired of it and left. That just built our reputation, because the ones who left told people about the band and how great it was and how it was supposed to be secret. We got to be like a legend for some people. Some of them even ran around trying to track us down."

Clementine sighed, tapping her fingernail on the glass over the woman in the photo. "But we never took advantage of the publicity. Some of us said Donny was crazy, and some said he was scared. Maybe he was a little of both. Maybe it was more about stage fright than being a perfectionist. But Donny just kept saying the band wasn't ready."

Reacher listened, mesmerized. He couldn't believe how similar the story was to Youforia's.

"And you know what?" Clementine squared her jaw and narrowed her eyes. "Some of us quit, but some of us stayed. We *believed* him, or maybe we were crazy or scared like he was." She smiled, gazing off into space.

Reacher leaned toward her, dying to know the rest. "Did you finally go public?"

Her smile faded, and she shook her head. "Pretty soon, it didn't matter if we wanted to be secret or not. The big band sound wasn't popular anymore. The times had passed us by."

Clementine turned from the picture on the wall to watch the musicians gathered around the bar. She slid her arm around Reacher's back as he followed her gaze. "Now all they have are their imaginary photos of the way things should have been. After all these years, they tell the same stories about each page every time. I think they even see the same pictures there."

"But not you," said Reacher.

Clementine laughed and rubbed his back. "I never said that."

At that moment, Eurydice broke away from the gang at the bar and strolled toward them. "Hands off my man, sister." Her face was flushed from all the laughing she'd done.

"I don't see a sign on him." Clementine hugged Reacher closer.

"How about if I put a sign on *you?*" Eurydice cracked her gum and sneered. "Either 'Out of Order' or 'Condemned.'"

"Sounds like a challenge," Clementine retorted. "How about it, young man? Would you like us to fight over you?"

But Reacher was in a daze and didn't answer. He kept watching the old men with the empty scrapbook as he struggled to digest the story Clementine had told him.

"What was that?" Eurydice leaned closer to Reacher, as if she were trying to hear something he'd said. "Well, okay, if you say so." She took his arm and tugged him away from Clementine. "He said he'd rather just pick me over you."

"Have your fun, Enid," said Clementine. "But if I were a few years younger, we both know I'd give you a run for your money."

Eurydice patted Reacher's arm. "We'd better get going. His kidnapper's waiting in the parking lot."

"Splendid," said Clementine. "Good luck with that."

Eurydice started to walk away, pulling Reacher by the arm. Then she stopped and turned back to Clementine. "Thank you," she said. "Thanks for your help."

Clementine sniffed and shrugged. "Just remember you owe me one. You know I'll collect."

"Yeah." Eurydice looked away, then back at Clementine. "You want to come along, for a change of scenery?"

"Change of scenery?" Clementine smiled ruefully. "That's what *dreams* are for, dear."

IN the cool night air outside the bar, it hit him.

Ever since his conversation with Clementine, Reacher had been in a daze. The daze had followed him through the enthusiastic goodbyes from the musicians and right out the door of Dusty's Wigwam, only to blow away a few steps later. For the first time, he realized something he thought he should've noticed much sooner.

"Your Favorites," he said, stopping in the parking lot in front of Dusty's. "Youforia."

"What is it?" asked Eurydice.

"This is too weird." He frowned and scrubbed a hand over the stubble on his scalp.

"What's weird?"

Reacher pointed at Dusty's. "Did any of that really happen? Clementine said something about dreams."

"What makes you think it was a dream?"

"Oh, I don't know," Reacher said sarcastically. "Maybe the band of old-timers playing at this hole in the wall to no one in the middle of the night? The scrapbook with the blank pages they all think have photos on them? Not to mention that their band is freakishly similar to *my* band. Even the names are alike! Your Favorites . . . Youforia. Youforia . . . Your Favorites."

"Wow," said Eurydice. "That *is* wild."

"Like you didn't notice."

Eurydice cracked her gum. "I didn't say that."

"I *must* be dreaming." He rubbed his eyes with the sides of his fists.

"No," said Eurydice. "Not a dream."

Reacher stopped rubbing his eyes and stared at her. "So you're trying to tell me that right along our route, there just happened to be a secret band with a name almost identical to the name of my own secret band?"

Eurydice nodded. "Lucky, huh?"

"So it's all a giant coincidence."

"Call it what you will, but those are real people in there, and they told you the truth." She stepped closer to him and cupped his chin in her hands. "Maybe you should ask yourself why it bothers you so much."

"I didn't say it bothers me." Reacher shrugged his shoulders to adjust his blue and black bowling shirt.

Eurydice gazed into his eyes, her face glowing red in the light from the neon sign. "All those wasted years, and now it's too late for those people." She paused. "But there's still time for you. There's still Maysville."

Softly, Reacher touched her hair. "Maybe I don't care anymore. There's such a thing as life without being in a band, you know."

She turned her head and kissed his wrist. "I don't like it when you lie to me."

"I'm sorry." He sighed. "So you think the band should go public in Maysville?"

"Here is what you need to know." Eurydice's face glowed with fresh intensity as she stared at him. She pressed her palm against his chest over his heart as she said the next words. "Your family was wrong about you, and you have nothing to fear."

Reacher frowned, looking puzzled. Eurydice smiled and kissed him on the lips.

Just then, a car horn honked, and both of them jumped. The triple headlights of the van flicked on, aimed in their direction.

"Sundra." Reacher watched as the van rolled across the street toward them. "I'll bet she saw us kissing."

"We'll tell her it was love at first sight," said Eurydice. "We couldn't help ourselves. Either that or I'm just a hopeless groupie with a thing for musicians," she added with a wink.

Back at the van, Reacher sat in the front seat beside Sundra. Without a word, she thumped him in the chest with *Fireskull's Revenant*. He took the paperback and flipped it open to where he'd left off. Looking over his shoulder, he winked at Eurydice in the back seat, then snapped on the dome light and started to read.

CHAPTER FORTY-FIVE

"COULD you not have picked a *better* time to come see me?" said Johnny Without as he fought off two enemy swordsmen at once.

In the middle of a raging battle, Scrier Inevitas floated above him, upside down, bobbing at the edge of his vision. Instead of falling straight down, her long black hair flowed all around her head like ribbons in a pool.

"If you and your foe do not unite, both your kingdoms shall be lost before the cock crows tomorrow." As always, her voice sounded as if she were speaking from the heart of a windstorm.

Metal clanged and clashed as Johnny parried the attacks of his enemies. He brandished a sword in each hand. As he flicked and swung the gleaming blades, his arms continuously changed shape, confusing his opponents.

"It's not that I do not believe you." He grunted out the words as he withstood a particularly vigorous advance. "It's just that I don't really have a *choice* right now! Did I happen to mention my kingdom's under attack at the moment?" One of his opponents' swords banged against

Johnny's gold breastplate, and he shunted the blade aside with a tricky twist and lunge.

"Your choice is clear," said Scrier. "Surrender."

With a cry of exertion, Johnny simultaneously swept aside both enemy swords and slashed their owners, one across the midsection, one across the chest. "So you are working for *him* now?" His fragmented voice changed constantly, making it sound like every syllable was spoken in a different tone and pitch by a different person. "For Fireskull?"

"I work for no one." Scrier dropped down in front of him so that he could see the grave expression on her face. "And I never lie," she said, bobbing back up out of the way.

"Then answer me this," said Johnny as one of his combatants lashed his blade perilously close to Johnny's throat. He had to deflect the enemy sword's next pass before he could resume talking. "If it is so important that Fireskull and I join forces, why is he attacking me?"

"It does not matter."

"It matters to me!" said Johnny as both opponents launched especially aggressive barrages. Fortunately, thanks to his distorted body, he literally had an eye on the back of his head; he could see and meet attacks from behind as well as in front of him, holding off both of Fireskull's men at once.

"There is still time," said Scrier. "If you surrender

now, your forces, combined with your enemy's, will be in position to repel the next threat. If you continue to resist, all will be lost by morning."

"If I surrender," said Johnny, "I will not live out the night! Fireskull has been waiting decades to kill me. He will not put off slaughtering everyone else in my kingdom, either!"

"There is still time," Scrier repeated. "You have been warned."

"I'll tell you what." Johnny unreeled blistering combinations of thrusts and slashes with both swords. "If you can guarantee that the citizens of my kingdom will not be massacred by Fireskull's troops, I will consider it."

Scrier fell silent. Glancing up between sword clashes, Johnny saw that she was staring into space as if deep in thought.

Finally, she spoke. "I cannot guarantee that. Perhaps you are right. Perhaps there can be no trust."

Gritting his teeth, Johnny fought off a flurry of strikes from both directions. "But I thought trust was our only hope."

"Then there is no hope," she said. "Your kingdoms are lost."

Slowly, she began to spin. Johnny realized that she was about to leave.

"When next we meet, you will have nothing left but

each other." Scrier spun faster and rose higher above the battlefield. Someone shot an arrow at her, but it shunted in a different direction when it got within a few feet. "When that happens, and you both have nowhere else to turn, I shall offer the same advice."

"Please, wait!" Johnny's head blew apart into bubbles that danced around and recombined.

"We shall see what your answer is then." Whirling like a weathervane in a tornado, Scrier suddenly shot straight up and disappeared into the bright orange sky.

With a burst of raging energy, Johnny stormed both of his opponents at once, his swords becoming glinting blurs of motion. The rest of him became a scream the size of a man, an enormous dark maw releasing his fury in an earsplitting blast.

Seconds later, he stood over the inert bodies of his enemies. His own body reverted from monstrous screaming maw to a form that was more or less normal for him— boulder-sized hands, accordion legs, and eyes orbiting his inflating and deflating balloon of a head. His gold breastplate, white tunic, and brown leather pants all reverted to their original forms along with him . . . and all were spattered with blood.

"She says that all is lost," he said, watching another enemy soldier stalk toward him. "Yet, as always, what choice do I have?"

It was while Johnny was preparing to fight this latest opponent that his chief aide and best friend, Shut Stepthroat, hollered from across the battlefield. "Look to the ridgetop! The ridgetop!"

Johnny stole a glance over and upward. Atop a ridge on the far side of the valley, he saw a single rider on ostrich-back. Light glinted off something that the rider was holding in front of his face.

"That is not one of ours!" said Shut. "And when was the last time Fireskull's troops rode *ostriches?*"

Johnny's heart pounded so hard that it leaped forward, pushing out a throbbing, heart-shaped piece of chest on a rubbery tether.

The ridge was directly above his beloved Castle Vanish.

"That's not one of ours," Lord Fireskull said to himself. "I do not think it's one of theirs, either."

Fireskull and his Lunatic Guard had just killed an eight-man patrol at the riverbank. After the attack, he had risen above the treetops with great flaps of his leathery wings, seeking fresh victims and signs of the overall progress of the invasion.

It was then, thanks to his elevation and inhumanly strong eyesight, that Fireskull had spotted the man on ostrich-back atop a distant ridge. Even from so far away, he could tell that the man's uniform belonged neither to his side nor to Johnny's, and was in fact completely unfamiliar.

As Fireskull rose higher for a better view, the man was joined by another rider . . . then another. And then, all at once, a line of riders rose up around the first three, occupying the entire length of the ridge.

"Reinforcements?" Fireskull wondered if Johnny's supporters from one of the eastern kingdoms had broken through the lines.

But even as he thought that, he knew it was wrong. He knew in his heart that the troops on the ridge had something to do with the new threat promised by Scrier.

Fireskull had refused her request that he join forces with Johnny. The only promise that he had made to her was to ruin every last square inch of Johnny's kingdom and turn every last one of Johnny's subjects into slaves, Lunatics, or sausage.

Now, as he gazed at the long line of unknown riders poised above Castle Vanish, Fireskull wondered if perhaps he had been a little hasty in refusing Scrier's guidance.

Someone on the ridge blew a signal on a bugle. Seconds later, the entire line of riders charged down the hillside into the valley.

TWENTY-NINE

IDEA

ONCE again, there was a parallel between Idea's life and *Fireskull's Revenant*. Like Johnny and Fireskull, Idea was encountering a long line of unknown riders, although in his case, the riders occupied cars, vans, SUVs, and campers, extending as far as his eyes could see.

Traffic was at a standstill on the flat rural two-lane road leading to Maysville, Kentucky. The first sign of the jam had come less than a mile ago, when Eunice had steered the green Beetle around a bend and nearly collided with the tail end of the lineup. Now the Bug inched forward, hemmed in by what seemed like an endless stretch of vehicles.

"Just look at them all." Idea fiddled nervously with the buttons of his shirt as he stared out the window.

"They're here because of you." Eunice was fixing her hair with both hands while she steered the car with her knees. "Because of what you created."

"Because of someone else *exploiting* what I created is more like it."

"But you still started it all," said Eunice. "You're the one with the magic touch."

Idea snorted, but he knew she was right about one thing: all that traffic was on the road because of Youforia.

Some of the cars had window or bumper stickers with slogans like I ♥ Youforia, Youforia = Euphoria, and I Believe in Youforia. People waved homemade signs asking if anyone wanted to buy or sell tickets. Car stereos blasted "Chapter 64" and other songs he didn't recognize.

Idea found it all mind-boggling and infuriating at the same time. On the one hand, he was blown away by the sheer enormity of the interest in his Internet hoax. On the other hand, when he thought of how strangers were making a fortune off the fans by pretending to be Youforia, he grew more and more angry.

"When is the show supposed to start, Bart?" asked Eunice.

"Seven o'clock tonight, according to Bud's tickies."

Eunice whistled with amazement. "You do realize it's only seven in the *morning* right now?"

Idea nodded. "It's going to take us all day just to get there."

"At least we know we're headed in the right direction," said Eunice.

"Lucky us."

She reached over and took his hand. "Try to relax," she said, smiling at him. "Everything's going to work out."

Immediately his mood softened. As angry as he was about the Youforia impostors, just thinking about kissing Eunice made him happy. "I hope you're right. It's just, now that I see what a big deal this is, I'm wondering if I even have a chance."

"A chance to do what?"

"I don't know." Idea stared out the window at a vast cornfield. "Like you said before, I don't own the rights to Youforia. Even if I tried to unite with the impostors like your digihoroscope said, I doubt they'd want me."

"Maybe," said Eunice. "Or maybe not. The important thing is, you're here. You're part of the equation. You might have more impact than you think."

Idea smiled at her. "Thanks for trying to make me feel better. And thanks for coming with me."

"Any time." She squeezed his hand.

Idea swallowed hard, then blurted out something he'd been meaning to say for a while. "I really like you and I hope you like me, too, Eunice."

A gap opened in front of the Bug, and Eunice eased the car into it. "Remember when the digihoroscope told you to 'unite'?"

"Sure," said Idea.

"What if it wasn't just referring to you and the impostor band?" said Eunice. "What if it meant that you should unite with someone else, too?"

"Like who?"

Eunice gave his hand a shake and released it. "*There's* a mystery for you. Let me know if you figure it out."

Idea felt himself blush. He wondered if she meant what he hoped she did—that he should unite with *her*.

Then, afraid to find out the truth right away, he grabbed *Fireskull's Revenant* from the dashboard and started reading.

CHAPTER FORTY-SIX

THE unknown army tore through the heart of the Kingdom of Without, crushing all opposition. Johnny's troops were like defenseless sheep, reeling in full retreat to the walls of Castle Vanish.

Fireskull's forces fared no better. The unknowns massacred most of them and drove the rest back across the border like mice into the Unrepentant Kingdom, ending the invasion.

And also beginning an invasion of their own. While one of their divisions laid siege to Castle Vanish, another charged toward Fireskull's own stronghold.

Fireskull had imagined he would be sitting on the throne of his enemy by the end of the day. Instead, he was soon fighting for his very existence on the doorstep of the castle he called home.

In a spearhead formation, the unknown army raced into the waiting ranks of Fireskull's elite Burning Legion, his last ring of defense.

Fireskull himself fought above and alongside his men,

swooping down on his leathery wings to hack off enemy heads. He battled with rage and grace, efficiently thinning the frontline while dodging barrages of spears and arrows.

All that he owned and ruled was riding on this one fight. The strangers on ostrich-back who had hurtled down from the hills were now poised to seize control of the seat of his power.

What truly grated on him was that he had no idea who the unknown army represented. The soldiers carried no banners or pennants. Their armor was uniformly blood crimson but bore no identifiable crests or emblems. Their bodies, when laid bare, had no brands or distinguishing physical characteristics that pointed to a patron or homeland.

They were truly ciphers, striking with equal savagery at Fireskull's and Johnny's kingdoms alike. They killed everyone in their path with indiscriminate brutality. They made no demands and offered no mercy.

Even if Fireskull had wanted to surrender, he would not have known to whom to do it.

A spear flashed toward him from the enemy ranks and he caught it with lightning quick reflexes. Instead of wasting it on one man, he drove it into the chests of one after another, punching it through armor breastplates with his inhuman strength.

An army of creatures like Fireskull, with strength like his and the power of flight, might have had some hope of turning the enemy. Unfortunately, the only other beings like himself that Fireskull knew of were half a world away or long dead. He had to settle for men to defend his kingdom—men who were exhausted from recent battles with Johnny's forces . . . and, frankly, men who would have been outmatched by the unknown invaders even had they been well rested.

Little by little, Fireskull saw the frontline press closer to his stronghold. Everywhere he turned, his soldiers fell to enemy swords or spears or maces.

Most discouraging of all, he saw the head of his chief commander brandished overhead on an enemy pike. This was none other than General Shunjoy Undercut, whom Fireskull had seen kill uncounted men with his bare hands, and whom Fireskull had always thought of as unkillable himself.

When he saw that head on the pike, he made a decision. It was a decision that he could barely stand to consider, a decision that just a few hours ago he could not have imagined ever making.

Swooping down, Fireskull released a blast of fiery breath that turned Undercut's severed head to a rain of ash. He unleashed another blast after that, cooking a dozen enemy soldiers like lobsters in their armored shells.

Then he swung around in midair and flew away from the battle. The shouts and screams and sounds of clashing swords and shields and armor faded behind him as he flapped off through the orange sky toward the red forestlands.

As he retreated.

And as he went, the words of Scrier echoed in his memory, adding to the shame that he felt. She had warned him.

And he had chosen, instead of following her advice, to twist her words to justify his own dark ambitions.

Even now, as he flew in full retreat from the battle and gave up his kingdom to the invaders, he managed to convince himself that Scrier shared the blame. After all, she knew him well enough.

She must have *known* he wouldn't listen.

THIRTY-ONE

REACHER

"**T**HE question now is, how do we get the lead singer to the concert?" said Sundra, swerving the van back and forth in the lane, as if it would do any good.

Reacher stared wide-eyed at the motionless sea of vehicles laid out before him under the green morning sky. For a band that was meant to be secret, Youforia was attracting the kind of turnout he would've expected for a major star.

The six northbound lanes of the Maysville beltway were packed solid with traffic, all pointed in the direction of Stowe Amphitheater. It was clear, given the abundance of Youforia stickers, signs, and T-shirts, that most of the vehicles were carrying concertgoers bound for the band's debut.

"I got another question for y'all," Eurydice drawled from the back seat, still pretending to be Elizadeath. "Is the *rest* of the band gonna make it to the show?"

"I have my doubts." Reacher ran a hand back and forth over the bristly white stubble on his head. The whereabouts of the band and its manager were unknown. He hadn't seen them since his abduction, and Eurydice said she hadn't seen them since an hour after that, when she'd left the motel to hunt for him.

They weren't answering their phones, either. During the drive from Dusty's Wigwam, he'd used the Youfers' confiscated cell phones to make what had seemed like a hundred calls to his bandmates, and not one of those calls had been picked up. The most he'd been able to do was leave messages on their voice mail.

"I guess we just have to hope they got one of your messages," said Sundra.

Eurydice cracked her gum. "But if they did, wouldn't y'all kinda sorta maybe expect 'em t' call back by now?"

"Maybe they were too busy," Sundra replied in a condescending tone. She'd been extra cold toward Eurydice since seeing the kiss in Dusty's parking lot. "Maybe they're already warming up at the amphitheater."

"Yeah, that must be it." Eurydice pressed her knee into the back of Reacher's seat.

He felt the pressure but didn't react. His eyes were glued to the six-lane sprawl of vehicles spread out around him.

He was having trouble getting used to the idea that most of the people in those vehicles were there because of him, that they'd come to see him sing and play with the band for the first time in public as Youforia.

Every time he imagined performing in front of all those people, he felt cold and nauseous. He pictured himself onstage, staring out at thousands of fans, screwing up the lyrics or the chords of a song while everyone booed.

It wouldn't be the first time he'd failed. Until he'd left home and gone on the road with Youforia, his life had been a pattern of repeated failures.

Since forming the band and escaping the people and places that had kept him down, he'd grown increasingly confident; but even so, it didn't always take much to push him back into the hole. Seeing so many people on their way to watch him perform, all of them expecting something special from the mystery band they'd been hearing about, was more than enough to do the trick.

What bothered Reacher the most, however, was the absence of the magic feeling. All along, since the band's beginning, he'd said that he wouldn't go public unless he got the magic feeling that the band was ready. Now that he was heading for Maysville, the magic feeling was nowhere to be found.

That was enough to convince him to try to avoid the failure he expected. "Let's get out of here," he told Sundra. "We'll be sitting here till Dogtober if we stay in this traffic."

Sundra scanned the broad river of motionless vehicles all around her. "Good idea." She cranked the steering wheel hard to the right and jerked the front end of the van into a gap between cars in the next lane.

The guy she cut in front of hit his horn, but Sundra ignored him and rolled across his lane. She hit her own horn then, getting the attention of the two girls in the car that was blocking the next lane over.

"Hey!" Sundra shouted out the window at them, wagging a thumb at Reacher. "Do you know who this is?"

The skinny blonde behind the wheel leaned out the window and squinted up at Reacher. "Not a clue."

"Who is he?" asked the brunette in the seat beside her.

"Reacher Mirage." Sundra nodded knowingly.

"Yeah, right," said the blonde. "And I'm Gail Virtuoso."

The brunette wasn't so quick to dismiss the idea. "Wait a minute." She frowned. "That *does* look like him, Wendy."

The blonde tilted her head to one side, reconsidering. "I don't know. He looks kind of like the photo on the website of Reacher at the barn jam, but not so much like the photo of him at the campfire."

"Sing something," the brunette suggested. "Like the chorus of 'Mr. In-Betweener.'"

Reacher sighed. He was more interested in finding out how there could be photos from the barn and the campfire on the web.

"Will you let us through if he sings a chorus?" Sundra asked the girls.

"If it's him," said the blonde.

"Believe me, we'll know," the brunette chimed in.

"Go ahead." Sundra gave Reacher's shoulder an encouraging shake.

He shrugged. "Okay, then. Here goes." He cleared his throat and sang the chorus from "Mr. In-Betweener," a song from his rock opera, *Singularity City*.

> "Where do I go when you turn the page?
> Am I alive when I'm not on the stage?
> Am I still me when I'm not on your mind?
> Do I still have a name when I'm left behind?
> When the puppeteer lets go of my strings,
> will I simply collapse in the wings?

And will anyone care what I feel like
when I'm in-between?"

When Reacher had finished, the blonde and brunette applauded and grinned. "Very nice," said the blonde. "Nice voice."

"But you don't sound a bit like Reacher Mirage," added the brunette.

"Because you tried so hard, though, we're going to let you through, anyway," said the blonde.

As the girls maneuvered their car to open a path to the side of the highway, Eurydice laughed in the back seat of the van. "Oh, that was sweet!"

Reacher grinned and laughed, too, the star-shaped port-wine stain on his right cheek dimpling into a crescent. "I just don't sound like myself today, I guess."

Sundra eased the van through the gap and took off down the shoulder. "I thought you did just fine." She sounded offended.

"Those girls'll never know how close they came to greatness," said Eurydice. "At least not till ya walk out onstage and they recognize y'all!"

"Yeah," said Reacher. "When I walk out onstage."

Even as he said it, Sundra whipped the Tucker down an exit ramp that Reacher hoped would lead to a final escape from the concert that was filling him with visions of disaster.

He tried not to think about it. Folding open *Fireskull's Revenant,* he tried to lose himself in the story.

Chapter Forty-Seven

SOLDIERS of the unknown army tried to execute Johnny Without sixteen times before he escaped.

Shortly after the end of the battle, they took him to the highest rampart of Castle Vanish to kill him, not that it mattered where they did it. Now that most every citizen of Johnny's kingdom was dead or in hiding, the only people watching were the other soldiers of their army.

Whoever the unknown invaders were, whatever their homeland or creed, they did not take prisoners. When they tried to execute Johnny, however, the killing machine stalled. Because of his constantly morphing body, conventional techniques were ineffective.

When the soldiers chopped his neck with an axe, Johnny's head dropped and rolled away, then rolled back and reattached itself. This happened three times before they tried something else.

When they plunged a sword through his torso, his body split around the blade, each half shrinking to become a miniature Johnny. The soldiers chased the Johnnys around until the tiny replicas finally danced back together and resumed their original, combined form.

They tried to suffocate him by stuffing rags in his mouth and nostrils, but his mouth and nostrils receded into his face and regrew on the back of his head. They slammed his head against a stone parapet, but it inflated on impact and bounced off without damage. They threw him off the rampart to the ground far below, and his body stretched out flat and floated slowly downward like a slip of paper.

When one simple plan after another failed, the soldiers turned to more ambitious approaches. They decided to tie each of Johnny's limbs to a different ostrich steed and have the ostriches tear him apart by running in different directions. Things did not work out as planned, though. First the soldiers had trouble tying Johnny's arms and legs because they enlarged and shrank unpredictably. When the soldiers finally managed to secure him to the ostriches and sent them running, the execution at last seemed complete: each bird tore off an arm or a leg, leaving only the head and torso still connected.

But then each severed limb suddenly turned to solid iron, stopping the ostriches in their tracks. The torso promptly grew new arms and legs.

By the time the soldiers got to their sixteenth attempt at killing him, Johnny noticed that they were slowing down. He was not surprised when they made the mistake that allowed him to escape.

With some difficulty, they tied him to a stake and stacked kindling all around him. While he squeezed and squirmed and strained against his bonds, the soldiers lit the kindling. Moments later, a bonfire roared around him, drawing ever closer.

When the fire was done with him, Johnny was a cloud of smoke and ash drifting into the sky.

Relieved that their work was finally done, the soldiers clapped one another on the back and went off to find something to eat. They planned to use what was left of the bonfire to cook their food.

Apparently none of them had considered the possibility that Johnny might yet be alive.

In fact, Johnny's consciousness survived in the cloud of smoke and ash. When the cloud had drifted far from Castle Vanish and passed over dense woodlands, his pieces flowed back together. His body became whole once more and fell, landing on a bed of leafy red treetops.

He lay there for a long time, letting the events of the day sink in while he gazed up at the bright orange sky. It was hard to believe that so much had happened in so short a time.

Although no official ceremony had marked his loss of power, he was no longer a king. An unknown enemy controlled his lands and wealth.

His armies had been slaughtered to the last man, or

close to it. His generals, from Fairforce to Knell to Paladine, had been hanged from the ramparts of Castle Vanish. His great and loyal friend Shut Stepthroat had been killed before his eyes.

He had nothing left except his own life.

It was not at all the way he had imagined things would turn out. He had always thought he would find a way to vanquish Fireskull, regain the Talisman of Integrity, and retrieve his two sons from the future.

Now, instead, an unknown enemy had triumphed, and Johnny was a fugitive. The enemy would not know that he was alive, but what good would that do him?

Scrier Inevitas had been right, as always. Johnny shuddered as he remembered her words.

When next we meet, you will have nothing left but each other.

At least he could take comfort in the fact that he would see Scrier again . . . if not a friendly face, at least a familiar one. On the other hand, her words suggested that he would see someone else again, too—someone very much unwanted.

You will have nothing left but each other, she had said. *Each other,* as in Johnny . . .

. . . and Fireskull.

THIRTY-THREE

IDEA

"**WHAT'S** the matter?" said the bearded man who was aiming the rifle at Idea's face. "Aren't you gonna say hi to your big brother?"

Eyes wide and hands held high, Idea stood in the middle of the men's bathroom at the gas station where Eunice had stopped. He had no idea who the bearded man was, and he was too scared to say anything.

"Now, that's a shame," the man continued. "I was expectin' a friendlier welcome than this." His beard was as black as the greasy hair curling out from under the band of his bright orange baseball cap. He had a short, upturned nose, big ears, and a wicked glint in his eyes.

Just then, the bathroom door opened behind him and two more men appeared, framed against an emerald backdrop. Idea blinked hard; was that the *sky* back there? Since when was it *green?*

One of the men was young, short, and excessively muscled, wearing expensive-looking mirrored sunglasses, a silk collared shirt with alternating blue and white vertical stripes, and white slacks. The other man, the one carrying the coil of rope, was ancient, scrawny, stooped, and mostly bald; he could have been in his seventies, eighties, or nineties, for all that Idea could tell.

"Hey, cuz," said the muscleman. "Long time no see."

"Surprise, surprise." When the old man sneered, Idea could see that he had no teeth. "Betcha didn't expect to see *us,* didja?"

Idea looked from one stranger to the other, then returned his gaze to the barrel of the rifle. The old man was absolutely right about all this being a surprise.

When he'd entered the bathroom, he hadn't expected to end up at gunpoint. But while walking out the door, he'd found the rifle barrel waiting for him, forcing him to back up.

In a way, it wasn't such a bad place to be, given that he was starting to feel like he might throw up soon. His stomach was churning with fear . . . and the onset of Deity Syndrome. The arrival of the gunman was just the kind of out-of-left-field plot twist that brought it on like an avalanche.

The old man closed and locked the bathroom door, then hobbled over to glare up at him. "Hey, moron." He smacked Idea's chest with the coil of rope. "Guess how we found you?" He pulled a folded piece of paper from the pocket of his gray flannel shirt and shook it open. Idea saw it was an advertisement for the Youforia show in Maysville.

"Idiot," said the grinning muscleman.

"Looks like you might miss the first number," said the bearded man.

"And the second and the third and the fourth," said the old man.

"Duuuuh!" The muscleman screwed up his features in an

expression of mocking stupidity. "I don't want my family to know where I am, so I'll put these *fliers* all over the place. They'll *never* find me now!"

The old man pressed his shriveled face so close to Idea's that Idea could smell his rancid breath. "What's that ya say, boy? You'd like nothin' better than goin' home to work the dairy farm?"

"Now, that's nice of you." The bearded man smiled and nodded.

"Selfless," added the muscleman.

"Now you done it. I'm gonna cry." The old man pretended to wipe a tear from his eye, then threw himself forward and hugged Idea.

"Why'd you go and do *that* for?" said the bearded man. "Now I'm gettin' choked up, too." With that, he loudly hawked up phlegm and spat it across the bathroom.

"I love ya, son." The old man pulled back from his embrace. "Now turn around so I can tie you up."

Finally Idea spoke. "You have me mistaken for someone else."

The old man looked at the other two men and they all grinned broadly.

"That's a good one," said the bearded man.

"Hi-larious," the muscleman chimed in.

"No, no." The old man shook his head. "Let's play along, boys. Why don't you introduce yourselves to this 'stranger'?"

"All right," said the bearded man. "My name is Planter, and I'm your brother."

"My name is Lifter," said the muscleman. "And I'm your cousin."

"I'm Daddy Naysayer," said the old man. "That just leaves you." He hobbled around behind Idea and spoke over his shoulder in a high-pitched voice, like a ventriloquist putting words in Idea's mouth. "Hello, Planter. Hello, Lifter. Pleased to meet you all. My name is Reacher. Reacher Mirage."

REACHER would have been better off if Sundra had listened to his directions. After she'd raced down the shoulder and off an exit in search of a shortcut to the concert, he had tried to give her the worst directions he could imagine.

Unfortunately, Sundra had a GPS app on her phone. The GPS had given perfect directions, and Reacher had gotten to Stowe Amphitheater in nothing flat.

After which, he'd walked right into his second abduction in twenty-four hours.

A yellow-T-shirted security guard with "Hector" on his nametag had snagged Reacher and the others at a checkpoint outside the amphitheater. Hector's yellow-shirted buddies had taken Eurydice and Sundra elsewhere, while Hector had led him straight to a huge white trailer.

As Reacher approached the trailer, he got the impression that the sky had shifted from green to blue, but he didn't dwell on it.

Hector ushered him inside, and a middle-aged woman with silver hair and a pink and black dress walked over to meet him. She wore a nametag that read "Loving Deity." "Idea! I was so worried!" She pecked him on the cheek. "I thought something awful had happened to my little boy."

"Idea?" Reacher frowned. Was she talking about the guy who'd been outing the band's secrets online and claimed to have created Youforia?

Suddenly a middle-aged man in a black suit with red pin-stripes and tie charged into the room from the back of the trailer. "All is forgiven!" Smiling, he hurried over and extended a hand. When Reacher didn't respond right away, the man grabbed his hand and shook it hard. "Glad you could join us, son." He had a neat black mustache and goatee, and his salt-and-pepper hair was tied back in a ponytail. His nametag read "Vengeful Deity."

"Thanks." Looking from one to the other, Reacher tried to figure out what was happening. Some kind of joke, maybe? Or did this Idea guy's mother and father really think he was their son? How was that even possible?

Just then, another man walked in from a doorway in the front section of the trailer. "I knew we'd catch up to you sooner or later." He had oily black hair, brown skin, and a huge hawk-like nose. "You led us on quite a chase, though." His nametag read "Bulab." Reacher thought he looked and sounded as if he was from India.

"A-minus." Yet another man emerged from the doorway up front, this one tall and silver-haired, with prominent cheek-bones, piercing blue eyes, and "Scholar" on his nametag. "You threw us off your trail back at the mall, but you posted on YoFace and Yapper that this was where you were headed. All we had to do was wait for you."

Vengeful shook his head and smiled. "Your mother and I would give you an A-*plus,* Idea."

"Absolutely," said Loving. "Not only did you stay a step ahead of Bulab and Scholar, but you turned that make-believe band of yours into a sensation at the same time."

Reacher stared at her. "Make-believe band?"

"Youforia, of course," said Loving. "You did such an incredible job marketing a nonexistent musical group that *thousands* of people have come to see them play!"

"Might have been nice to get a financial piece of all that." Vengeful said it offhandedly, then shrugged. "Still, you've accomplished something wonderful here."

"Thanks." Now that Reacher realized who the strangers thought he was, he decided it would be smart to play along and learn more. Maybe they could even lead him to the real Idea Deity.

"As a matter of fact, we'd like to propose something to you," said Loving. "Scholar?"

Scholar pressed a button on a remote control and a screen slid down from a slot in the ceiling. Bulab flipped open a laptop on a table and switched on a projector beside it.

"We propose that you harness the popular support you've created," Idea's mother continued. "And use it to spawn a grass-roots political organization."

Scholar touched a button on the remote control and a slide appeared on the screen. The slide featured a multicolored bar graph with the title "Youforia Party Projected Growth."

"A viable third political party is possible," said Vengeful.

"And we would be in the driver's seat. Just look at this projected growth rate."

"Next slide," said Loving. The image on the screen changed to a single-panel cartoon that showed two men sitting at a bar with drinks in front of them. The caption under the cartoon read "Is it possible for a never-was to become a has-been?"

"You've brought us around, son," she said. "Your running away was the best thing that ever happened to us."

"You don't want to end up like this." Vengeful pointed to the cartoon on the screen. "I say take this bull by the horns and put it to work for you."

"You have a ready-made audience pouring in to see your make-believe band," said Loving.

"Why not give them a *real* band?" Vengeful adjusted his ponytail. "You could adopt the identity of the lead singer, Reacher Mirage."

"We'll buy the other musicians you need," Loving added. "And we'll handle sign-ups for the Youforia Party."

Reacher stared at them, dumbfounded. If he understood correctly, they wanted him to pose as their son, Idea, posing as himself, Reacher Mirage.

"Next," said Loving. The new slide featured a pyramid emblazoned with the words TOP OF MIND balanced precariously atop the head of a grinning cartoon man. "Getting to the top of someone's mind can take a tremendous amount of work."

"But you've already achieved it," Vengeful went on. "Now is the time to turn that market penetration into a fledgling power structure."

"Bulab!" called Loving. "Show him the costume!"

Bulab lifted a garment bag from the back of a chair. He unzipped the bag and peeled it away, revealing its contents.

Vengeful walked over and threw an arm around Reacher's shoulders. "Now *that's* a rock 'n' roll suit!"

Reacher rubbed the white stubble on his scalp as he stared at the glittering multicolored outfit that Bulab was holding up for him to see. It was a jumpsuit with white fur trim and a neckline that looked as if it would plunge all the way to his navel. It was striped with every color in the rainbow and looked skintight except for the super-flared trouser legs.

"It comes with white boots!" said Bulab.

"And a red satin cape," added Vengeful.

"Try it on," urged Loving.

Just then, a knock on the trailer door got everyone's attention. Reacher sighed with relief.

"Go ahead." Vengeful nodded at Hector the security guard. "See who it is."

Hector gave Vengeful a disgruntled look, then turned and opened the trailer door. "Yeah?" He blocked Reacher's view with his broad back.

"Stage manager." The voice was that of a young woman. "We're trying to find the band's lead singer."

"You're in luck!" said Vengeful. "Let her in, Hector."

Hector moved aside, and the young woman stepped up into the trailer. "Thank you."

As soon as he saw her, Reacher thought she was beautiful. She had big blue eyes, an upturned nose, and chest-length blond hair with a single braid running through alternating black and white beads. Her smile was crooked and smirky, but good-natured. "Like I said, we're looking for the lead singer." She carried a clipboard and wore a headset and microphone wired to a box clipped to her belt. "You seen him?"

Reacher shook his head, but Loving and Vengeful both nodded on either side of him. "You've come to the right place," said Vengeful.

The longer Reacher looked at the stage manager, the more familiar she seemed. He couldn't put his finger on it, but he knew that he'd seen her somewhere before.

"We've got his costume right here." Loving waved at Bulab, who held up the rock star suit.

The stage manager turned to look at the outfit. It was then that Reacher realized why she looked so familiar.

Another face was tattooed on the back of her head, framed by black hair instead of blond. The backside of her outfit looked like a second front half; her blouse was white on the front side and black on the back, while her pants were black on the front and white on the back.

"That's quite a costume," said the stage manager.

"Excuse me, dear," interrupted Loving. "What did you say your name was?"

The stage manager reached out to shake hands. Her fingernails were painted with black and white yin-yang symbols. "Eunice," she said. "Eunice Truant."

THIRTY-FIVE

IDEA

"I'M telling you," said Idea. "I'm not Reacher Mirage."

Behind him, Daddy Naysayer went right on wrapping his wrists with rope. "Oh, we believe you, we believe you. This just happens to be how we treat *all* complete strangers."

"Reacher Mirage doesn't even exist," Idea insisted. "He's nothing but a fictional character."

"An *objectionable* character, is more like it," said Lifter Mirage.

"An *idiot* character," added Planter Mirage. He and Lifter shared a laugh, though the rifle barrel Planter was aiming at Idea's face never wavered.

"Get the truck," Daddy said sternly, looking at Lifter. "Back it right up to the door."

"Okey-doke." Turning, Lifter pulled open the men's room door and strolled outside.

Idea's stomach twisted, and chills coursed through him. Once again he thought he could see the hand of a malevolent author at work, manipulating him with implausible plot twists. A full-blown Deity Syndrome relapse was under way.

"There's some guy *pretending* to be Reacher Mirage," he offered. "Maybe that's who you're looking for."

"There's some guy pretending to be *me,* too," said Daddy. "He's the one out lookin' for the guy pretending to be *you.*"

Planter snickered and kept the gun level.

As he looked at it, Idea wondered if he'd reached the end of his story. Was this the chapter he'd been dreading, the one he'd seen predicted in omens revolving around the number 64? It certainly seemed his death was imminent.

If so, he had nothing to lose. He decided it was time to play the one card he had left up his sleeve.

"My family has a lot of money," he said. "One phone call would get you whatever you need."

"Maybe the family *in* your head has money," scoffed Daddy. "But the family pointin' a gun *at* your head is another story."

Idea felt sweat rolling down his sides and back. "My name is Idea Deity. I made up Reacher and the band for a hoax website. Maybe that's why you think I'm him."

"Nice try, boy." Daddy gave a last tug on Idea's bonds and walked around in front of him, snickering. "You *wish* you were somebody else."

Just then, the door swung open. Planter quickly lowered the rifle, and everyone turned to see who was there.

The young woman in the doorway had narrow green eyes and a thin, sharp face. Her full lips were painted bright red, and braids of jet black hair fell to her shoulders.

She wore a brown smock with the gas station's emblem on

the chest. She leaned on the handle of a mop in a wheeled bucket of water.

As soon as Idea saw her, he thought she looked familiar, though he couldn't quite place her.

" 'Scuse me," she said. "Are you guys about done in there? I gotta clean, y'know."

"In a minute." Planter held the rifle behind him, concealed along the length of his leg.

The woman rolled her eyes. She was chewing a piece of gum, and she cracked it three times. "Look. You've been in there forever. The manager said find another gas station."

Daddy was standing in front of Idea, trying to keep the woman from seeing he was tied up. "What's your name, miss?"

"Eurydice Tarantella," said the woman.

"Miss Tarantella," said Daddy. "Have you ever heard of a shovel-feel-like?"

Eurydice blew a bubble. It burst, and she drew it back into her mouth. "What the heck's a shovel-feel-like?"

Daddy chuckled. "You're about to find out."

"Behind you!" Idea shouted as he spotted Lifter running up behind Eurydice, a shovel poised like a baseball bat on his shoulder.

In that instant, as Eurydice turned around, Idea recognized her. He recognized the face that was tattooed on the back of her head, that is.

It was framed by long blond hair. A single braid descended from one temple, threaded through beads of alternating black and white.

THIRTY-SIX

REACHER

REACHER felt like a clown as Eunice Truant led him away from the trailer in the skintight rainbow-striped white-fur-trimmed rock star jumpsuit.

He was sure he looked ridiculous, although no one in the parade behind him seemed to notice. Loving and Vengeful chattered about business, followed by Bulab, who mumbled in a foreign language to Scholar. Hector, the yellow-shirted security guard, said nothing.

"Right this way, folks," Eunice said over her shoulder as she briskly walked along. "We only have an hour and a half until showtime."

The group passed other trailers and trucks parked in the concourse under the vast bowl supporting the amphitheater's seating. Roadies shouted and hauled equipment on carts, cutting back and forth across the access lane in front of them.

As Eunice hurried forward, Reacher leaned toward her and spoke in a low voice. "Eurydice? Is that you?"

"It's *Eunice*, honey." She smiled. "Rhymes with 'newness.'"

She looked away, but Reacher kept studying her features. Her face, with its blue eyes, dimples, and blond hair, resembled the face tattooed on the back of Eurydice's head. In turn, the face on the back of Eunice's head, with its green eyes, sharp nose, and black hair, reminded him of Eurydice's.

Eunice turned the group down a short tunnel leading to the field in the heart of the amphitheater. They emerged in open sunlight behind the stage, blinking up at the mountains of speakers and the huge scaffolding on which the lights and video screens were hung.

Reacher gazed at the scene in wonder, but not because of the stage setup. The blue sky was far more amazing to him, so different from the green sky he was used to.

"Here we are, superstars," said Eunice. "Welcome to the debut concert of the world's best-known unknown band, Youforia!"

"Not bad." Vengeful stepped past Eunice for a closer look at the speaker equipment.

"Excuse me." Loving also pushed forward, pointing at the nearest tower of scaffolding. "Why don't we put some banners up there for the show?"

"Not sure, Mrs. Deity," Eunice replied. "But I can find out."

"Would you, dear?"

Vengeful marched off along the edge of the stage. "Could you also look into the pyrotechnical situation? I don't see enough flash pots up front."

"Just a minute, please," called Eunice. "I have a question first."

Vengeful stopped and turned impatiently. "What's that?"

"How would you like to be backup singers tonight?"

Idea's father grinned and hurried back. "Are you *kidding?*"

"Not at all," said Eunice. "We've had a hard enough time tracking down the band and lead singer. Now we need backup vocalists."

"I *was* in a garage band as a kid." Vengeful smoothed his ponytail. "I kind of had a Morrison-Plant-Daltrey thing going."

Eunice raised her clipboard. "What's your name again?"

"Vengeful Deity. Do you need me to spell that?"

"Nope." Eunice scribbled on her clipboard. "What about you, ma'am?"

Loving shrugged and shuffled her feet. "Oh, I couldn't. I'm not qualified at all."

"Okey-doke." Eunice turned to Bulab. "What about—"

"Unless you count being lead soprano soloist at state chorus in high school four years running," said Loving. "And my lead roles in twelve professional opera productions starting at the age of seventeen."

"Sounds good to me." Eunice scribbled on the clipboard. "Now, if these other two gentlemen have—"

"I've also sung with several symphony orchestras," Loving continued.

"Yes, thank you," said Eunice. "I've already written your—"

"And I starred in the touring company production of—"

"What about you, sir?" Eunice said to Bulab.

Loving huffed and glared at Bulab, who ignored her.

"I sing along with my car stereo."

"Perfect." She scribbled some more. "And you?"

"I have no musical interest or ability whatsoever," said Scholar.

"You're in." Eunice made a final note, then attached the pen to her clipboard with finality. With one yin-yang–painted fingernail, she flipped a switch on the box on her belt and spoke into the tiny microphone that wrapped around from the headset's earpiece to her mouth. "This is Eunice. I've got our backup singers."

Loving laced her fingers together and beamed at Reacher. "This is so *exciting.*"

"Yeah?" Eunice listened to her headset earpiece. "Okay. All right. No-no, that's fine. No, that's . . . we'll get started right away. Got it." She switched off the box and grinned. "Listen up, everybody. I'm supposed to get you people suited up and onstage in fifteen minutes."

"This will be something to remember." Vengeful smiled at Reacher. "Your mother and I will be part of your world debut."

"I can't wait." Reacher forced a smile with great effort.

"Hector!" said Eunice. "Take these four to dressing room A. Tell Eville she needs to have them ready to go on in fifteen."

Hector frowned. "Who?"

"Dressing room A. Now go-go-go!" She shooed them all away, then spun to face Reacher. "And *you,* come with me!"

"We'll try not to upstage you, son!" called Vengeful as Hector herded him and the others toward an exit tunnel.

"We'll try not to steal the spotlight!" Loving added.

Even as they said it, Reacher knew they would do the exact opposite if given the chance.

As they disappeared into the exit, Reacher followed Eunice

through another tunnel that led back to the concourse under the seats. They walked along the curve of the concourse a little ways, then crossed the lane and hurried through an open gate in the chainlink fence that circled the amphitheater. A yellow-shirted guard on the other side waved as they hustled past him.

"So, Stage Manager Eunice," said Reacher as he trailed her across the parking lot. "Will the concert happen out here? For that matter, where *is* here?" He spread his arms wide. "What's with the blue sky and green grass?"

Eunice headed straight for a 1960s-era green Volkswagen Beetle that was parked nearby. "Get in." She threw open the driver's side door and ducked inside.

Reacher opened the passenger's door and hesitated. "Is the rest of the band here? You said you had a hard time tracking them down, but does that mean you *did* track them down?"

Eunice started the engine. "I can take you to them, or I can take you to someone else. Someone you've been wanting very badly to meet."

"Who?"

When she told him, he dropped down into the seat without another moment of hesitation. She threw the car into gear and sped out of the amphitheater's parking lot.

THIRTY-SEVEN

IDEA

IDEA had never thought of himself as brave, but there he was, with his arms tied behind his back, fighting a man with a gun.

Eurydice Tarantella had gotten things rolling by stopping Lifter from hitting her in the head with a shovel. Whoever she really was—two-faced reverse twin of Eunice; maybe Eunice herself in disguise—her reflexes had turned out to be lightning fast, her aim perfect, her strength surprising.

She'd spun around at Idea's warning, wrapping her fingers around the handle of her mop and hoisting it up out of the bucket. She'd swung the mop around in an arc, spattering Daddy Naysayer and Planter with filthy water.

Lifter had gotten worse than a shower, though. She'd smacked him full in the face with the gray mop head, interrupting his charge.

As the mop struck Lifter's face, Eurydice had lashed back a sneakered foot, kicking the bucket toward Daddy and Planter. It slammed into Daddy's shins with a crack, launching the gray water all over them.

She'd then shoved Lifter back with the mop, and he'd dropped the shovel and tripped over a curb, tumbling down onto the parking lot pavement.

In the men's room, Daddy had quickly recovered. Knocking aside the bucket, he'd charged outside and leaped onto Eurydice's back, wrapping his arms around her throat.

She had flipped the old man over her head and onto the ground with no trouble, but his attack had given Planter time to fix her in his rifle sights. It was then that Idea had gotten brave.

Realizing Eurydice was about to be shot, he'd impulsively thrown himself against Planter. Instead of pulling the trigger, Planter had fallen against the wall, then shoved Idea away and swung the rifle barrel around to aim at his chest.

Luckily, a shout from outside had gotten Planter's attention just then. Stealing a quick glance, Idea had seen that Lifter and Eurydice were having a sword fight with the shovel and mop. While Planter watched the battle, the rifle shifted, and Idea was in the clear.

That was why, now, he ducked his head and hurled himself at Planter. His hands were tied, but he still managed to sweep aside the rifle and drive a shoulder into Planter's chest, knocking the wind out of him.

Idea drew back and flung himself forward again, heaving his full weight into Planter's chest and abdomen. The next time he pulled back, though, Planter came to life, kicking and swinging.

He landed a good one with his steel-toed boot. Idea stumbled back, falling over the toilet and cracking his head against the wall.

Cursing, Planter jammed his rifle butt into Idea's gut. "You *will* pay for that, brother." He threw in another blow for good measure.

Wincing in pain, Idea looked out the open door. He saw Daddy sneaking up on Eurydice as she blocked another strike from Lifter's shovel with her mop.

"The old man's right behind you!" he shouted.

"No fair helpin'." Taking off his orange ball cap, Planter leaned down and placed it on Idea's head. "Now mind your own business." He yanked the cap down over Idea's face.

Planter left him there like that, wedged between the toilet and the wall with his hands bound, unable to remove the sweaty hat. Idea strained to listen, trying to piece together what was happening. He heard shouts, clatter, grunts, rustling—but, thankfully, not the gunshot that he dreaded.

Unfortunately, the cap did more than block his view of the fight. Pulled tightly over his nose and mouth, it heated up as his exhaled breath collected inside it. His face felt warmer with each passing moment, and breathing became more difficult. The fiery orange color just seemed to make matters worse, reinforcing the sensation of building heat.

Then, all of a sudden, the cap seemed to catch fire for real.

For a moment, Idea's field of vision was filled with a wall of flame. Orange tongues of fire danced and flickered, radiating intense heat. Beyond the flames, he glimpsed what he thought were trees and rolling hills, spreading out far below him. It was as if he were flying, looking down at a landscape as he passed over it . . . a landscape shrouded by a wall of flame.

Or maybe, he thought, the wall of flame wasn't so far away. The heat, after all, was intense.

Maybe the flames surrounded *him* instead of shrouding the landscape. Maybe they were *part* of him.

As if he were Fireskull.

The vision brought a new possibility to mind. With Eurydice's help, he'd survived the fight with Daddy Naysayer, Planter, and Lifter. So maybe he wasn't doomed to die in a book about his own life, like he'd thought. Maybe his destiny awaited in the pages of a different book, one he was reading, one with striking similarities to aspects of his own life experiences.

The fact that he was picturing himself in Fireskull's body, in Fireskull's world, seemed to back up this theory. It sent his Deity Syndrome into instant overdrive, making him spin out of control in his flight over the landscape.

Then the wall of flame disappeared. Eunice Truant smiled down at him, holding the orange cap in her hand.

"Eunice?" said Idea. "What happened to Eurydice?"

Eunice's eyes widened and she giggled. "Whoops!" Then she stuffed the ball cap back over Idea's face.

A second later, the cap again lifted, this time revealing dark-haired Eurydice's smiling face. "Peek-a-boo!" she said. "Come out, come out, wherever you are."

"Man." Idea looked around, but he saw no sign of Eunice in the room. "That was just weird."

"*Tell* me about it." She helped him to his feet. "How those three idiots manage to run a lawn mower, let alone a dairy farm, is beyond me."

Idea looked outside as she untied his wrists. "Where are they, anyway?"

"In that dumpster over there." She cracked her gum twice. "I figured it was the best place for them."

Sure enough, Idea could see arms and legs hanging over the side of the big black dumpster across the parking lot.

"By the way." Eurydice slipped the rope from his wrists and tossed it in a corner. "Thanks for the assist."

Idea brushed off his black button-down shirt. He was surprised it hadn't gotten torn in the fight. "You beat all three of them?"

"One was an old-timer," she said. "The other two were morons. It wasn't really a fair fight."

"Morons with a shovel and a rifle," Idea corrected.

"But still morons." Eurydice grinned. "Morons who got beat by a girl. I'd wake them up and rub their noses in it if we weren't running so late right now."

Idea followed her into the parking lot. Looking around, he saw more of the emerald sky he'd glimpsed earlier, and patches of *pink* grass to boot. "Late for what?"

Eurydice stripped off the brown gas station attendant's smock and tossed it into the dumpster on her way past, revealing a half-and-half outfit underneath—black blouse and white pants in front, white blouse and black pants in back. "Here's the deal." She flung open the door of a white van and hopped up into the driver's seat. "I can take you to the concert, or I can take you to meet someone who will change your life."

Idea frowned as he opened the passenger's side door. "Change it for the better?"

Eurydice blew a pink bubble and popped it. "That's up to the two of you."

Idea hesitated. He was inclined to trust Eurydice because of her apparent link to Eunice. But the fact remained, she was still a stranger to him. He'd never met her before she'd interrupted his attempted abduction.

"I need to know more," said Idea.

Eurydice sighed. "If you want to meet him, we have to leave *now*."

"Then hurry up and tell me who he is."

"Get in," she said, cracking her gum, and he did. After she told him to whom she was offering to take him, he made his choice without hesitation. The tires of the van squealed as it surged out of the gas station's parking lot, heading in the opposite direction from Stowe Amphitheater.

IDEA

THE name of the diner was Seconds. The motto, painted in white letters across the front windows, was YOU'LL ALWAYS COME BACK FOR SECONDS!

The long narrow building sat five miles outside Maysville, clad in glass and stainless steel, shining alone among the endless pink fields. Seconds reminded Idea of diners in movies about the 1950s. It was in such great shape, though, he couldn't tell if it had been around since then or had been built a week ago.

The parking lot, as Eurydice rolled the van into it, was nearly full. Idea thought that this must mean the food at Seconds was good, but he knew he was too nervous to enjoy it.

His mind was fixed on the meeting that was about to happen. The more he thought about it, the more agitated he became. If Eurydice was right, this would be what everything had been leading up to. This would be the time for answers.

Eurydice parked the van and they walked to the front of the diner. "After you." She held the door and waved him inside. A bell jingled as it closed behind them.

"Hey, Splitter!" Eurydice called, waving and smiling at a cook looking out from the kitchen.

+ **201** +

"Hey, Eudora!" Splitter saluted her with a stainless steel spatula. "Long time no eesay!"

"Ain't that the uthtray!" Eurydice spoke in pig Latin like Splitter had. "Can I abgray an oothbay?"

Without warning, a waitress swept past. "We've got a booth right over here." Her voice was a smoker's croak. "Now move it or lose it."

"I love you too, Mixie," said Eurydice. "Aterlay, Ittersplay," she said to the cook.

"You betcha," said Splitter.

"Coffee?" Mixie said gruffly as they took their seats.

"You want coffee?" Eurydice asked Idea.

Idea shook his head. He was nervous enough without adding a caffeine rush.

"One, please." Eurydice cracked her gum.

But Mixie was already walking away. "Get it yourself," she muttered, stuffing an unlit cigarette into her mouth as she headed toward the exit. "I'm on break." With that, she threw open the door and marched outside, lighting the cigarette on the way.

"Order up!" Splitter plunked plates of meat loaf and mashed potatoes on the sill of his service window. When no one came to pick them up, he looked at Eurydice. "Whadda ya say? Once more for old times' akesay?"

"Why not?" Eurydice got up and glided behind the counter to scoop up the plates of food.

"Thanks, eetheartsway," said Splitter. "Table six. The booth in the ornercay."

Eurydice whisked across the diner and deposited the plates

in front of the elderly couple in the corner booth. "Just remember," she told them. "*I* get the tip when you're done."

Then she walked back behind the counter and poured herself a cup of coffee. "Now you need to get up, hon," she told Idea. "Move to the other side of the booth."

"Why?" Idea asked.

"Because the seat you're in is taken."

Idea scowled. "What're you talking about? It was empty when we came in."

Eurydice cracked her gum three times fast. "Just because you can't see someone sitting there, that doesn't mean the seat is empty."

"**Y**OU'RE telling me he's right there"—Reacher pointed at the red vinyl seat across the table—"but he's *invisible?*"

"You can't see or hear him," said Eunice, sitting beside Reacher on the bench facing the door of Seconds.

"Can he see me?" he asked. "Can he hear me?"

Eunice shook her head. "Neither one."

Reacher blew out his breath and threw himself against the back of the seat. "Okay, first of all, this is hard to believe, to say the least," he said, fiddling with the buttons of his green and white bowling shirt. "Secondly, if it's true, how am I supposed to meet this guy?" Eunice had had the bowling shirt and a pair of jeans in the back of the Beetle. Reacher had changed in the men's room of a gas station on the way to Seconds, tossing the ridiculous rock 'n' roll suit in the trash.

"You speak through me," said Eunice. "Tell me what you want to tell him, and I'll pass it along."

"Pass it along how?"

"He has someone with him who can see and hear me," she explained. "Just like I can see and hear her. She'll tell me what he says, and I'll tell her what you say."

"Just like that, huh?"

"It's the only way." Eunice shrugged as she played with her blond braid. "For now."

Just then, Mixie came over with two cups and a full pot of coffee. "Here you go, you two," she said sweetly, beaming as she put the cups on the table and poured steaming black coffee into them.

"Thanks," said Eunice.

Mixie dropped a handful of creamers on the table and patted Eunice's arm. "You just let me know if there's anything else I can get you, dear."

At that moment, the cook roared Mixie's name from the kitchen, and she scurried away. His voice echoed through the diner as he berated her yet again for being too slow.

Eunice glared in the direction of the kitchen until the shouting died down. Then she turned back to Reacher. "You want to kick things off?"

"You mean talk to the thin air over there?" Reacher couldn't help sounding skeptical.

"Now's your chance to speak to him," said Eunice.

"If he's right there, why can't we see each other?" Reacher waved at the empty seat across the table.

"Optical illusion."

"What?"

"Shh." Eunice leaned over the table and stared intently into the space on the other side of it. She remained silent for a moment, then smiled.

"She's singing a song for you," said Eunice. "It goes like, 'Eurydice, Eurydice. She is the perfect woman.'"

Reacher's eyes widened.

"Also, she wants to know if you've got that magic feeling yet. She's had it since the first time she saw you."

Reacher rose halfway off his seat. "Eurydice?" he said, gaping at the empty seat on the other side of the booth.

"Yeah," said Eunice. "She says to quit screwing around, because she doesn't have all day for this."

Reacher extended an arm across the table and swept it back and forth in the empty space.

Eunice cleared her throat. "Neither do I. And neither do you."

 +

FORTY

"**THERE** you are!" said Eurydice after silently staring at the empty side of the booth.

"What?" said Idea.

"That was the first thing she said to you when you first met." Eurydice tossed a jet black braid over her shoulder. "'There you are! Fancy meeting *you* here!'"

Idea realized she was right about Eunice's first words to him . . . so, perhaps she was also right about the empty side of the booth not being as empty as it seemed. Either that, or Eurydice and Eunice had been comparing notes behind his back.

Eurydice stared into space again, then chuckled. "Are you that good a kisser?" she said to Idea. "Sounds like you made a big impression at that rest stop outside Cincinnati."

Again Eurydice had come up with information that only Eunice should have known. "So she's over there with him, is that what you're saying?" Lifting the bangs from his eyes with the edge of his hand, Idea squinted at the empty seat across from him. "And I can't see or hear them because . . . ?"

"Because the stars are out of alignment," said Eurydice. "And you have too much processed sugar in your diet."

Idea sighed. "You two have a lot in common."

She cracked her gum and pointed across the table. "Reacher Mirage is sitting right there. What do you want to say to him?"

Idea frowned thoughtfully. He would feel ridiculous talking to empty space. . . . But he could not entirely dismiss the possibility that Eurydice was telling the truth. After all, she seemed to be linked with Eunice, and he'd seen for himself that Eunice had some kind of mysterious abilities when she'd switched faces in the mall in Indianapolis.

Besides, Idea really did have a lot to say to the guy who was pretending to be his creation. He thought of a question and opened his mouth, but Eurydice cut him off.

"Too late," she said. "He beat you to it. He wants to know why you've been claiming that you made up his band."

"*That* got a rise out of him." Eunice laughed as she watched the empty bench across the table. People in the next booth were staring at her as if she were crazy, but she didn't seem to notice.

She watched and listened attentively to the emptiness, then turned to Reacher. "Idea wants to know why you and your friends have been pretending to be the band that he made up."

"Tell him I don't know what he's talking about," said Reacher. "I never even heard of him before yesterday, and Youforia's been together for *years*."

Eunice told her unseen contact what Reacher had said, then waited for a reply. "He says you stole his idea and are using it to rip people off."

Reacher folded his arms. By now, he'd forgotten all doubts

about carrying on a conversation with someone he couldn't see. "Oh yeah? Well, here's what I want you to tell *him* . . ."

"I won't repeat what he said." Eurydice looked disgusted. "There's no need for that kind of language."

"He can curse me out all he wants," said Idea. "But that won't change the fact that he's a *thief!* He stole my intellectual property!"

Eurydice relayed Idea's message and waited for a response. "In a nutshell"—she cracked her gum—"Reacher would like to see you prove it."

"Idea says he can show you computer log files dating back to the beginning of Youforia," said Eunice. "The files detail all activity related to the Youforia website and will verify that his claim predates your own."

Reacher snorted. "Speaking of websites, ask him where he got all that personal information about my band that he posted on YoFace, Yapper, and his website. While you're at it, ask him *why* he felt the need to violate our privacy like that."

"I made it all up!" Idea rubbed the three moles on his left cheek with the tip of his index finger. "You can't violate someone's privacy if he's a fictional character!" As he said it, he felt a twinge of Deity Syndrome—an ache in his stomach, a flicker of dizziness, a quick chill up his spine.

"Reacher says he's as real as you are," said Eurydice. "So are Wicked, Chick, and Gail."

"Oh, sure," Idea snapped. "The people *claiming* to be them are real. The people who stole their identities from my website."

"What if he's telling the truth?" said Eurydice, asking him a direct question instead of passing along his message to the other side.

"The truth is, *I* made up everyone in the band and everything about them," said Idea.

"Okay." Eurydice nodded. "But what if *he's* telling the truth, too?"

FORTY-ONE

REACHER + IDE

"**WHAT** are they saying over there?" Reacher asked. It had been a few moments since the last response from Idea.

"She's saying that maybe there are different truths for different people," said Eunice.

Reacher frowned. "I don't understand."

"What's true for you isn't necessarily what's true for somebody else, is it?" Eunice reached over and grabbed the ketchup bottle from the condiment rack along the windowsill. "You might say that this ketchup is red. Someone who's colorblind might say it's gray. You'd both be telling the truth based on what you perceived, right?"

Reacher thought about it. "Sure. What's your point?"

"What if he didn't steal your ideas for the band?" said Eurydice. "What if he didn't see your website or social networking posts until long after he'd formed *his* band?"

"But he *must* have seen my website first," Idea insisted. "How else could he have come up with a band called Youforia with members who are exact copies of the ones I described on my site?"

Eurydice cracked her gum. "Maybe the two of you are connected."

"At the amphitheater, did you think it was odd that four people thought you were Idea?" Eunice asked. "Four people who knew him well?"

"Sure," said Reacher. "But things happened so fast, I didn't get much of a chance to think about it."

"Idea had a similar experience," said Eunice. "Your father, brother, and cousin all thought he was you."

"My parents thought he was me?" Idea asked. "Bulab and Scholar, too?"

Eurydice nodded. "What do you think the chances are that was just a freak case of mistaken identity?"

"What are you getting at?" Reacher asked.

"Has it occurred to you that maybe you're not enemies after all?" said Eunice. "That maybe you're important to each other for a different reason?"

"Like what?"

"You tell me." Eurydice blew an orange bubble, then popped it and drew the gum back into her mouth. "What could you do for each other?"

Idea considered the question, staring at the spot where he imagined invisible Eunice might be sitting. "When Eunice and

I asked the digihoroscope what I should do when I met the phony Youforia, it said to 'unite with your enemies.'" He paused to think for a moment. "Eunice said maybe that meant I should team up with the phonies and make them the real Youforia."

"There's just one problem with that," said Eurydice. "Reacher wants to keep his band a secret."

"Then why did they set up this big debut concert in Maysville?" Idea asked.

"What makes you think Reacher did that?"

"Idea says he didn't set up the Maysville show," said Eunice.

"Then who did?"

"Who knows?" Eunice shrugged. "I guess it could have been anyone."

"It definitely wasn't me," said Reacher. "I'm not ready to take the band public yet."

Lightly, Eunice laid her fingertips atop Reacher's forearm. The glossy black and white nails gleamed in the sunlight from the window. "You're *afraid* to take the band public, you mean."

Reacher met her gaze, then looked away. "Yes."

"If neither of us set up the concert, I know who did," said Idea. "I know why this is all happening."

"Tell me." Eurydice cracked her gum twice.

Idea's heart pounded, and his stomach twisted. "It's *him*. The same one who makes us do everything."

"God?"

Idea shook his head. "I've always had the feeling that some-one is pulling our strings. Like we're in a novel, and we have no control over what happens."

Eurydice placed a hand on his shoulder. "This feeling. Is it fear?"

Idea flicked his fingertip over the triangle of moles on his left cheek. "Yes."

"You're afraid you'll let everyone down," said Eunice. "Because your family has always told you that you're a failure. Because they've treated you like one all your life."

Reacher stared at his clenched fists on the table and nodded.

"Other people have always run your life, haven't they?" said Eurydice.

"Right," said Idea.

"Even when you ran away, you knew they would catch you sooner or later."

Idea stared out the window. "So what?"

Eurydice cracked her gum twice. "So what if I told you that you could change everything?"

"Change everything how?" said Reacher.

"Make everything right," said Eunice. "The two of you." She gestured at the empty seat across the booth.

"I don't get it."

"I can give you the chance," she said. "But the two of you have to agree to do something."

"Agree to do what?"

"Work together," said Eurydice. "Agree to work together instead of against each other."

"Work together on what?"

"Why not assume it's something that could do you some good?" Eurydice blew a lemon yellow bubble with her gum, then popped it. "Why not take a chance?"

Idea stared at her. "What does Eunice say?"

"Tell him I can't tell him what to do," Eunice said to the empty space across the table. "The same goes for you," she said to Reacher.

"To be honest," said Reacher, "I really don't know what you're talking about."

Eunice took his hand. "Do you wish your life was different?" she asked, staring deep into his eyes.

Idea answered without hesitation. "Yes."

"And if I offered you the chance to change your life, would you take it?" asked Eurydice.

Reacher thought it over, then shrugged and nodded. "Sure. Why not?"

"Even if there are no guarantees?" said Eunice. "Even if the outcome is in your hands?"

"Nothing in life is guaranteed anyway, right?" said Idea.

"And will you promise to work *with* Reacher instead of *against* him?" Eurydice asked. "No matter what?"

"How could I promise that if I've never even *met* him?" said Reacher. "All I know is that he posted personal information about my band on the Internet, and he thinks *I* ripped *him* off."

"You've talked about how what he says and what I say can both be true," said Idea. "And about how maybe we're connected in some way . . . but I still don't know for a fact that he didn't steal Youforia from me. I don't even know for a fact that he's *here*."

"And how do I know you're telling me the truth?" asked Reacher. "I barely *know* you."

"I want to talk to Eunice," said Idea.

"I want to talk to Eurydice," said Reacher.

"Ten seconds," said Eunice and Eurydice. "You have ten seconds to tell me yes or no. Yes, you want the chance to change things, and you promise . . .

" . . . to work with Idea . . .

" . . . to work with Reacher . . .

" . . . no matter what happens; or no, you don't want to do it. Maybe I'm full of crap, in which case, what do you have to lose?" Eunice and Eurydice paused, raising their eyebrows. "And maybe I'm telling the truth, in which case, why miss out on such a great opportunity?" They both lifted their hands with all fingers extended.

"Ten . . . nine . . ." They flicked down one finger at a time to match the count.

"This is ridiculous." Idea shook his head.

Reacher rubbed the white stubble on his scalp. "What's with the time limit?"

"Eight," said Eurydice.

"Seven," said Eunice.

"I mean, this is just a hypothetical question, right?" said Idea.

"Six," said Eunice.

"Five," said Eurydice.

"Okay," said Reacher. "I'll play along."

"Four," said Eunice.

"*If* such a thing were possible," said Idea, "I guess I would say . . ."

"Three," said Eurydice.

"Yeah," said Reacher. "Yes. I'll do it."

"Two," said Eunice.

"Yes," said Idea.

"One," said Eurydice, cracking her gum.

A moment later, when Mixie hurried back to the table, Eunice and Reacher were gone. In the middle of the table, a ketchup bottle sat atop a five-dollar bill.

"That sweetheart," Mixie said to herself, slipping the money into her apron pocket. "This will go to charity." She patted the pocket, unable to bring herself to keep such a big tip for doing so little work.

When Mixie finally got around to glancing at the booth, Eurydice and Idea were gone. Pennies, hundreds of them, were spread all over the table.

"Oh, good." Mixie stuck a fresh cigarette in her crinkled sneer. "A nice tip." Smoking was banned in the diner, but she lit the cigarette, anyway.

"Thanks a lot, sweetheart." Mixie said "sweetheart" like it meant something nasty. "You'll get yours."

When she got done counting all the pennies, she found there were exactly five hundred of them.

CHAPTER FORTY-EIGHT

REACHER

WHEN Reacher opened his eyes, he was running full tilt through a forest. His initial shock at leaping suddenly into that situation was compounded when he looked down at himself.

His legs appeared to be whirling blurs of motion, as if he were churning forward on spinning wheels instead of human appendages. Above the whirling blurs, his torso appeared to consist of a huge coil that expanded and contracted as he ran.

His hands were just as bizarre. The right one had become a flesh-colored bubble the size of a cabbage. The left looked as if it were formed of solid diamond, with each finger tipped in a gleaming scimitar claw.

Startled, Reacher stumbled midstep and rolled head over feet through the brush. He came to a stop at the base of a red thick-trunked tree, barely avoiding bashing his skull against it.

As he sat there for a moment, trying to get his bearings, he saw that his body had changed. Instead of whirling blurs, he had legs again . . . although one was two feet shorter than the other and covered in thorns. His coiled torso had become a glowing, molten glob that was oozing onto the forest floor around him. His right hand had changed from bubble to brick, and his left hand had completely disappeared.

Then, right before his eyes, his body shifted again. It seemed to be in a constant state of metamorphosis, although it never felt other than normal to him.

He watched his arms become legs, and his legs become spaghetti. He watched his right hand turn to liquid, and his left hand reappear and spontaneously rotate all the way around on his wrist.

It didn't take long for him to realize why the bizarre phenomena seemed so familiar. He knew whom his new body reminded him of before he heard his pursuer call him by name.

"I know you're out there," a man said from somewhere nearby. "Surrender or die, Johnny Without."

CHAPTER FORTY-NINE

IDEA

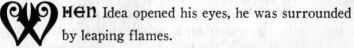

WHEN Idea opened his eyes, he was surrounded by leaping flames.

Fire raged in every direction, flaring bright orange and throwing off intense heat. The flames made a roaring sound like a rough wind, overlaid with a hissing, spitting crackle.

He spun around but could find no path to freedom through the blaze. Beyond the fiery wall, he saw undamaged trees and brush, just a few feet away, yet unreachable.

Slowly he extended a hand, hoping to judge his distance from the flames. In the process, he was surprised twice.

First, his hand grew no warmer as it reached out, though it appeared to be moving within or beyond the curtain of flame.

Second, his hand looked not at all like he had come to expect it to look. It seemed to be much bigger and was encased in a black metal glove with spikes on the knuckles and wrist.

He brought the gloved hand back toward him and

turned it, flexing his fingers. Raising his other hand, he saw that it, too, was within or beyond the curtain of flame and packed into a spiked metal glove.

It was then that he remembered the vision he'd had under Planter Mirage's orange ball cap back in the men's room at the gas station. He'd thought at first that he was surrounded by a wall of fire, beyond which he could see sky and a landscape. Then he'd realized the flames were much closer, that they might be part of him.

Now he knew it for sure. However he moved, the flames moved with him. When he looked at anything— hands, trees, anything—he saw it through the orange, flickering haze of firelight. And when he reached up to scratch his head, there was blistering heat and nothing solid to scratch. When he drew his hand away, he saw that the heavy black glove was smoking.

Even without looking in a mirror, he knew what had happened. He had become Lord Fireskull.

And if that was true, he was inside *Fireskull's Revenant,* just as he'd come to suspect after surviving his brush with death with Daddy Naysayer and the boys. Which meant that maybe he wasn't destined to die as himself after all.

Instead, he would die as Fireskull.

CHAPTER FIFTY

REACHER

As the wailing crimson-armored soldier charged toward him with sword held high, Reacher wished that he could catch up on his reading.

He knew without a doubt that he'd become Johnny Without from *Fireskull's Revenant*. He guessed that he'd landed in the world of that novel, but he didn't recognize the scene in which he was now immersed. He didn't know what was happening or what was due to happen next, all of which he thought he would've known if only he'd finished reading the book.

Since he didn't have a copy at hand to consult, Reacher realized he would have to improvise. Maybe as things progressed, he could get a better idea of what was going on and how to deal with it.

If he survived, that is.

Fortunately, he knew that inhabiting Johnny Without's funhouse body gave him an advantage. In the last chapter of *Fireskull's Revenant* that he'd read, Johnny had survived sixteen attempted executions, thanks to his constantly changing form.

Still, as confident as Reacher was that he could survive the charging soldier's attack, he felt a surge of fear and adrenaline as the gleaming sword swung toward him. Instead of waiting calmly to test his new body's resistance to harm, he rolled out of the way of the sword strike at the last instant, barely dodging the blade.

Suddenly, although he didn't make a conscious effort, his body compressed widthwise and stretched out lengthwise into the form of a snake. The new form felt perfectly natural and controllable, as if he'd lived in it since birth.

Grunting, the soldier hauled up his sword for another strike. While the blade was in mid-downswing, Reacher the snake shot out of its path and darted between the soldier's armored legs.

Before the soldier could turn, Reacher rose up behind him, instantly changing from snake to man and growing to twice his original height, then three times, then four. He was already at ten times his original height by the time the soldier turned.

Raising the visor of his crimson helmet, the soldier craned his neck, his gaze sliding higher and higher. When he finally caught sight of Reacher's head far above the writhing red treetops, he shook his own head, turned, and walked away.

Reacher helped him along, kicking him with his enormous foot and sending him tumbling through the brush. Every time the soldier got to his feet and took a few steps, Reacher gave him another kick . . . until something else drew his attention.

Out of the corner of his eye, he glimpsed a hovering figure. Just as he turned for a closer look, his body suddenly plunged down out of the treetops, snapping back to normal size.

Dazed by the sudden, drastic change, Reacher ended up sprawled on his back in one of his own giant footprints, staring up at the orange sky through a huge hole that he'd torn in the tree canopy.

While he lay there, the figure he'd glimpsed drifted down toward him, turning slowly as an autumn leaf.

It stopped right above him, feet pointed to the sky, face inches from his own. Her familiar gaze locked with his, and her black hair—loose now, not in braids—fell all around his head.

"Eurydice?"

"Call me Scrier." When she spoke, she sounded like Eurydice in the middle of a windstorm.

She reached out to touch his face. Her fingernails, like Eurydice's, were painted like yin-yang symbols. But instead of the dark half being closest to the tip on one hand

and the white half closer on the other, hers alternated. The dark half was closer to the tip on one finger, then the white half on the next finger, and so on.

She closed the last few inches and pressed her lips to Reacher's for a lingering kiss.

CHAPTER FIFTY-ONE

IDEA

FLYING came naturally to Idea, as if he'd always been Lord Fireskull, and he was thrilled by it. Flapping his leathery wings with the ground dropping away from him, he was overwhelmed by a feeling of pure freedom and an elation that he'd never imagined possible.

It was quite a change from the way he'd felt just a short time ago. After realizing that he'd been transformed into Fireskull, he'd experienced a full-blown Deity Syndrome meltdown. Throughout his life, the fear that he might be a character in a novel had been enough to make him physically ill; once he knew with absolute certainty that he'd become a fictional character, the sickness had been truly overpowering. In the throes of it, he'd lain squirming and trembling on the ground for a seeming eternity, spitting up gouts of flame.

Eventually, the attack had passed, fading like a storm in the distance. Idea had still felt queasy when he'd gotten up off the ground, as if the syndrome could rise again at any moment. But the sensation had faded as he distracted himself by experimenting with Fireskull's abilities.

The local foliage had suffered as he'd tried out Fireskull's flaming breath and great strength, burning swaths of forest with a sigh and knocking over red-tentacled trees with a flick of his wrist. None of that, however, could compare to the thrill of unassisted flight.

He climbed higher into the bright orange sky with each flap of his wings, then angled his body and glided forward. Warm air rising from below filled his wings, holding him aloft like upraised hands.

Diving down, he skimmed the surface of a pond, then shot back up into the heights. He looped around and spun in circles until he was dizzy, then did somersaults and cartwheels in midair. When a yellow-feathered long-necked bird that was bigger than he was flapped past, he zipped after it and matched its speed, his fingers brushing the tips of its wings.

Gracefully Idea rolled in and out of foamy clouds, feeling as if he were in a beautiful dream of flight. If he could have felt the white wisps of cloud vapor caressing his face, the experience would have been complete. But since his skull was afire, that wasn't likely to happen.

Great sweeps of his wings lifted him above a high ridge. On his way over the crest, he dipped down and touched the head of a green and gold deerlike creature with writhing antlers. The beast raised its head and met his gaze with what seemed like an expression of indignant surprise.

And when Idea turned and looked at what lay beyond the ridge, he experienced a surprise of his own.

A scene of destruction spread over the vast plain that rolled out from the base of the ridge. Everywhere, in every direction, the vegetation was trampled, the ground churned up, the houses afire. The bloody corpses of people and animals littered the ground beneath rings of screeching, slow-flying buzzard-things. Armies of men in crimson armor marched in tight ranks, their movements synchronized, flowing like carpets over the sea of bodies and debris.

At the heart of it all, plumes of smoke pumped from a giant black castle, blotting out the sun. Crimson-armored soldiers heaved furniture and people from the ramparts, which piled up in mounds along the base of the castle walls.

Hovering just past the ridgeline, Idea stared at the wasteland below. He'd never seen anything like it outside of a movie or video game. All at once, he was gripped by amazement and outrage . . . as well as another sudden revelation.

Until that moment, Idea had known only that he'd been dropped into the world of *Fireskull's Revenant*. He hadn't known exactly *when* in the novel he'd arrived.

Now he knew. He was at or shortly after the point where he'd left off reading the book.

The unknown army had just conquered Fireskull's

kingdom. Fireskull had flown away from the battle, retreating into the forestlands. The enemy was bound to try to track him down.

In other words, it wasn't a great time to be Fireskull.

What came next, he didn't know. He hadn't finished reading the novel and hadn't peeked ahead, either. Now that he was trapped in the book, he wished he'd read the rest of it, after all.

Slowly he turned and flew away from the wasteland. He dropped below the ridgeline on the other side as soon as he could, plunging out of sight of the multitude of soldiers on the plain.

He needed time to think, time to figure out what he should do next. He would get as far from the ruined heart of the kingdom as he could and hole up in a cave until his situation made some kind of sense.

At least, that was what he planned to do, until he saw the woman gliding toward him.

Her gleaming white gown wrapped around her as she slowly corkscrewed through the air, angling down from higher altitudes over the forestlands. Her arms were extended straight out from her sides like the wings of an airplane, and her long blond hair swirled around her head like ribbons around a Maypole.

Idea watched her, mesmerized. As she drew closer, he realized who she must be in the world of the novel. Then he recognized her as someone from what he'd always thought of as the world of reality.

She was Scrier Inevitas, of course, the sorceress in *Fireskull's Revenant*. She was also, unmistakably, the same woman who'd kissed him at the rest stop along the highway near Cincinnati.

"Eunice!" He flapped his wings to fly toward her.

"You may call me Scrier." Her voice sounded just like Eunice's, but surrounded by howling winds.

"It's good to see you." Idea reached out and caught her by the shoulders. "I missed you."

"I cannot kiss you," she said. "Not the way you are now."

Idea was glad she'd said that, because he *had* been thinking of trying to kiss her. Even with his vision veiled by flame, he'd momentarily forgotten that his head was made of fire.

"I guess being Fireskull isn't so great after all," he said.

"It is still good to see you." Scrier/Eunice placed a palm against his gleaming black breastplate. Her fingernails were painted with yin-yang symbols but the dark half and white half alternated from finger to finger in being closest to the tip. "I would recognize you anywhere, in any disguise."

Idea smiled and gazed at her for a moment, then grew

more serious. "Can you tell me what's going on? How did I end up inside the novel I've been reading?"

"It's your chance to make everything right," she replied. "Remember what Eurydice said?"

"No guarantees," he recalled. "The outcome is in my hands."

"And one other's," said Scrier/Eunice. "You promised to work with him, no matter what happens."

"So Reacher is here, too," Idea said as another piece of the puzzle clicked into place. "Where is he?"

"We will find him." Scrier/Eunice folded her hands around his massive metal gauntlet. "But first I must tell you the secret that led to the downfall of your kingdom."

Chapter Fifty-Two

Reacher

As riders approached from both directions on the road, Reacher held his breath and hugged the ground under the bushes. His Johnny Without body was not exactly made for prolonged concealment; at any moment, it could expand to enormous size or spin like an out-of-control stopwatch needle or shatter like glass into a billion glittering, squawking shards.

It wasn't a matter of *if* his body would undergo a disruptive transformation, but *when*. He just hoped it wouldn't happen until he'd seen what he'd come to see.

Scrier/Eurydice had led him to this spot and told him to hide in the brush along the road. She'd said, "If you are patient, you will learn the answer to a mystery. You will see the face of the man who conquered your kingdom."

Before he could ask any questions, she'd kissed him and spiraled up out of sight above the clouds. Reacher had waited a while before anyone approached his hiding place. It could have been minutes, though it had felt much longer because of his struggle to hold still. He'd been changing the whole time, constantly shifting shape and position.

When he saw the riders coming, he redoubled his efforts and got himself partly under control. . . . But he knew it wouldn't last.

Two groups of riders on ostrich-back now trotted toward each other. Each group consisted of five men in identical crimson armor, clustered around a sixth man who looked different from the rest. The man in the middle of one group wore a helmet that looked like a human skull and a black leather uniform festooned with medals. The man in the middle of the other group wore a cloak of rough brown cloth like burlap; a hood concealed his face.

The two groups met and stopped several yards down the road from Reacher. He pushed aside a clump of leaves so he could see them from a low angle. He had a clear frontal view of the man in the skull helmet and black uniform, but he could only see the hooded man from behind.

Fortunately, they were close enough that he could hear their conversation without difficulty.

The man in black removed his helmet and bowed low on his ostrich. The crimson-armored men around him did the same.

"Sire," he said. "May all the world bask in the light of your perfect love."

"Rise, General Deathcrave," said the hooded man. "What news of Fireskull?"

General Deathcrave straightened. In that instant,

Reacher got a good look at him for the first time, and he immediately recognized him.

Deathcrave had a broad jowly face with twinkling eyes and a shaggy brown mane. His skin was flushed and sweaty, and short braids descended from his bushy puff of beard.

Reacher was stunned. The surprise must have had some effect on his physiology, for he felt his body changing and stirring as he lay there. He struggled to hold himself together. A few leaves rustled, and then his body settled. But he knew better than to assume it would stay calm.

"Fireskull is on the run," said General Deathcrave. "Colonel Sweat is leading a task force in hot pursuit."

As the general spoke, Reacher couldn't believe his ears. Not only did Deathcrave look just like Wicked Livenbladder, lead guitarist for Youforia, but he sounded just like him, too.

In fact, the hooded man also sounded familiar, although Reacher could not yet place his voice.

"As long as Fireskull is at large, my victory is incomplete," he said.

"Sweat shall destroy him." Deathcrave never looked directly at the hooded man as he spoke. None of the other men looked at him, either.

"I have another mission for you," the man continued. "Bring me Johnny Without."

Deathcrave started to look up, then caught himself and kept his eyes trained downward. "Without is dead. Burned at the stake."

"In his present form, Without cannot be killed," said the hooded man. "You should have awaited my arrival before authorizing an execution."

"I am sorry." Deathcrave bowed his head lower. "It has always been our law that the kings of conquered lands shall be killed before they can set eyes on you, Secret King. Even I am not fit to behold your glorious face."

"Find Without and bring him to me," said the Secret King. "I know a way to destroy him."

Again Reacher became agitated, and a series of changes rippled through his body. One leg turned freezing cold, as if it had become ice, while the other leg felt as if it were either numb or gone. One hand turned hard and heavy as solid rock, while the other tingled and fluttered with electrical current.

Reacher closed his eyes and tried to relax. As his breathing slowed and steadied, his body felt more normal, and he began to think he would be okay.

Then he opened his eyes and saw his bare foot squirming past his face, about to wriggle out onto the road.

Without thinking, he grabbed the foot and yanked it back, ruffling the brush in the process. The foot jerked in his grip, nearly escaping, and he shook the brush again trying to restrain it.

With the foot clamped hard against the ground, Reacher watched the riders on the road. The conversation had ended, and everyone was looking around as if they'd heard something and were trying to locate its source.

He held his breath. General Deathcrave and the armored riders looked in every direction except the right one. But the Secret King turned to look back over his shoulder and down.

Reacher could have sworn the Secret King's gaze went right to him. His heart pounded. He felt the rippling and tingling that always heralded a new transformation, and he clenched his teeth and tried hard to will it not to happen.

His foot twitched in his grasp.

The Secret King pulled back his hood, revealing his face. Finally his gaze slid onward, but not before Reacher got a look at him and understood why his voice had sounded familiar.

His face was thin and chiseled, with high cheekbones and bright blue eyes. His wavy hair was silver.

The Secret King could have been the twin of Youforia's manager, Sty Latherclad.

At first, Reacher was surprised. As he thought about it, though, he decided that coming across Sty or someone who looked like him in the world of *Fireskull's Revenant* wasn't so surprising, given the circumstances. If Reacher could become Johnny Without, and Wicked could become General Deathcrave, it almost made sense that Sty would also play a role in this place. In fact, Reacher fully expected to encounter others here who resembled people he knew back home.

He was still pondering this as the Secret King and the other riders stopped looking around for the source of the rustling noise he'd made.

"Must have been a squid-rat," said Deathcrave.

"Enough delays," said the Secret King. "Field your men and find Without. Do not return until you have him in custody."

"Yes, Your Majesty." Deathcrave's eyes remained fixed on the ground.

"And whatever you do," the Secret King added, "under no circumstances allow him to unite with Fireskull."

"Yes, Your Majesty."

"My prophecy must be upheld. Its accuracy must never be called into question."

"Understood, Your Majesty," said Deathcrave.

It was then that Reacher realized the Secret King had another identity.

As he and his soldiers rode off in one direction, and Deathcrave and his group rode off in the other, Reacher thought back to the text of *Fireskull's Revenant*. One man was described in the novel as having handsome features and silver hair and wearing a hooded cloak made of rough brown cloth. One man was depicted delivering a prophecy that Johnny and Fireskull had to be kept apart or the world would end.

Apparently, the Secret King, who looked and sounded like Sty Latherclad, was also Highcast the Prophet.

Chapter Fifty-three

Idea

THE guy forcing the sword toward Idea's throat looked just like Bud System, except for the blood-red armor and the murderous glint in his eyes.

Bud was the fat man in Chicago who had tried to sell Idea "tickie-tickies" to the Youforia concert. Bud's double, who called himself Colonel Sweat, had far more harmful intentions.

Sweat and a group of armored warriors had ambushed Idea and Scrier/Eunice in a gorge. She had just finished telling him the secret of who had conquered Fireskull's and Johnny's kingdoms and how he'd done it.

Idea hadn't been very surprised by the plot twist that Scrier/Eunice had revealed. Milt Ifthen, author of *Fireskull's Revenant,* had made it pretty obvious from early in the novel what the identity of the leader of the invaders would turn out to be.

Scrier/Eunice had explained that Highcast the Prophet, also known as the Secret King, had discouraged an alliance between Fireskull and Johnny, an alliance that could have successfully opposed him, by predicting the world would end if they ever again met face-to-face. He'd used similar false prophecies many times before that, driving wedges between other kingdoms, which he then had been able to conquer. Fireskull's and Johnny's had fallen just as easily; it hadn't taken much effort to pit the long-standing enemies against each other.

As thoroughly as the Secret King had defeated Fireskull, however, he'd still felt the need to send Colonel Sweat to eliminate him, which had been a smart move. Scrier/Eunice had assured Idea that he and Reacher could still triumph if they joined together.

Scrier/Eunice had also told Idea that she would lead him to Reacher, and the two of them would join forces. As she'd promised back in the diner, they would have the chance to change their lives, as long as they worked together.

Before Idea could press her for more details on how exactly his life could change, Colonel Sweat and his team had attacked.

"Yield, Firefool." Sweat grunted as he pushed his silver sword against Idea's black sword. "Why drag this out?"

The Fireskull body that Idea now inhabited was physically powerful, but Sweat still managed to force the crossed swords forward. Idea redoubled his effort, pushing both blades back toward Sweat . . . and Sweat regained the advantage again with a sudden heave.

The swords lunged toward Idea. He only managed to stop them when his hands were at his shoulders.

"Ha!" said Sweat. "I've cut into you!"

Idea felt no pain, but he suspected Sweat was telling the truth. From the position of his hands, which were gripping his sword, he was pretty sure the edge of the blade had intersected the black leather collar at his throat.

The absence of pain was a good sign, though. Given the fact that his head and neck were made of flame, he had a feeling that he would be fine and could still win this.

He let the sword press a little more into his throat, then exhaled a puff of flame-breath in Sweat's face. It was strong enough to singe his hair and skin and send him stumbling backward.

Idea followed up with a stiff kick to Sweat's chest, landing the colonel on the ground with a clatter of armor. When he tried to get back to his feet, Idea swung a black gauntleted fist against the side of his head, knocking him unconscious.

Towering over the body of Colonel Sweat, Idea realized he had the power to kill him, and probably should. Killing Sweat would mean one less enemy to face in the future. Murdering someone in the pages of a novel wouldn't even be considered a crime, and it might be no more of a sin than gunning down computer-generated foes in a video game.

Nevertheless, he couldn't bring himself to do it. He inhabited Fireskull's body, but his morals hadn't changed. If he could avoid killing, he would.

There was a rustling sound behind him, and Idea turned, expecting to see an enemy soldier attacking. He saw Scrier/Eunice instead. She hovered two feet above the ground, blond hair and white gown rippling, although no breeze was blowing.

"Others will pursue Reacher," she said, her voice rising amid the sound of rushing wind. "We must get to him without delay."

Along the length of the gorge behind her, Idea saw the six armored warriors who had accompanied Colonel Sweat. They were all frozen in place, caught in battle poses with swords, maces, or bows raised.

Idea pointed in their direction. "What did you do to them?"

A small smile flitted across Scrier/Eunice's face. "I *know* you've seen human statues before."

Idea stared at the frozen men a moment more, then returned his full attention to her. "Do you know where to find Reacher? Is he nearby?"

She nodded. "I do have a connection to him. And he is not nearby. He is miles away, in the Kingdom of Without."

"Which has also been conquered by the Secret King," said Idea.

"Yes," she said. "It will be a dangerous journey, even if you fly."

He sighed, emitting a jet of orange flame from his fiery mouth. "But working with Reacher is the only way I can get a chance to change my life."

"Exactly. If you are going to meet with him, you must leave immediately. I cannot keep these men frozen indefinitely."

Idea stared at her for a long moment, considering what she'd told him and what she'd meant to him in the world outside the novel. He felt removed from her now, and not just because he couldn't kiss her. She seemed different—colder and more self-contained. Although Idea wasn't changing his behavior to match his new body, Eunice seemed to become more like Scrier with each passing moment.

"All right." He unfurled his leathery black wings to their full span. "Let's go."

"Fly as fast as you can," she said. "Watch for attacks from below."

With a flap of his wings, Idea rose from the ground. "Do you realize we've been on the run since the moment we met?"

"We are near the end now."

"The end of what?" he asked, still flapping, still rising. "Our lives?"

"No." Scrier/Eunice's long blond hair fluttered as she climbed into the sky along with him. "The book."

CHAPTER FIFTY-FOUR

REACHER

"**H**URRY," said Scrier/Eurydice, floating alongside Reacher through the forest. "You must get to him before the search parties find you." Her black tresses flowed across her face as if carried by a river current.

"No kidding," Reacher said sarcastically. "I'm doing the best I can." He'd been jogging at a brisk pace through the forest until his left foot had turned into a block of stone five times its original size. Now jogging was out of the question; moving forward at all was a struggle.

They'd been on the run since he had witnessed the Secret King's meeting with General Deathcrave. After the King and his minions had ridden away, Scrier/Eurydice had popped up and told Reacher that he had to get to Idea as quickly as he could.

Ever since, she'd been driving him hard through the forests and fields, right up to the point of exhaustion. After all his Johnny Without body had been through that day, it was no wonder he felt ready to drop. Battling the forces of Fireskull and the Secret King, in addition to surviving sixteen execution attempts, was enough to wear out even a man with an indestructible crazy-quilt body.

"How much farther?" Again he was startled by the bizarre sound of so many different voices coming out of his mouth, changing with every syllable.

"It depends on how much closer Idea comes," said Scrier/Eurydice.

"He's traveling, too?"

"At the moment, he is headed in our direction."

Reacher wasn't surprised that she seemed to know Idea's whereabouts and movements. She claimed to have a link to him, and Reacher believed her. It was much easier for him to believe that *anything* was possible, now that he'd been zapped into the world of a fantasy novel.

"The faster you go, the sooner the two of you will meet," Scrier/Eurydice continued. "Depending on how much the Secret King's forces slow you down when they strike."

"You mean *if* they strike?"

"They will strike," she said. "Your speed right now will mean the difference between fighting a handful and fighting an army."

Reacher stumbled to a halt as his legs turned into coiled springs. "I'll take the handful," he said, putting the springs to use by bounding forward in giant, bouncing leaps.

CHAPTER FIFTY-FIVE

IDEA

One minute, Idea was flapping along through a clear orange sky, following Scrier/Eunice as she spiraled ahead in the distance. The next minute, a cloud of arrows lifted out of the writhing red treetops below, flashing straight toward him.

He unleashed a blast of fiery breath, transforming many of the arrows into ash. The ones that got through whistled past him, narrowly missing his wings.

Idea flapped faster, increasing his speed. The archers below revised their aim and sent up another cloud of arrows.

He burned those, too, and kept speeding up. He heard more arrows launching behind him, but he was out of range. Safe for the moment.

That was what he was thinking when the spear shot through his left wing.

It came from below without warning, piercing the center of the wing. He howled, and the spear kept going, leaving behind a ragged, gaping hole.

He hadn't thought Fireskull's body would be so vulnerable, but the hole had a disastrous effect. In addition to kicking up a storm of pain, it destabilized him, making his flight unsteady. When someone on the ground a little further on put an arrow through the other wing, it completely threw him off balance.

He called out to Scrier/Eunice as he wobbled, fighting to stay aloft. She doubled back and flashed toward him, corkscrewing as fast as the spinning bit on a power drill.

But when she reached him, she didn't try to stop his fall. "This isn't working," she said as she dropped down beside him. "You are still too afraid of being controlled by other people. You aren't ready to join with Reacher."

"Help!" Idea reached for her, but she stayed just out of reach. "Can't you see I'm *falling* here?"

"It is time for you to run the Gauntlet of Realities. That will better prepare you for the work ahead." She snapped the fingers of both hands.

There was a blinding flash of light. Suddenly, Idea stopped falling.

And found himself lying in bed.

He blinked, realizing the blazing veil of Fireskull's vision was gone. Heart pounding, he looked around. He was in a bedroom, but not in any home he'd ever known.

To one side, a beige curtain hung a few feet away, running the length of the bed. He heard someone cough behind it; in the dim light, he could only make out a vague silhouette of a man reclining in another bed.

Turning, he saw a bunch of wilted flowers in a fluted plastic vase on a bedside table. Past the flowers, through a doorway, he saw women in multicolored hospital scrubs hurrying back and forth.

Then he heard a familiar voice.

"Do you need more pain meds?" It was a man's voice. "Here." He felt someone press a cylindrical object into his hand. "Just hit the button, remember?"

Idea looked in the direction of the voice. He was shocked when he saw who was sitting there, and not just because it would be shocking to see *anyone* sitting there after being transported into a novel and back out again without warning.

He was shocked because the man beside his bed was his father, Vengeful. Even more shocking was the fact that Vengeful was touching his hand gently and smiling with genuine warmth.

"Use as much medicine as you need," he said. "Whatever it takes to kill the pain."

Idea saw tears in Vengeful's eyes. He looked away, directing his gaze at Idea's legs under the sheet on the bed.

It was only then that Idea realized he couldn't feel them.

Chapter Fifty-Six

REACHER distinctly heard rock music in the background as the five crimson knights who encircled him all thrust the points of their swords at him at once.

He realized he was about to die. His unpredictable Johnny Without body always picked moments like this to change to rubber or smoke or stone. But this time, his shape-shifting mode had inexplicably gone offline. In less than a heartbeat, the five swords would pierce his chest as if it were a wicker basket.

He sucked in a breath, preparing to die. Before the knights could kill him, though, they went into ultra-slow motion.

Then, Scrier/Eurydice's head dropped in front of him, upside down. "You're not ready, either. Still too weighed down with fear."

He gaped at the swords as they crept toward him. "Maybe because so many people are trying to *kill* me?"

"You need to run the Gauntlet of Realities. Once you've shed the extra baggage, you'll be ready to move on to the next phase with Idea." She snapped the fingers of both hands and was gone in a flash of light.

At that instant, someone struck a guitar chord—D minor. Then another—an F—and another.

If the crimson knights heard the music, they showed no sign of it. The swords continued to crawl inward, gleaming tips sliding toward his chest.

Then, all of a sudden, all five swords swung up to point at the sky. The crimson-armored warriors stomped around him, footsteps hitting what sounded like hardwood instead of dirt.

The guitar chords continued, coming more rapidly to match the rhythm of their armored boots.

Looking down, Reacher saw that the ground had become a stage. Row after row of varnished, honey-gold boards had replaced the dusty earth. He also saw that his original non-shape-shifting body had replaced Johnny Without's. Instead of Johnny's gold breastplate, white tunic, and leather leggings, he was back in his green and white bowling shirt and blue jeans.

Looking up, he saw that the sky had vanished, too. Instead of the bright orange vastness and single sun of Johnny Without's world, rows of bright white lights glared amid nightlike darkness.

As the chords continued, Reacher suddenly recognized their arrangement. He knew exactly what had come before and what would come after them, for a very good reason.

The chords were the intro of a song that he'd written.

Even as he realized that he was listening to "Surrenderphobe," from his rock opera, *Singularity City,* the crimson knights stopped circling and lowered their swords. They remained bowed with sword tips touching the floorboards in a perfect ring, and Reacher got his first unobstructed look around the new environment into which he'd been flung.

As his eyes adjusted to the cascade of light from above, he saw that he was indeed on a stage. Beyond its front edge, fanning outward and upward, an enormous audience stared back at him from the shadows of a great concert hall.

Frozen, Reacher gaped at the sea of faces. It was the audience he'd always dreamed of, and dreaded—vast beyond belief, attentive, judgmental.

Someone moved in front of him onstage, diverting his attention from the crowd. It was someone he knew well, playing guitar just a few feet away.

"Hey!" whispered Wicked Livenbladder, in all his fierce, furry glory. "You're supposed to *sing*, remember?"

Reacher shook his head to clear it.

Wicked glared. "I'll play the last few bars again. This time, don't miss your cue!"

Someone in the audience cleared his throat. Someone else laughed softly. Reacher's darkest nightmares were coming true, the ones in which he failed and fell apart in front of a giant unforgiving crowd.

The ones that had made him keep Youforia secret for so long.

His heart pounded and his stomach twisted. Wicked ducked away and took up the last bars of the intro once more.

Reacher closed his eyes and drew in a deep breath, trying to steady himself. He dragged a hand slowly back over the rough white stubble on his scalp. He couldn't do it. He couldn't sing in front of all those people.

He opened his eyes as Wicked hit the last note of the intro. He turned to walk offstage, to get away from yet another moment of failure.

And everything around him changed again.

Suddenly he was in some kind of old-fashioned nightclub. A huge sign in silver script on the far wall read *Swing Room*. Couples sat at candlelit tables on semicircular tiers facing him. Everyone smoked cigarettes and had a glass of wine or beer or a mixed drink in front of them.

And every man and woman wore clothes and hairstyles straight out of the 1940s.

Reacher himself wore a black tuxedo and bow tie. At a blast of horns that made him jump, he spun around and saw a big band behind him. The trumpet bells and trombone slides gleamed like solid gold as they pointed in his direction.

Then he heard a voice and spun in the other direction.

A man in a white tuxedo pointed a conductor's baton at him. He had a long thin face with a pencil mustache, enormous teeth, and a great, oily forelock.

"Ladies and gentlemen!" shouted the conductor. "Presenting the newest and greatest singing sensation of them all, here to perform the hit song 'Tangerine'! Soon to be *your favorite*, Richie Mirage!"

Glancing down at the lettering on one of the music stands behind the conductor, Reacher knew who the man must be.

Suddenly he remembered the poster in Dusty's Wigwam, the poster from long ago advertising the big band called Your Favorites.

The bandleader on the poster had been identical to the man who'd just introduced him. There could be no doubt.

The man with the forelock and mustache was the one and only Donny Basquette.

FIFTY-ONE

IDEA

ACCORDING to his father, Idea had been heavily medicated for three full days, flowing in and out of consciousness. Before that, while driving drunk at night, he had crashed into a utility pole, totaling his car.

And leaving him paralyzed from the waist down.

It was a terrible feeling, not being able to move so much of his body. He hated being at the mercy of other people for even the simplest of tasks . . . being totally dependent on his parents, the very people whose control he'd struggled to escape in the life he remembered from his reality.

But these versions of his parents were not identical to the ones he'd left behind. Amazingly, this Vengeful and Loving Deity actually seemed to care about his needs and want to spend time with him.

His father watched TV with him and joked about the shows they saw. His mother brought him fresh ice water and Jell-O and fixed his pillow and straightened his bedclothes. Neither of them spoke in any but the most caring and reassuring way about the accident and its consequences.

"Don't worry," said Vengeful. "We'll work things out."

"Focus on getting better," said Loving. "One day at a time. Think about how lucky you are just to be alive."

"We know how lucky *we* are," Vengeful assured him, patting his folded hands. "We came very close to losing you forever."

"We never want to come that close again," Loving added with tears in her eyes. "We love you so much, son."

Idea couldn't help but get choked up when he heard such an outpouring of affection.

"We want you to get well again." Loving gently pushed his hair up out of his eyes. "We want you to make the most of the gifts you've been given."

"Gifts?" Idea tensed. In the nightmare of a reality that he knew best, his parents had constantly pressured him to use his "gifts."

Loving smiled down at him. "Your sense of humor. Your creativity. Your kindness."

Idea relaxed. "Oh."

"You made a mistake," said Vengeful. "You'll have to live with it for the rest of your life, but maybe you can make the world a better place in some small way because of your experience."

Idea's heart pounded, but it had nothing to do with Deity Syndrome. He was overcome with a feeling of love for the mother and father he'd never known before in quite this way.

They were the parents he'd always wanted. They showered him with unconditional affection instead of trying to control him.

Now that he saw how it could be, a great weight was lifted from his heart. All his life, he'd been pushed and driven by people with power over him. He'd been terrified that he'd never break free.

He'd even come down with a syndrome that had grown from the same roots. He saw it clearly for the first time: his fear of being controlled by a malevolent author wasn't much different from his fear of being controlled by malevolent parents. Together, these fears had kept him on the run, always looking over his shoulder. Always afraid that his parents or an author would destroy him.

Maybe it was time to stop feeling that way. Maybe it was time to let go of the fear.

Idea reached out from the hospital bed, spreading his arms wide to embrace his parents. They moved closer, beaming with joy, and he wrapped his arms around them.

Then, he felt a jolt of pain in his neck and cried out.

Immediately, Loving and Vengeful disentangled themselves from him. He howled again as a second jolt followed the first.

"Here." His father forced the cylindrical painkiller device into his hand. "Give yourself a shot of this."

"It'll help, sweetheart." His mother stroked his head as he writhed in agony.

Idea resisted their advice for as long as he could. He wanted to stay awake and savor the perfect parents who'd come to him here, the mother and father of his dreams.

But, finally, the repeated flashes of pain became too much. He screamed and heaved his head from side to side on the pillow. If he could have moved his legs, he would have thrashed them uncontrollably on the bed.

He squeezed the painkiller button three times. Within moments, the pain subsided, and he grew drowsy.

"Better?" Loving touched his forehead with the back of her soft hand.

He nodded and smiled weakly.

"You'll be okay," said Vengeful. When Idea turned to look at him, he had a proud, sad smile on his face. "You'll be just fine."

Slowly, a warm wave washed over Idea. He slid under the surface of it, then bobbed back up to awareness again. Apparently, some time had passed, for Vengeful was reading a newspaper at the foot of the bed, and Loving was nowhere to be seen.

Rolling his head to one side, he saw a thick paperback book on the bedside table. It was a familiar book, one he would've recognized by its thickness and battered cover even if he'd been unable to read the title on the spine.

The wave rushed over him again. The last thing he saw before closing his eyes was *Fireskull's Revenant*.

When next he opened his eyes, the book and the room were gone. His parents had disappeared. The hospital gown was gone, too, and he was back in his black button-down shirt and jeans.

He sat upright in a swivel chair of simulated black leather. A gray-cased computer monitor squatted on the woodgrain computer desk in front of him. The desk was chipped in just enough spots for Idea to glimpse the pale pressboard underneath the veneer.

To either side of him, scrambled piles of papers, binders, and file folders bulged over the edges of tables set at the height of the chair's armrests. A tabletop fan hummed away on a two-drawer file cabinet to the right of the desk, caressing his face with its light breeze.

The room itself was bright, with light from a ceiling fixture radiating off the white plaster walls. Apparently it was night-time, for no daylight leaked between the warped blue slats of the cheap plastic venetian blinds on the room's two windows.

A cursor blinked on the monitor in front of him. His fingers rested lightly on the keyboard in his lap. The cursor sat at the end of the following lines of text:

> A cursor blinked on the computer screen in front of Idea. His fingers rested lightly on the keyboard in his lap.

"**C**'MON, kid!" Donny Basquette whispered in Reacher's ear. "You're makin' me look *bad* here. Start singin'!" With that, Donny shoved the bulky microphone stand into his hand.

The jostling was enough to rouse Reacher from his daze. For the past few moments, as Your Favorites played the intro to "Tangerine" over and over and over again, he had stood between the big band and the audience, alternately staring at one and then the other.

He was having a hard time getting used to the fact that he had apparently traveled back in time to what looked like the 1940s. Especially since, just minutes before, he'd been dropped in the middle of a performance of his rock musical, *Singularity City*. And minutes before that, he'd been running and fighting for his life as Johnny Without in the orange-skied fantasy world of the novel *Fireskull's Revenant*.

He was having trouble keeping up.

"Sorry, folks," Donny Basquette said with a huge grin, displaying his enormous, gleaming teeth. "Young Richie here kept waitin' for the kazoo solo, only he forgot we left the kazoo player in Kalamazoo last week!" Everybody laughed. "Now that we've got that cleared up, let's welcome Richie Mirage one more time!"

As everyone in the audience clapped and cheered enthusiastically, Donny turned to the band and waved his baton to start "Tangerine" again. He flashed Reacher a bloodshot glare that said, *Sing or you'll be sorry!*

Reacher didn't want to do it. The same old stage fright curdled up from his belly and stuck in his throat.

He couldn't bear the thought of failing in front of the crowd. He could practically hear the catcalls now, roaring through the nightclub.

Daddy Naysayer had been right all those times he'd called him a loser. He knew it in his heart. Why even *try* to be something else?

Unless . . . this time, it didn't matter. Because he was far away from the people who'd talked him down, in a place and time that might not even be real. If they *were* real, they were so far in the past that his success or failure would have no bearing on what he thought of as the present.

Whatever he did here, *it wouldn't matter.* So what if he sang off key? So what if people booed him off the stage? He had nothing to lose.

Except a couple teeth, maybe, if Donny punched him in the face, which was looking pretty likely. Flushed and clenched with rage, Donny shook his baton at him. He looked like he was ready to beat him over the head with it.

Shaking, Reacher took a deep breath and opened his mouth. And there it was.

His voice. Not at band practice, not in disguise, not in front of kidnappers who'd turn him in for a reward if he didn't perform. His voice, loud and clear, unencumbered by worries about failure or success.

He was actually singing along to "Tangerine," even though he didn't know more than a single word of the lyrics. He accomplished this by singing that one word the whole way through the song, bending and stretching and mumbling it to disguise it as best he could.

Apparently, he didn't screw up the song too badly. The elegant men and women in the nightclub smiled at their tables, sipping drinks and nodding in time with the band.

Before long, Reacher found himself getting into it. He swayed to the rhythm and became more animated, using gestures and facial expressions to enhance his performance.

"Tangeriiine," he sang. "Tan . . . gerine gerine. Tangerine gerine . . . gerine geran geriiine."

Although he was only singing one word over and over, he began to feel like young Frank Sinatra in an old movie, playing to an adoring crowd of sophisticates in an Art Deco nightclub. He combed fingers through his hair and strutted from side to side with microphone in hand, making plenty of eye contact, particularly with the women.

When the band roared into the bridge, drowning him out, he moved off to one side, clapping to draw applause for Your

Favorites. As he took a good look at the musicians, he recognized several of them, including Mooney Claptrack, who had to be in his early twenties and had a monstrous black mountain of hair atop his head instead of a wispy silver comb-over. A scrawny hawk-nosed guy playing the xylophone gave Reacher a proud ecstatic grin and he knew right away that he was none other than Laszlo Taper.

When the band had finished playing the bridge, Reacher broke in again, singing as he strode back to his spot in front of Your Favorites.

"*Tan-tan gerine, oh ta-an-gertan.*" He really belted it out. "*Tingeran tan t-tangerinetin . . .*"

"*My heart belongs to Tan . . . ger . . . iiine!*" sang everyone in the audience, joining together for the ending that they all knew by heart.

Oily black forelock jumping, Donny frantically whipped his conductor's baton back and forth. Your Favorites extended the number, pouring on a Latin rhythm that accelerated with each passing moment.

Reacher put down the microphone and danced, one hand on his stomach, the other hand up in the air, hips swaying to the feverish samba. People in the audience cheered, and his heart raced with pure joy.

In that moment, the fears that had kept him from unveiling his secret band to the world faded even further. As everyone in the audience got up and danced and applauded, he closed his eyes, blissfully drinking in the noise and excitement.

Then suddenly it all cut off at once.

He had a powerful feeling of vertigo, as if he'd lost contact with the floor and no longer knew which way was up. His stomach wrenched, and he couldn't catch his breath.

When his eyes shot open, he was lying on his side in soft pink grass under a sunny green sky. The tuxedo was gone, and he was back in his bowling shirt and jeans.

A baby crawled over the grass toward him, a smile playing over its chubby features.

A young woman's voice called out from not far away. "Reacher!" she said. "Reacher!"

Surprised, Reacher lifted his head and looked up. A beautiful woman with long red hair ran up and hoisted the baby off the lawn, curling it into her bare freckled arms.

As soon as she had the child in her arms, the woman backed away from him. She watched him cautiously, then turned her attention to the infant.

"That's right, baby boy," she said in a sweet high-pitched voice. "You're all right now."

The baby gurgled. The woman extended an index finger, and the baby reached out and grabbed hold of it.

"You're gonna be just fine," she continued. "You don't have to worry about a thing, my little Reacher."

FIFTY-THREE

IDEA

THE title on the top sheet of the stapled stack of papers was "*My Favorite Band Does Not Exist* Chapter Outline."

Idea trembled as he reached for it and began to read page one.

Six paragraphs flowed down the page, each representing a different chapter. The first, under the heading "Chapter 1," started with this: *Idea Deity meets Eunice Truant in Niagara Falls and runs from people who he says are agents of his parents.*

The section designated "Chapter 6" included this: *While camping with Eunice, Idea has an attack of Deity Syndrome (the unshakable belief that he's a character in a novel and his fate is pre-destined and out of his control).*

Idea turned the page and read onward, stroking the three moles on his left cheek with his fingertip. The outline included more details of his recent life; everything from escaping Bulab and Scholar in the mall in Indianapolis to being held at gunpoint in a gas station men's room by Daddy Naysayer, Planter, and Lifter. The outline also described events in the lives of Reacher Mirage and Eurydice Tarantella ... as well as Lord Fireskull and Johnny Without from *Fireskull's Revenant.*

When he got to the part about reading the chapter outline, he stopped, afraid to go further. Afraid to find out what was going to happen next.

He held the outline in his hands, wondering what secrets it contained. Especially in Chapter 64. Somewhere in those pages, he had reason to believe, the exact moment and nature of his death were spelled out. Someone had put it there . . . and put him *here* to find it.

He knew exactly who it must be: his old enemy, the puller-of-strings . . . the one who made his heart pound and his stomach twist and waves of nausea rush through him. The cause of his Deity Syndrome.

Idea was sitting in the chair, at the desk, in the home of the mysterious being whose presence he'd always felt but never seen or heard.

He could think of no other explanation. Who else would have up-to-the-minute details of Idea's life typed in outline form? Who else would have sticky notes with messages like "Idea has what Reacher lacks & vice versa" affixed to the monitor and desk? Who else would have the power or the twisted sense of humor to bring him here in the first place?

Who else but the malevolent author of his life?

Lifting his bangs from his eyes with the edge of his hand, Idea looked around and finally caught a glimpse of the guy behind the scenes. Three framed eight-by-ten photos were arranged on the plaster wall, alongside a window in a corner of the room. Each photo centered on the same person, a guy with sandy brown hair, beard, and mustache.

The guy looked young, perhaps in his twenties. In one photo, he stood in front of the famous Big Ben clock tower in London, England. In another, he wore a tie-dyed T-shirt and stood by a city lamppost bearing street signs labeled "Haight" and "Ashbury." In the third, he stood in the prow of a boat afloat in gunmetal gray water, surrounded by milky mist.

A sticky note was attached to the frame of each photo. The note on the London photo read *"Hi!"* The note on the photo of the intersection of Haight and Ashbury Streets read *"Make yourself at home!"*

The third note, the one on the photo of the boat, was a bit wordier. *"Just please, whatever you do,"* it said, *"don't change the novel manuscript on the screen while you're here. That's all I ask."*

Immediately Idea turned his attention to the words on the computer monitor. Now that the manipulator had asked him not to alter them, he could think of nothing else but doing exactly that.

He thought that maybe doing so could influence his reality. He realized, of course, that it could also be a trap of some kind. The manipulator's note had so blatantly alerted him to the manuscript's vulnerability to tampering that it had practically *begged* him to meddle with it.

Still, if Idea had any chance of altering the outcome of his circumstances, he had to take it. If it didn't work, what did he have to lose by trying?

He put down the outline and placed his fingers on the keyboard. The last words before the cursor on the screen were: He placed his fingers on the keyboard.

He hit the "Enter" key, and the cursor shot down to start a new paragraph. Frowning, he thought for a moment . . . and then he began.

Suddenly, he typed, the walls of the room shifted from dull white to glossy red.

When he put a period at the end of the sentence, what he'd described became a reality. He blinked, and the walls were red.

He smiled and typed some more.

Then, the room was gone, and Idea was on a tropical beach. The computer was still on its desk in front of him, magically humming away though its power cords connected only to sand and thin air.

As soon as he hit the last period of the paragraph, Idea found himself in the scene he'd just described. He sat in the swivel chair on the soft white sand of a beach, facing the sparkling blue-green fringe of the ocean. The computer on the desk in front of him worked fine, even though its cords hung unconnected.

Having proven the power at his fingertips, Idea leaned back to consider his next move. He thought he should make the most of it, changing his life to the way he wanted it to be in one giant overhaul.

What better way to put Deity Syndrome behind him once and for all than to take control of the very force that had been controlling him? What better way to break free of the author than to write his own story?

His fingers rattled over the keys, and words appeared on the screen . . . but he stopped suddenly. Leaning forward, he stared at the screen, mystified by what he saw there.

Idea had meant to type this: Eunice Truant appeared in Idea's arms.

Instead, these words appeared on the screen: Alone, Idea floated off into space.

Although his surroundings didn't change immediately to match the words on the screen, he began to panic. Quickly, he hammered more keys on the board, trying to undo what he feared was about to happen.

But it wasn't space at all, he thought he typed. Idea stayed right on the sunny beach, and Eunice appeared in his arms. She kissed him and told him she loved him and wanted to make love to him.

Just like the last time, what appeared on the screen had nothing to do with what he'd typed:

In ancient times, old and burdensome Eskimos were cast adrift on ice floes to die. In the far future, Idea Deity, 173-year-old burden extraordinaire, was in the same predicament.

Idea was too old to work as a space miner anymore. All he did was use precious resources that the young miners aboard the starship *High Ground* needed to survive. So they left him behind on an asteroid with no way to escape. And the oxygen in his breathing tank wouldn't last much longer.

"No!" he yelled, but it was too late. The computer and desk winked out of existence. The blue sky, beach sand, and ocean vanished, too.

He found himself standing on dry gray dust, surrounded by the starry blackness of outer space.

He was wearing a space suit, and it was running out of oxygen. So much for taking control of his own story.

FIFTY-FOUR

BABY Reacher laughed in his mother's arms as the man on the ground sat up and rubbed his head.

"Are you all right, mister?" The woman looked concerned but kept her distance.

"Yeah." Reacher managed a polite smile, although his head was still spinning from his transfer to this place. "Thanks for asking."

The baby chose that moment to babble and flutter his hand, flapping his tiny fingers against his palm.

"Oh, look." The woman beamed at the child in her arms. "Reacher's waving at you. Hi-bye, baby boy! Hi-bye!"

Grown-up Reacher laughed and stared. He didn't want to put off the woman, but he couldn't help but be fascinated by her and the baby. The possibilities of who they might be and what that might mean to him were so incredible that he could hardly grasp them.

With such a unique first name in common, he found it hard to believe there was no connection between him and the infant. Further, he thought it was possible that he'd traveled through time to get here. He seemed to have done it before, to get to the

Swing Room in the '40s, so why not now? The woman's clothes and hair had an unmistakable retro look, from between two and three decades ago.

As hard as it was to believe, he thought that little Reacher might actually be the infant version of himself, which meant that the baby's mother might be his own mother as a young woman.

Just the thought of it made him shiver.

"If you're sure you're all right, then," the woman said pleasantly, turning to move away.

Reacher got to his feet. "I'm good." He dusted himself off, then decided to test his theory. "I'm . . . Donny," he said with a friendly nod, trying to sound casual. "What did you say your name was again?"

"Dreamer," said the woman. "Dreamer Mirage. Nice to meet you, Donny."

"It's nice to meet you, too." Reacher had a hard time keeping his excitement from showing. He'd guessed correctly about the woman's identity. Although she'd died in his early childhood, and he didn't remember her well, there could be no mistaking that name. He doubted there was another woman named Dreamer with a baby named Reacher in the entire world.

She was his mother.

"Well, I'd better get back to the picnic." Dreamer bobbed her head toward a set of tables arranged on the fringe of the sunny, pink park. A portly gray-haired woman was setting up Tupperware containers on one of the tables, helped by two little boys. Reacher guessed the woman was his grandmother, and the two boys were his brother, Planter, and cousin Lifter.

Reacher's heart raced. He wanted to keep talking to his mother for days. He wanted to tell her everything. He wanted to ask her a lifetime of questions. He wanted to wrap his arms around her and cry tears of joy on her shoulder.

But she hadn't invited him to join her at the picnic.

"How old is little Reacher there?" he asked, trying to prolong the conversation.

"Ten months and ten days." Dreamer smiled at her baby and swung him around for another look.

"He sure looks like a happy baby."

"He's had a sweet disposition from the start," she said. "Just like his father, I always say."

Remembering Daddy Naysayer, the overbearing tyrant who had raised him, Reacher thought she couldn't be serious. "His father?"

A sad look clouded her bright green eyes. "He was a wonderful man," she said softly. "He died in the war."

Reacher felt as if someone had slugged him in the stomach with a brick. It took all his willpower not to let his casual façade fall away and reveal an expression of eye-popping, jaw-dropping shock.

He swallowed hard and clenched his fists to control his emotions. "He . . . died?"

Dreamer's gleaming red hair fell forward as she nodded.

"I'm so sorry," Reacher said quietly. "That's terrible."

Baby Reacher blinked at him with a look of bewilderment. He pumped his chubby arms and squirmed with increased agitation.

Reacher's heart pounded like a fist against a door. "What was his name?"

"Purpose." Dreamer looked at the ground as she spoke. "Purpose Mirage."

Reacher rubbed his scalp and cleared his throat. He was having more trouble keeping his cool with each passing moment.

Apparently his father wasn't the man he'd always thought he was. Where, then, did Daddy Naysayer fit into the picture?

"It must be hard for you," he said softly. "Do you have help, at least?"

She looked up, tucking her red hair behind her right ear. "My mother." She nodded toward the gray-haired woman at the picnic table. "And my stepfather."

"What's his name, if you don't mind my asking?"

Dreamer's eyes narrowed the slightest bit, as if the questions were making her suspicious. "Hark Naysayer. And what did you say your last name was, Donny?"

Reacher felt dizzy. He would have sat down if there had been anywhere else to sit but the ground.

"Basquette." His voice sounded a million miles away. All he could think about was what his mother had just told him.

In the space of five minutes, the fundamental facts of his life had completely changed. He'd always thought Daddy Naysayer was his father. Daddy Naysayer had always treated him with contempt and told him he was worthless and stupid and doomed to failure. Since these opinions had come from his supposed father, Reacher had taken them to heart.

Now he knew that Daddy Naysayer had not been his father

at all. His father, it turns out, was a wonderful man named Purpose, a man with a sweet disposition, a man who had died in the war.

A man he'd never met.

After his mother and grandmother had died when he was young, Reacher had been brought up by Daddy Naysayer. His entire life had been shaped by that twisted, slave-driving bully. His own brother had been thoroughly warped and turned against him.

And all along, as the fear and self-hatred had wormed their way into Reacher's soul, he'd unknowingly possessed the weapon to eradicate them. All along, he'd secretly possessed the father's love he had craved.

Now that he knew it, he could let go of even more of the fear that had held him back for so many years.

"Mr. Basquette?" Dreamer stared at Reacher with a funny look on her face. "Are you sure you're all right?"

He rubbed his temples. He was feeling dizzy again all of a sudden. "Maybe I need to sit down after all. Would you mind if I sat at your table over there?"

Dreamer shook her head. "That's fine. I'll fix you an iced tea."

She walked off toward the table and Reacher fell in step behind her. He was thrilled to have the chance to ask more questions . . . and just to be able to spend time with his mother.

Then his right foot turned into a rolling sphere the size of a bowling ball. His left foot turned into four identical feet fanning out from the base of his leg.

+ + +

Reacher was back in Johnny Without's body, his bowling shirt and jeans replaced by Johnny's gold breastplate and brown leather leggings.

Dreamer and the baby were gone.

In their place, five crimson-armored warriors stomped around him in a circle, swords pointing up at the blazing orange sky.

As he shook off the shock of the sudden change in scenery, the warriors stopped circling and swung down their swords to point at him. Then, with a guttural battle cry, they charged toward him all at once.

Which was when he heard a familiar voice in his ear.

"Quickly!" shouted Scrier/Eurydice, hovering alongside him. "Fight your way past them and don't stop running. You're almost there. You've almost reached Idea!"

FIFTY-FIVE

IDEA

IDEA sat cross-legged on the surface of the asteroid, watching the gauge on the wrist of his space suit. The needle flicked from the green zone into the red, indicating that the oxygen in his tanks was more than half gone.

For all intents and purposes, the gauge was a timer counting down the minutes until his death. When the oxygen ran out, he would die.

The asteroid rolled in its orbit, and the gray and black bulk of the mining ship *High Ground* came into view. As she glided off toward another asteroid, he tipped his head back and saw the distant yellow disk of the sun. He raised his fist and shook it as if the sun were to blame for his misfortune.

"I hate you!" he said, and then he hesitated because he didn't recognize his voice. It had become a 173-year-old man's voice, raspy and cracking and rough. He couldn't see what he looked like, but he guessed that, like his voice, he'd been physically transformed.

"I *do* hate you!" He knew he was using up his oxygen faster by shouting, but he didn't care. "You're a real *jerk*, you know that?"

The only answer was the faint hiss of the oxygen injectors in his helmet.

"You suck!" he continued. "Putting me through all this crap . . . for what? So you can get your rocks off?"

His anger built and boiled within him. He got to his feet and threw a rock in the sun's direction. As soon as he did it, sharp pain shot up his wrist and into his shoulder. . . . Arthritis, maybe?

He shrugged it off. "Well, screw you! I'm *sick* of being manipulated. And as for this dumb death-in-space scene . . . *up yours!*"

Idea had finally had enough. He'd been running scared for too long, afraid he was trapped in a book with an unhappy ending. Afraid of a malevolent author who twisted his every thought and word and action.

But now he felt more angry than afraid. He was sick of being knocked around, tired of running away instead of fighting back.

Visiting the author's office had taken away some of his fear. He'd realized the author was just a guy instead of a terrifying unknown force. He wasn't a god.

Maybe he wasn't as powerful as Idea had imagined. Maybe Idea could still take control of his own story.

Maybe all he needed was a good plot twist.

"Your story *stinks!* It needs a rewrite!" He began fumbling with the helmet of his suit, trying to break the seals and twist it off. "Now, send me somewhere I want to be! I *know* you don't want me to take this off and *die!*"

The only answer he got was the hiss of the oxygen.

Grunting, he wrenched at the helmet, but it wouldn't turn. He had trouble working with the bulky gloves, and there was the added impediment of the arthritis pain in his hands.

Finally, though, he found what felt like a catch, a switch near the base of his throat. "Last chance! Get me out of here *now!*"

No answer.

Idea hesitated. There might be no coming back from what he was about to do. If the author refused to let him control the story, he might be killing himself for real.

But even if he did, would it be worse than letting some guy at a keyboard continue to run his life? Would Idea rather go on being somebody's puppet, or take control of his own existence?

He popped the catch. The seal broke with a soft hiss, and he lifted off his helmet.

Immediately, he felt a great pressure surging from within, as if he were about to explode in all directions. All around him, the distant stars winked with cold white light in the unforgiving void.

Chapter Fifty-seven

Reacher

REACHER exploded into thousands of droplets, which squirted through the eyeholes and breathing vents in the crimson knights' armor, blinding them and cutting off their air supplies. With much grunting and clatter, they dropped to the ground, writhing and prying at their helmets.

When they were all unconscious, Reacher's droplets spurted back out and recombined to form his body.

He didn't get much time to savor his victory, though. He'd been standing over his defeated foes for only a moment when Scrier/Eurydice dropped down in front of him.

"Run!" she said. "You're almost through the Gauntlet!"

"Okay, okay," he said, irritated that he'd been yanked out of a dream-come-true visit with his long-lost mother and tossed back into this violent realm. "How much farther did you say it is?"

"Just run! Both of you are almost out of time!"

Reacher turned from the five unconscious knights and ran in the direction she was pointing. He took four steps before everything around him changed.

Without warning, he was back in a tuxedo in front of Your Favorites in the Swing Room. He stumbled to a stop, and a spotlight caught him in its glare.

"Back by popular demand!" said Donny Basquette, sweeping an arm in his direction. "Ladies and gentlemen, your favorite, Richie Mirage!"

The audience applauded as the band roared into the intro for "Tangerine." Reacher stepped forward and bumped into the microphone with an amplified thump, nearly knocking it over.

Just then, a black-haired woman at a table in the back jumped up, cupped her hands around her mouth, and hollered over the music and applause. "This way! Keep running!"

Reacher recognized the voice right away. Shading his eyes against the spotlight, he recognized her face, too.

He turned to Donny Basquette and shrugged apologetically. "Gotta see a man about a horse," he said, and then he leaped off the stage and darted through the audience.

The band kept playing as he ran. On his way through the staggered tiers of tables, he saw Scrier/Eurydice waving him on from her spot at the back of the room.

She pointed at the exit, and Reacher ducked through it. "Go! Go!" she urged as he passed. "Don't stop for anything!"

The next thing he knew, he was careening across a stage to the sound of pounding drums and screaming guitars.

CHAPTER FIFTY-EIGHT

IDEA

GASPING for breath, Idea opened his eyes just in time to see two spearheads plunging toward his chest.

He was alive and off the asteroid! He'd forced the author to change his story!

Unfortunately, he'd also ended up back in Fireskull's body, sprawled on the ground, about to be killed. So the author might get the last laugh, after all.

Idea flung himself to one side just as the spears closed in. As he did so, he bowled over one of the two crimson knights trying to kill him. The knight toppled over backward, dropping his weapon and crashing down with a resounding *clang*.

Before the other knight could take a stab at him, Idea belched a gout of flame in his direction, super-heating his armor and sending him reeling.

Idea scrambled to his feet and scanned the surrounding forest. The last thing he remembered from his time as Fireskull was being shot down by spears and arrows. If he was picking up anywhere near where he'd left off, he anticipated more attacks in the immediate future.

Sure enough, he heard the crackling of multiple footsteps running through the underbrush. Zeroing in on the noise, he saw three more crimson knights hurrying toward him with swords held high.

At that moment, an arrow whizzed past him and impaled a tree just a few feet away. His first thought was to take to the air, but when he tried to unfurl Fireskull's wings, bolts of agony lanced through his body.

Apparently the sky was off-limits to him for now. The wounds to his wings were too severe.

Not everyone was grounded like he was, however. Just as he drew his wings back in, Scrier/Eunice dropped from above, her face less than a foot from his own and upside down. Her appearance was so sudden and close that she made him jump.

"Run!" she said, her blond hair streaming all around like ribbons underwater. "You're almost through the Gauntlet. Reacher is not far, but you must hurry!"

"That'd be great"—Idea pointed toward the onrushing knights—"except I've got a few obstacles heading my way, in case you haven't noticed." Just then, another arrow flashed by, and another.

"Do not let them hold you back," Scrier/Eunice urged. "There is barely enough time as it is."

"Easy for you to say."

"You must work together," she said. "You must unite. Now run! I told you not to stop!"

As Scrier/Eunice drifted up and away from him, Idea watched the knights approach and considered the situation. Now that he'd taken a stand against the author, he didn't want to let anyone else control him. Yet he'd always trusted Eunice; she hadn't steered him wrong before.

He decided to continue to follow her lead. Squaring his shoulders, he took his first steps toward the approaching knights. From a walk, he moved up to a jog, then broke into a run.

The crimson knights charged toward him, howling battle cries and swinging swords. Idea ran faster, belching out blasts of scalding flame.

They crashed together in a blaze of fire and clashing metal. Swords and spears clanged against armor in a blur of rage and brutality. The air filled with sparks and blood and shrapnel.

Idea fought with impassioned fury, determined to seize control of the battle, just as he'd turned the tide on the asteroid. He spun and kicked and breathed fire, driving off his opponents in short order.

In that moment, he felt like he could do anything. He felt like he had taken control of his life and would never give it up again.

The author could throw any challenge his way and Idea would conquer it. He would add his own twist to the plot and rewrite the outcome to suit him. Deity Syndrome would no longer keep him on the run, afraid that he had no control over his story.

As for Chapter 64, and the omens of his death? Bring 'em on! The love of his parents in the alternate reality hospital had empowered him. The triumph in rewriting his destiny on the asteroid had given him the confidence he'd needed. He felt like *nothing* could hold him back ever again.

Nothing except the two dozen crimson knights who suddenly stepped out of the forest.

"Your presence is required," said one of the knights. "We have come to escort you."

Idea lowered his sword. So he wasn't *completely* in control, after all. "Where to, exactly?"

"To an audience with the Dread Lord of this and all lands," said the knight. "Our master, and *yours* now, too. He will be the judge of your fate, Fireskull."

"That's nice." Idea sighed, releasing a jet of flame. "What's his name again, did you say?"

"The Secret King."

FIFTY-EIGHT

REACHER

AS soon as he hit the stage and heard the lead guitar screaming and the bass guitar booming and the drums thundering
in a particular crescendo, Reacher knew he was just in time for
the big finale of *Singularity City*.

The crowd in the giant concert hall roared as he crossed the
stage. Gaping at the audience, he slowed his run to a jog, then
a walk—which was a good thing, because Wicked Livenbladder
leaped up to block his path.

The crescendo reached its peak and suddenly cut to silence.
Reacher knew it was the exact instant when he was supposed to
sing again, reprising the main theme, "Coming to Life."

It was a moment meant to illustrate Impulse Devilcare's
final triumph over the world that tries to crush his spirit. It was
supposed to be the emotional high point of the rock opera, with
Impulse starting softly and building with the band to a surge of
jubilant power.

The weight of the entire show rested on this moment. Looking offstage, Reacher spotted Scrier/Eurydice in the wings, mo-
tioning for him to get moving, to come toward her. Instead, he let
his gaze roam the stage, fixing on each member of the band in

turn: hairy Wicked; bald, scarred Chick; redheaded fireball Gail. All of them wore identical expressions—wide-eyed, switched-on, waiting.

Hopeful.

He knew the right thing to do was to keep running, but he stood his ground and took a deep breath. He couldn't let this moment pass without tasting it.

Closing his eyes, he began to sing.

> *"Come to life,*
> *your life will come.*
> *Come to life*
> *and touch the sun."*

As the pitch of Reacher's voice rose, Wicked began to strum his guitar softly.

> *"Come to stay,*
> *we'll make our way.*
> *Come to see,*
> *and be with me."*

His voice continued to rise, and the guitar slowly climbed along with it.

Gentle as a heartbeat, Chick's bass joined in, pulsing under both of them.

> *"D-don't you know that two two heads are better . . ."*

Gail jumped in, skimming a light rhythm just under the surface, adding heat to the slow build.

"... *better* ... *better* ..."

Everyone stopped and held for exactly one beat, then crashed down with a single huge chord.

"Better much better than one!" wailed Reacher, and the band rocked hard and loud and wild enough that they were perfectly poised on the brink between divinity and completely falling apart.

The audience went crazy. Every last person in the monstrous concert hall leaped up at once, screaming and dancing and waving.

And Reacher himself felt a rush of triumph and joy unlike any he'd ever known before. Like Impulse Devilcare in *Singularity City,* he'd finally defeated the forces that had held him back for so long. He'd silenced the voices of Daddy Naysayer and everyone else who'd called him a failure; he'd crushed the fear underneath a mountain of fresh confidence built on the love and faith of his mother, his *true* father, and the audience at Dusty's Wigwam in the 1940s.

Scrier/Eurydice had run him through the Gauntlet of Realities, and he'd come out the other side a better person, no longer so afraid of failure that he'd continue to spend his life hiding from the world.

Pumping his arms in the air, he grinned at the crowd, basking in their adulation, letting it permeate every cell in his body, every beat of his heart, soaking in so deep that he would never be without it.

Then, out of nowhere, someone punched him in the face.

As he plunged back and down, he saw that the concert hall and band and stage were gone. Above him, the sky between the red tentacles of the trees was orange again.

Luckily, he was also back in his shape-shifting Johnny Without body. Instead of hitting the ground hard and hurting something, he passed through it, leaving only his face sticking up from the surface.

Wicked's evil twin, General Deathcrave, towered over him, eyes bulging with murderous rage from the sockets of his skull-shaped helmet. "No more running. It's the end of the road for you!"

With that, he bent down and rammed a fist into the ground below Reacher's face. Reacher felt fingers like iron ingots close around his throat, and then he was being hauled up out of the dirt.

"Look, worm!" Deathcrave hoisted him into the air and shook him by the throat. "You have a visitor!"

The Secret King walked toward them with arms outstretched. The hood of his rough brown cloak was down, giving Reacher full view of his uncanny likeness to Youforia's manager, Sty.

"Do not look at him!" Deathcrave shook Reacher violently. "No mortal is fit to gaze upon his magnificence!"

"That's all right," the Secret King said with a friendly chuckle. "Let him look. He'll be dead soon enough."

It was then that Reacher remembered what he'd heard the Secret King say earlier, on the road where he'd spied on him: *Find Without and bring him to me. I know a way to destroy him.*

A chill raced through his entire body, making him shiver uncontrollably from head to toe.

"And here comes someone who'll be glad to see him go." The King clapped his hands.

Three figures emerged from the woods—two crimson knights and a man with a flaming head.

"Lord Fireskull!" shouted the King. "You're just in time!" He pulled a gold-plated cylinder from a loop on his belt and twirled it in his hand. "I'm about to kill your greatest enemy."

Chapter Fifty-Nine

Idea

THE Secret King looked just like Idea's greatness coach, Scholar, so it was strange watching him kill Johnny Without. As Idea gaped, the King twisted one end of the gold cylinder like the tip of a kaleidoscope. There was a sound like a rushing wind, and Johnny's head distended, stretching out to a point that was sucked toward the mouth of the device.

"Hey, Fireskull. Come on over and see what a little black magic can do!" The King gestured for Idea to join him. "Or should I say, a little *black hole* magic."

At first, all Idea wanted to do was get away from the brown-robed maniac who was sucking Johnny Without into the gold-plated cylinder. He had a hunch that if he stuck around, he might be the instrument's next target.

Just as he made up his mind to try to run for it, however, someone changed that decision.

A flutter of motion in the sky above the clearing caught his eye, and he looked up. Scrier/Eunice floated over Deathcrave, Johnny, and the Secret King, hanging upside down and pointing an index finger at them. She turned slowly on the vertical axis of her body, rotating on the point of her fingertip.

Her mouth moved, and at first, Idea didn't hear anything. Then a sound of whispering wind hissed past his ear, carrying her words. "Johnny is Reacher. Now is the time."

Idea thought he was the only one who'd heard her words, because no one else reacted. He also thought he understood the full meaning of what she'd said.

Just as his mind inhabited the body of Fireskull, Reacher must be inhabiting Johnny Without. This must be the time that Eurydice had foretold, the time when Idea and Reacher would have to work together to change their lives.

Or just plain save them. With each passing second, Johnny's head was stretching out to a finer point and being sucked closer to the mouth of the black-hole gun.

The Secret King chuckled. "Don't be shy, Fireskull. Come and give me a hand over here."

Idea moved to stand at the King's side.

"Reach up here, will you?" The King poked his chin toward the cylinder that he gripped with both hands.

Heart pounding, Idea reached for the weapon. Once he took hold of it, he could release Johnny from its power and turn it against the Secret King and Deathcrave.

But the King switched gears on him. "On second thought"—he moved the gun out of reach—"do you know what I really need you to do?"

"What?"

The Secret King pushed his face to within a few inches of Idea's. "Take that sword of yours and hack Johnny up into smaller pieces that'll fit better through the black hole."

CHAPTER SIXTY

REACHER & IDEA

Even though Reacher's eyes were hyperextended with the rest of his head, making everything look like stretched-out reflections in a fun-house mirror, he could still see Fireskull draw the sword from his scabbard.

Over the roaring sound that had filled his ears since the Secret King had first turned the black-hole gun on him, he'd heard the King tell Fireskull to chop him up. Any other time, Reacher would have been certain that Johnny Without's body could survive such a hack job by instinctively changing shape.

This time, though, he wasn't so sure. The gun seemed to diminish his powers, making him vulnerable.

Fireskull raised the sword and took a step toward him. Reacher wondered if his mind would die when the body he inhabited in the novel was killed.

In desperation, he made an effort to get control of his shape-shifting abilities. He could hardly concentrate, what with the roaring wind and his head being pulled like taffy.

Just as he gave up, he felt a diamond-hard spike erupt

from the center of his left palm. Immediately, he closed his fingers around the spike to hide it from his captors.

Fireskull stepped closer, and Reacher tensed. As soon as he was close enough, but before he could swing the blade, Reacher would pump the spike into the middle of his chest. There was no time for mercy; he knew in his heart that he had to kill or be killed.

Fireskull took another step closer. Reacher pulled back his arm.

Then, suddenly, he heard a woman's voice through the roaring wind in his ears. "Fireskull is Idea. Now is the time."

A flicker of movement in the sky above the sword caught Reacher's attention. Scrier/Eurydice hovered there, spinning slowly, feet pointing at the ground.

"Work with him," said her voice in his ear. "He will not harm you."

Scrier/Eurydice had not yet steered him wrong, but it wasn't easy to believe her with Fireskull standing before him, about to swing a sword in his direction. Reacher's survival instinct urged him to drive the spike into Fireskull before another second could pass.

If only he could somehow prove what she had just told him. If only he could know for a fact that Fireskull was really Idea Deity in disguise.

Suddenly, it came to him. He thought of a sure-fire way to prove who was in charge of that flame-shrouded body.

Just as Fireskull looked ready to swing the sword, Reacher opened his mouth.

And he sang.

CHAPTER SIXTY-ONE

IDEA & REACHER

IDEA was about to attack the Secret King with the sword when Johnny Without started to sing. In that moment, any doubt he still had that Reacher was inside Johnny exploded into a billion pieces.

Idea knew the song by heart. After all, he was the one who'd written it and posted the lyrics online.

It was "Mr. In-Betweener."

"Where do I go when you turn the page?" sang Reacher, his constantly changing Johnny Without voice distorted by the effects of the black-hole gun. *"Am I alive when I'm not on the stage?"*

The Secret King laughed. "Singing at death's door, eh? Better make it quick!"

"When the puppeteer lets go of my strings, will I simply collapse in the wings?" Reacher continued. *"And will anyone care what I feel like—"*

"When I'm in-between!" Idea brought the sword down hard on the black-hole gun.

The Secret King let go of the gun as the sword crashed through it. The two halves of the golden cylinder tumbled to the ground, spilling silvery glitter and shards of glass. A dark swirl the size of an apple also spit out and leaped upward . . . the very black hole that had powered the weapon.

As the gun let go of him, Reacher's head snapped back to normal, flinging him forward into Idea. The spike in the palm of his hand came within inches of Idea's heart as he was knocked down, missing him by pure luck and stabbing the ground instead.

Expecting an immediate attack, Idea shoved Reacher aside as soon as the two of them hit the dirt. It quickly became obvious, however, that the attack wasn't coming . . . at least, not in the way he'd expected.

As Idea gazed up, he saw that both Deathcrave's and the Secret King's backs were turned and they were looking at the sky. Above them, blond-haired Scrier/Eunice and black-haired Scrier/Eurydice tumbled willy-nilly around the dark swirl that had emerged from the ruined black-hole gun.

CHAPTER SIXTY-TWO

IDEA & REACHER

"**A**DMIT it," the Secret King said to the Scriers as they orbited the misty black swirl in the sky. "I surprised the heck out of you just now, didn't I?"

Scrier/Eunice and Scrier/Eurydice silently wheeled around the swirl, their gowns hopelessly twisted and tangled about their spinning bodies.

"I *wanted* the black-hole gun to break. I wanted the black hole to be released." He snapped his fingers, and the Scriers spun faster. "It was all about capturing *you*."

Idea and Reacher—still in the bodies of Fireskull and Johnny—cast confused looks at each other, then got up off the ground. Reacher was still a little shaky from having his head stretched, and Idea steadied him with a hand on his arm.

"How long has it been, my dear?" said the Secret King.

The Scriers glared at him as they tumbled past. "Layermaster Telltale Halcyon," Scrier/Eunice said evenly.

"It has not been long enough," Scrier/Eurydice added.

Idea frowned up at the Scriers. "You *know* him?"

"Yes," said Scrier/Eunice. "We are of the same noble order."

"The Way of the Chain." Scrier/Eurydice smiled. "Passers between all the worlds of the slipstream. Travelers of the infinitely expanding Chain of Realities—times, dreams, nightmares, and stories. Protectors and guides of those caught in the leaks and collisions between them."

"Like you and Reacher," explained Scrier/Eunice. "One boy snapped in two by a break in the Chain, reaching out through your band, Youforia, to find the other half you'd lost."

"Because of *him*." Scrier/Eurydice pointed a finger at the King. "The greatest among us, the Layermaster himself. He turned his back on the precepts of the Way, broke apart a billion billion realities and used the pieces to build his own Moment."

"The greatest Moment there ever was or ever could be!" The King pumped his fists in the air triumphantly. "A never-ending Moment of perfect paradise mingling the greatest wonders of every reality, era, dream, and story that ever existed!"

"You should not have built it," hissed Scrier/Eunice. "It was not worth the cost of shattering so many worlds."

"What's done is done." The King shrugged. "But you couldn't leave well enough alone. You had to find a way to ruin it. So you split yourself in two and latched on to these broken boys who could reach between worlds." He shot a glare at Idea and Reacher. "You drove them into a book with the power to undo my greatest achievement."

"Is that true?" asked Reacher, looking up at the two women swirling above them. "Is that why we're here?"

"It is." Scrier/Eurydice nodded. *"Fireskull's Revenant"* was designed as a fail-safe measure to ensure the survival of the Chain in the event of a catastrophe. It was written by a member of our order under the pen name Milt Ifthen."

"Fireskull's Revenant is an omniversal text," continued Scrier/Eunice. "A book existing in exactly the same form in every reality. Its unique resonance across all worlds allowed it to survive the Shattering of Realities unchanged— and to become the seed of their restoration. It carries an echo of the imprint of the original Chain."

"This echo will be of use to the two of you," said Scrier/Eurydice. "Now that you are ready to handle it."

Suddenly, General Deathcrave let loose a roar. "How much longer must we listen to these two? Can't we kill them any faster?"

The Secret King laughed and patted Deathcrave's shoulder. "The end will come soon enough, General. Let's savor their last pathetic bleatings. I believe we should stop and smell the roses whenever possible."

Idea ignored the King and General and stayed focused

on the Scriers turning above them. "But why us?" he said. "What about your fellow members of the Way of the Chain?"

"All dead." Scrier/Eunice looked grim. "Killed in the Shattering. Except my sister and me, and Milt Ifthen." She glanced at Layermaster Halcyon, who smirked back at her, and sighed. "I needed to find others who could cross between worlds. The two of you, through your link, had the beginnings of such power. For that, you were unique in all the Chain."

"You were already reaching into each other's worlds without knowing it," continued Scrier/Eurydice. "Idea, you sensed Reacher's existence and glimpsed Youforia's career. You unconsciously pushed your online posts into Reacher's world, making the band's secrets public."

Scrier/Eunice pointed at Reacher. "You, on the other hand, accessed details of Idea's life and incorporated them into *Singularity City*. The character Impulse Devilcare was based on Idea."

Scrier/Eurydice brought her hands together, interlacing the fingers. "We hoped to awaken the power you both possessed to its fullest potential by uniting you, and helping resolve your conflicts."

"Our first attempt to push you together failed, though." Scrier/Eunice shook her head. "You traded places instead. Idea, you ended up in Reacher's world, facing his stepfather, brother, and cousin. Reacher, you traveled to Idea's world and encountered his parents."

"But we straightened things out at Seconds," explained Scrier/Eurydice. "We shifted you both into *Fireskull's Revenant,* then sent you through the Gauntlet of Realities to prepare you for the work ahead."

Idea shook his head, trying to process the information. "So the jumps between times and places weren't literary devices? I'm *not* living in a book—other than *Fireskull's Revenant,* I mean?"

"That is correct," said Scrier/Eunice.

Idea frowned. "But what about the author whose office I visited? He wrote things about me, and then they *happened.*"

"That was Milt Ifthen." Scrier/Eunice nodded. "Guiding you with his gift for weaving fiction that shapes reality."

"But I thought he was malevolent," said Idea. "Evil. Trying to control me."

"He was only ever benevolent," said Scrier/Eunice. "He guided your life for the greater good of the Chain."

Before anyone could say another word, Layermaster Halcyon spun and knocked Idea to the ground. Reacher reacted fast and jumped Halcyon, only to be thrown down on top of Idea like a sack of potatoes.

Halcyon laughed and kicked them both for good measure. "Enough questions!" He gave each of them one more solid kick, then turned away. "Keep these two out of my way, will you, Deathcrave? Break what you like, but leave the killing to me."

"Yes, Majesty."

"Now, where were we—" Halcyon fell silent as soon as he looked up at the Scriers.

Deathcrave looked skyward, too, giving Idea and Reacher a chance to untangle themselves. As they helped each other up from the ground, they also looked up and saw that the scene in the sky had changed.

Scrier/Eunice and Scrier/Eurydice no longer tumbled chaotically around the swirling black hole. They spun around it with hands joined and bodies flattened, turning rhythmically like the blades of a propeller.

The longer Idea watched them, however, the more clearly he saw that they weren't holding hands at all. Their hands had actually *merged*, becoming undifferentiated knobs of flesh and bone.

Scrier/Eunice and Scrier/Eurydice were melting together.

Chapter Sixty-Three
Reacher & Idea

"Not again!" Halcyon's voice filled with rage as he gaped up at the joined Scriers.

"What are they doing?" Deathcrave sounded mystified.

"Uniting," said Scrier/Eunice.

"*Re*uniting," Scrier/Eurydice corrected. "We are the halves of a whole."

"As are you, Idea and Reacher." Scrier/Eunice smiled down as she spun past them.

"You were never meant to stand alone," said Scrier/Eurydice.

As Reacher gazed up at the turning women, he saw that their arms were now fused together at the elbows. In a matter of moments, if the combining didn't slow down, their heads would be touching.

"Together, we will not be defeated," Scrier/Eurydice proclaimed.

"Neither will you, Idea and Reacher," said Scrier/Eunice. "United, you will possess the power to undo the Shattering, erase the Moment, and restore the Chain of

Realities. Layermaster Halcyon cannot stand against you."

"Enough is enough!" Halcyon drew a glowing sword from a scabbard that hung at his hip. "Deathcrave, I'll separate the Siamese twins up there while you butcher their idiot pets."

"Yes, Majesty." Deathcrave drew his own enormous broadsword and moved toward Idea and Reacher.

"Idea and Reacher," said Scrier/Eunice. Her head and Scrier/Eurydice's were already fused together up to the eyes. "You must unite!"

"You have traversed the Gauntlet of Realities," explained Scrier/Eurydice. "In so doing, you prepared yourselves for this union. You shed much of what was weighing you down."

"Idea, you are no longer afraid of being controlled," continued Scrier/Eunice. "Reacher, you are no longer limited by fear of failure. At last, you both are ready to merge your strengths and usher in a new era by restoring the Chain."

"Stand together and focus your thoughts," said Scrier/ Eurydice. "It will happen."

Just then, Deathcrave swung his broadsword. Idea and Reacher leaped away, barely avoiding the hissing stroke of the heavy blade.

A second later, it whisked back at them, again barely missing as they jumped away. Deathcrave paused, sword loose at his side, and sized them up, then grinned. He jammed two fingers between his lips and let loose a shrill whistle.

Six knights in crimson armor charged out of the surrounding woods, swords and maces and shields raised high.

"Now we'll have some fun, hey?" Deathcrave slashed the broadsword through the air as he marched toward Idea and Reacher.

Reacher nervously looked around as the knights closed in from the fringes of the clearing. In a moment, he and Idea would be completely surrounded. Johnny Without's shape-shifting body might provide some kind of defense or escape, but it would be unpredictable at best.

His heart pounded. Looking up, he saw that Scrier/Eunice and Scrier/Eurydice were melded together almost down to their waists. With a furious howl, Halcyon hauled back his glowing sword and hurled it at them like a spear. The blade shot upward like a missile, its point racing toward the middle of their merged bodies . . . but it never struck its target. When it got to within a few feet of the Scriers, it melted away in midair, falling back to the ground as a shower of shimmering metal rain.

The clanking of the crimson knights grew closer. Reacher turned just in time to evade another swing of Deathcrave's broadsword.

Then, he reached out a hand toward Idea. "What do you say?"

"Unite, huh?" said Idea.

"It might be our best chance right now."

Snarling, Deathcrave unleashed two more swift swings of his sword, driving Reacher and Idea back several steps closer to the approaching knights.

"Are you in or out?" Reacher asked. He could hear the crimson knights closing in around them.

"In!" Idea grabbed ahold of Reacher's arm.

Immediately Reacher felt his body change. He focused his thoughts on the process as much as he could with Deathcrave still swinging away and the knights clattering in from all sides.

Looking down at his arm, Reacher saw that Idea's hand was already melting into it.

He also saw the ground fall away from him just as Deathcrave was taking another swing. As their bodies fused, he and Idea floated upward, out of reach of the broadsword. A heartbeat after they left the ground, the crimson-armored knights stampeded onto the very spot where they had just been standing.

"Something just occurred to me," said Idea as his upper arm merged with Reacher's. "This must be Chapter 64."

Reacher relaxed. To his surprise, the only thing that he felt from the uniting process was a tingling warmth and an all-over tugging sensation. "Like Youforia's song 'Chapter 64'?"

"I was afraid I'd die in Chapter 64," Idea said. The

merging process was speeding up; he and Reacher were joined at the shoulder.

"Just like the guy in our song," said Reacher.

"This must be it." Suddenly, Idea and Reacher rushed together, becoming a single body from the neck down. "But I'm not afraid anymore. I accept it."

"Good for you," said Reacher.

"This is when I die," said Idea, just as his head began to melt into Reacher's. "This is Chapter 64."

Then there was a final tug, and one guy drifted in the sky where two had been.

A girl floated over to him and lightly kissed his forehead. Her hair was half blond and half jet black. Her features were a combination of Eunice's and Eurydice's—an upswept nose, sharp cheekbones, round chin, full lips.

"I don't know about Chapter 64," she said softly, stroking his face. "But I *can* tell you the next chapter of your story will have a very happy ending."

Chapter Sixty-Four
Idea & Reacher

THE new guy floated in the blazing orange sky, bobbing gently on an errant breeze. His eyes fluttered open at the touch of Eunice/Eurydice's lips against his.

And a wave of pure joy rolled through him. He'd kissed her before, but it had never felt like this. It had never felt so good, so totally perfect. Like something in a dream.

Pulling back, she held his face in her hands and gazed at him, smiling. "You're beautiful." She kissed his forehead, his eyes, his nose, his cheek. "The way you were always meant to be."

"So are you." He smiled back at her. He turned his head one way, then the other, kissing each of her hands.

She frowned a little, looking concerned. "How do you feel?"

"Strange. But good." How else could he describe it? He had the memories of two people in his head, yet somehow he was one. Idea and Reacher had ceased to exist as separate people—had died, in a way—but it felt perfectly natural. It felt right.

As if this was what he'd been waiting for all his life. His *lives*.

He pulled her close and kissed her again.

The new guy glanced down at Halcyon as he screamed and shook his fists with rage. He looked very small from so far up. "He can't hurt us?"

"Not anymore." She grinned. "He'll be swept away in the Restoration."

"So how do we do it, exactly? How do we put the worlds back the way they're supposed to be?"

"Follow my lead." Eunice/Eurydice kissed him again on the lips. "As always."

"Then what?"

She frowned. "What do you mean?"

"Will we stay like this? The way we are now?" He spread his arms and gazed down at his new body. "Or will we change again?"

"We will *always* change," she said. "But you will never again be broken in two. You will live one life in one body, experienced from one point of view."

"What will that life be like?" he asked.

"Something altogether new. Better than you can imagine."

"Will I remember any of this?" he said.

"Yes. Only you and I will remember." She tipped her head and narrowed her eyes. "Unless you'd rather not?"

"Don't you dare." He hugged her tight in the dancing light of Halcyon's energy blasts splashing harmlessly from below. "Don't you *dare* make me forget you. Forget *us*."

She pushed her fingers through his hair—half black, half white, split down the middle—and whispered in his ear. "Are you ready? *Really* ready?"

He smirked. "What if I'm not?"

"Then . . . nothing. Nothing changes. *He* wins." She hiked a thumb at Halcyon. "And the worlds go on as they are now—fragmented, chaotic, incomplete."

He thought about it for a long moment. "How hard will it be?"

She shrugged and nodded. "I won't lie to you. It'll be pretty intense. After all, we're talking about setting the entire Chain of Realities right again."

Idea Deity might have run away because he felt like she was trying to control him. Reacher Mirage might have been too afraid of failure to try to restore the Chain. But together, after all they'd been through, there wasn't a doubt between them.

They'd triumphed over the things that were holding them back. Now there was nothing they couldn't handle. Nothing *he* couldn't handle.

"I'm ready," he said. "Bring it on."

"I love you," she whispered, and then she took his hands. "Let's do this."

Slowly at first, they started spinning and rising. Down below, Halcyon screamed harder, but his voice just got further away.

"Reach out with your mind," she said. "Focus on the world around you. Be aware of every bit of it."

He did as she said. He heard the wind, saw the writhing red trees, felt the heat of the sun. He tasted the dust in the hot, dry air, smelled the ozone from Halcyon's energy blasts. He tried his best to hold all these sensations and more in his mind, to be aware of it all at once.

"Now look deeper," she told him. "Push beneath the surface."

He tried. Grimacing, he concentrated on piercing the layers he could detect with his senses. He strained to break through and connect with whatever lay underneath.

But he couldn't find it. "Nothing. I'm getting nothing."

She squeezed his hands. "Relax. I'll show you the way." Then she leaned forward, tipping her forehead against his. "Open your mind to me."

He wasn't quite sure how to do that, but he tried. He imagined his brain was a flower, and then he pictured its petals opening wide.

Suddenly there was a burst of light inside him, and he felt her presence in his head. There was warmth, and wisdom, and power, and love. Then he felt her do something, and there was movement. Like the sun rising over the horizon, the true face of the world of *Fireskull's Revenant* rolled into view.

Underneath the clutter of sights and sounds and smells and tastes and touches lay a glittering filigree of light, an intricate pattern of countless swirling strands in a state of constant shivering flux.

"I see it now!" Even as he said it, he couldn't quite grasp the entirety of what he saw. It was too big, too complex, too *everything*. Parts of it were impossible for him to see at all, as if they extended into dimensions beyond the ones he could comprehend.

"It's the shape of the Chain." Her voice was hushed, as if even she were in awe of what she saw. "An echo of the pattern of the worlds as they once were, and could be again."

His breath caught in his throat. He could not look away from his mind's-eye view. "It's beautiful."

"All we have to do is retrace the pattern throughout the existing, shattered Chain."

"Is *that* all?" He let out a nervous chuckle.

She squeezed his hands tighter. "Follow me." She kissed him. "Do what I do."

A flicker of old fears bubbled up from deep within. "What if I can't handle this?"

"Trust me." She grinned. "You're a natural."

"All right." Glancing away from his mind's eye, he looked around. The two of them were still spinning and rising. They were so high in the sky that the buildings of Johnny's and Fireskull's kingdoms were tiny shapes, the people too small to be seen.

With her mind still linked to his, she spun them faster in the bright orange atmosphere. "Hold on, my love."

He felt her mind stretching, reaching out in all directions, pulling him along with her. The filigree pattern of the original Chain clung to them as they whirled, the glowing strands wrapping around them like thread on a skein.

They twirled across the sky, reeling in the imprint of a billion billion worlds, times, dreams, stories, songs. He felt it gather around them like a butterfly's cocoon, light as gossamer although it was infinitely complex and concentrated, a map of something too massive to be mapped.

When they had enough of it, they stopped spinning. The two of them drifted aloft for long moments, bundled up together in their shelter in the sky, feeling it pulse around them. They laughed as it twinkled and sparked and sang, talking to them in millions of images, thoughts, and languages.

Then, she pressed her lips against his. As they kissed, she helped him reach out with his mind and take aim in all directions, fixing his sights on all points in the Chain.

It was like aiming at every drop of water in the ocean at once. It was almost too much for him; he was drowning. But then a wave of calm swept through him, and he was in control. He felt like this was what he'd been born to do, what he'd waited all his life for.

The cocoon quivered, straining to break free. They held it there a second longer, making sure their aim was true.

And then they let go of it. The pattern burst outward in a big bang of blinding radiance, sizzling through the damaged Chain, instantly repairing it.

In the heart of the explosion, the guy who'd once been Idea and Reacher and the girl who'd been Eunice and Eurydice floated in each other's arms, locked in an intense kiss. Then, the blast wave folded back in on itself, and they were gone, washed up on the shore of a new reality.

EPILOGUE

"**H**ELLO?" said the young man at the entrance as the rickety door swung open. "Johnny Fireskull?"

Two young women crowded behind him, peering into the steamy darkness of the shanty barroom. "Is he in there?" the ponytailed brunette said in a half whisper. "You see him?"

"Johnny?" The other girl, a blonde with pigtails, raised her voice over the sounds of the jungle, calling into the barroom. "We're from California."

Of the five grimy men in the room—four sitting at the bar and one standing behind it—not one looked up at the visitors' arrival.

"Let me *see*," said a guy behind the first three newcomers. "I can't *see*."

"Okay, kids," said another voice, a woman's, from outside the shanty. "What did I say about respect?"

Suddenly everyone fell silent. The four visitors crowding the doorway moved to either side, clearing a path.

The woman walked between the parted young people into the barroom. "It would be a shame if you came all the way to the heart of the Amazon and got sent home without a glimpse of the greatest rock legend in the world."

The woman looked and sounded older than the other four visitors, who were all in their late teens. She was tall and slim and wore a khaki shirt and pants with her backpack and hiking boots.

The color of her hair was split down the middle, blond on the left side and jet black on the right.

"Sorry, Eureka." The guy who'd first opened the door wiped sweat from his brow with the back of his arm. "We're just excited."

"It's been a long trip," said the ponytailed brunette.

"I can't believe we're finally here!" the blonde chimed in.

Eureka Armslength smiled and nodded. "I can appreciate that. But remember, show respect. Follow my lead."

She shouldered out of her backpack and put it on the floor, leaning it against the wall. Turning, she spoke in the direction of the four men sitting at the bar.

"Johnny," she said. "I bring pilgrims from afar. Of the many who try to find you every day, these four musicians are the first in six months to succeed."

The men at the bar shifted. Two of them sipped cans of beer, but no one turned around to face Eureka and the pilgrims.

"They have solved the mysteries, passed the tests, and remained united," Eureka continued. "They have proven themselves worthy."

One of the men at the bar drained a soda and crushed the empty can in his fist. He tossed the crushed can into a trash bin and wiped his mouth on the sleeve of his denim shirt.

Then he turned around on his rickety wooden barstool and smiled.

He looked as if he were in his thirties, about the same age as Eureka. He was broad-shouldered and fit, but with a slight bulge of belly swelling the black T-shirt he wore under the unbuttoned denim overshirt.

The purple smudge of a star-shaped port-wine stain occupied his right cheek. A patch of three moles arranged in a triangle occupied the left.

He took off his hat, revealing hair that was two different colors, split down the middle—black on the left side, white on the right.

The four teens gasped in unison when they saw his face.

Eureka gestured at the man with the two-toned hair. "This is Johnny Fireskull," she said solemnly.

Johnny chuckled. "And who are my guests today?"

Eureka waved her four charges into the barroom. They lined up inside the door, and Eureka went to the first one on the left.

"Sarah Overnight." Eureka placed a hand on the brunette's shoulder. "She's a bass guitarist."

"Nice to meet you, Sarah," said Johnny.

Sarah beamed and shuffled her feet self-consciously.

Eureka went to the next in line, the young man who'd first opened the door. He was tall and thin, with ebony skin and shoulder-length dreadlocks.

"Unwise Parable." Eureka touched his arm. "A drummer."

"Nice to meet you, Unwise."

The young man nodded and smiled. "You'll never know how great it is for me to meet you."

Eureka moved on to the guy who'd been stuck outside when the others had crowded the door. "Stray Gonestar," she said. "Keyboardist."

"My pleasure, Stray," said Johnny.

Stray was heavyset, with orange stubble on his scalp and a triangular red goatee on his chin. Sweat ran down the sides of his round face in the hot, humid barroom. "Same here, Mr. Fireskull," he said with a little bow.

"And Grief Neverwait." Eureka placed her hand on the shoulder of the blond girl with pigtails. "Lead guitar."

"Nice to meet you, Grief."

Grief couldn't stop smiling. "Thanks for having us."

"Thank you for coming," said Johnny. "Thanks for going to so much trouble to get here."

"No trouble at all," Stray said ruefully, and everyone laughed.

"Really?" Johnny chuckled. "Then, maybe we need to make it harder."

The four teens emphatically shook their heads and said that no, he didn't need to make the trip any harder.

Johnny got up from his stool and walked over to stand in front of the pilgrims. For a moment, no one said anything.

"It's always like this." Johnny rubbed the back of his neck. "A little awkward, right? I mean, you were never a hundred percent sure you were going to find me, were you?"

"There was never a doubt in our minds," said Stray, and the pilgrims all laughed.

"Well," Johnny said, "I'm not dead." He spread his arms wide. "And you're among the handful of people in the whole world who know it."

"I still can't believe this," said Grief. "It's like a dream or something."

Johnny slid his hands into his pants pockets and rocked on the balls of his feet. "Tell me about it," he said, smirking at Eureka.

"Can I ask you a question?" said Unwise, adjusting his dreadlocks.

"Fire away."

"It's probably the same one you get asked a lot," the teen said. "Why did you do it?"

"Do what?" Johnny asked. "Drop out? Fake my own death?"

"All of it."

Johnny smiled. The star-shaped port-wine stain on his cheek dimpled into a crescent. "Love the music, hate the strings attached. It's pretty much that simple."

"But if you want to stay out of the spotlight, then why let us find you?" Unwise asked. "Why let anyone find you ever?"

"It's because of something I learned a long time ago." Johnny turned a meaningful look toward Eureka. "A secret's no fun unless you share it."

"Wait a minute," said Stray. "Isn't that from one of your songs?"

Johnny shrugged. "If it isn't, it *should* be."

Just then, Eureka raised her arm and tapped her wristwatch. "It's about that time."

Sarah, the bass player, got a panicky look on her face. "You're not sending us home already, are you?"

"No, no." Johnny shook his head. "In fact, you have a big night ahead of you."

"Big night?" said Grief.

"There's a gig down the river," said Johnny. "You'll be my band. I'm calling you 'Newforia.'"

The four pilgrims exchanged wide-eyed looks.

"You're kidding," said Stray.

"Dead serious," Johnny replied.

"Oh . . . my . . . god." Grief looked like she was about to explode into a million blond-pigtailed pieces.

"We're going to play a gig with Johnny Fireskull!" said Unwise.

"*The* Johnny Fireskull," Sarah added, tears running down her face.

"This better not be a dream," said Unwise.

"Oh . . . my . . . god," Grief repeated.

"Come on, everyone." Eureka herded the pilgrims toward the door. "Let's go get ready for the show. We'll see Johnny again soon enough."

Just when she seemed to have them all headed for the doorway, Sarah ducked to one side and rushed back over to Johnny. "Could you play us a song first?"

"Well," he said. "I really have to get ready for tonight, too."

"Just one song," Sarah pleaded. "We've come so far, and

the only thing that kept me going all that way was the thought of hearing you sing in person."

Johnny sighed and scratched his chin. He looked at Eureka, who shrugged, and then at the four teenagers. They watched him with a level of expectant tension so high that he could have sworn he felt the physical pressure from their stares pushing him backward.

"Sure," he said. "One song."

The pilgrims hurried away from the door and arranged themselves on stacked crates in a corner of the barroom. Johnny got the bartender to loan him the beat-up acoustic guitar from the backroom, and then he pulled up a stool and started playing.

"This one's for a couple of girls I used to know back home," he said, winking at Eureka.

She smiled back at him and nodded as he began to sing:

> *"Where do we go when you close the book?*
> *Will you ever come back for a second look?*
> *Will we live out our lives in a parallel place,*
> *or when you put us aside*
> *will we just fade away?*
> *Will we know any better inside?*
> *Will we feel anything when we die?*
> *Is there a sequel in store*
> *or no more*
> *or no more*
> *when we get to the end?"*

ABOUT THE AUTHOR

ROBERT T. JESCHONEK'S stories have appeared in magazines and anthologies around the world, including those in the *Star Trek* series published by Pocket Books. He has also written several podcasts, numerous e-books, and a Twitter serial, as well as stories for DC Comics. He lives in Johnstown, Pennsylvania, and this is his first novel. You can visit him online at www.thefictioneer.com.